King of Rabbits

Karla Neblett

King of Rabbits

WILLIAM HEINEMANN: LONDON

1 3 5 7 9 10 8 6 4 2

William Heinemann
20 Vauxhall Bridge Road
London SW1V 2SA

William Heinemann is part of the Penguin Random House group of companies whose addresses can be found at global.penguinrandomhouse.com.

First published by William Heinemann in 2021

www.penguin.co.uk

A CIP catalogue record for this book is available from the British Library.

ISBN 9781785152481

Typeset in 13.5/15.5pt Perpetua
by Integra Software Services Pvt. Ltd, Pondicherry

Printed and bound in Great Britain by Clays Ltd, Elcograf S.p.A.

The authorised representative in the EEA is Penguin Random House Ireland, Morrison Chambers, 32 Nassau Street, Dublin D02 YH68.

Penguin Random House is committed to a sustainable future for our business, our readers and our planet. This book is made from Forest Stewardship Council® certified paper.

For my dad, Ivan Neblett … I told you I would get our surname on a book, I just thought and hoped you'd be here to see it. I miss you so much.

For all of our lost boys.

CHAPTER I

15 December 2005

Doesn't everyone start life happy?

I did.

The biggest tree in Middledown Woods is a pine tree. I lean against it now in our den, pulling rope over my scarred palm so that it burns. When we were little, me and Saffie came here and rubbed pine needles in our hands so they smelled wild, like the grey rabbits. Mum's hair smelled like Dark and Lovely moisture cream. My two favourite smells.

I was happy till I was six.

I sit down with my back against the tree. There's a spot I always sit where I've cut off a branch and made a seat on the moss between some roots. Nan gave me a waterproof tartan blanket – that's for the floor – and three pillows to match – they go at the bottom of the trunk so it's comfy to sit. The lower branches reach around me and into the room, which I cut out from the inside of a laurel bush. I drop the rope. My hand aches. The trunk is rough so I pull up Dad's old sleeping bag to stop the tree scraping my spine. The sleeping bag is covered in blim-burns. From one of the tree branches, I pull off needles and rub them same as Nan crumbles flour and margarine between her fingers to make rock cakes.

It's pitch black outside. I have a torch hanging from a branch. The laurel-bush den is covered in old tent fabric, military camouflage nylon, to keep the rain out, and along each side I've used cupboard doors from the old kitchen to make strong walls and stop the wind getting in. It's warm in summer, but at this time of year it's freezing.

Squeeze my eyes, breathe in deep.

I feel trippy. No sleep for days.

Deep pufferfish breath.

Open my eyes, watch shadows swirl, see branches flicker against moonlight through the small openings. Listen to the tawny owl. Imagine it flap, flap, flapping over to the Grey Tower at the edge of the woods that looks over the valley.

Feel sick. Everything's too much. Like the sensory overload I get when Richie makes us play Grand Theft Auto.

Close my eyes. Mind keeps running over the same old shit. How it was then. How it is now. How I need to get away.

When I think back, it started the day after I first had the dream; it felt familiar and completely twisted me up. I'd not been to Cranston for a while. That day after the dream I went, and ended up calling Leah.

Usually if I talk to Leah, something's up. She'll call me, send a card or come home to take me for lunch at the Hilcombe Teapot, where they serve fuck-you-up-strength triple-shot cappuccinos. She's sophisticated like that – doesn't tremor after caffeine. Leah reaches out. She worries. When she's on one, she can't sleep. Like me. We have insomnia in common. When I text her in the middle of the night she always replies. Leah told Mum I'd called her, said I didn't sound right. As if Mum could do anything about a bad dream. No one knew about the dream, though. It would have surprised Leah. Really, I guess, I wanted her, but she had important stuff on. She's the clever one. The only one in the family gone to uni.

There's only one reason I go to Cranston.

5 November 2005

It took three and a half hours and three buses to get to the prison. It's on the outskirts, down a side street in a residential area off the main road – it's a feeder road from the centre. There, I was a stranger. It's well far from home. The building is made from red bricks. In Middledown it's all yellow painted council houses or stone cottages. Soon as Mum let me on a bus without her when I was ten, me and the lads went to Cranston. They helped me find the prison. We'd printed off a map at school when we were in Year Six. After that I'd pop there now and again, stare at it and wonder what it would take to break down the walls – a cannon ball, an army truck, Nan's slicing tongue?

That day, my fingers were numb from cold. I stood smoking a roll-up and thinking how miserable the red bricks looked; it reminded me of school – neat, boring, suffocating. Actually, the wall round the outside was so tall, with spiralled barbed wire on top, I could only see the top of Her Majesty's behind it. If I wanted to climb that wall I'd use a rope and a grappling hook. When climbing, it helps if a mate gives you a shove, not in a gay way, but like a firm shove on the ass so that then whoever's already on top of the wall or branch can pull you up.

I was tired. That dream. I was annoyed I'd forgotten my toothbrush because I wanted to go straight to Yasmin's and crash there – my bag, actually Jade's old school bag, had everything in: boxers, Lynx, a ten bag and my phone charger. Everything except my toothbrush. Prick.

I threw the roll-up at the street lamp I was kicking before I called Leah.

Emphasising the 'O' so I knew she was well glad I'd called her, she answered, 'Hello,' then added, 'I was just thinking about you.'

'Really? What were you thinking?'

'After we last spoke, I wanted to check you were OK.'

'What d'you mean?' I tried to remember what we'd been talking about. Derelict buildings? There was an abandoned manor house out the other side of Vells that I'd discovered when I was walking old Wheeler's dog.

'You said you'd been in isolation at school.'

'Oh that.'

'Oh that, he says.'

I knew she'd be rolling her eyes.

'You don't know how clever you are,' she said.

I began to regret calling her, maybe she was in rant mode, and jealously watched two men drinking pints on the pavement outside the pub over the road. One had an arm in a sling and his mate offered him a peanut; all he could do was open his mouth as his mate threw one at his face. It bounced off his chin and rolled on to one of the double yellow lines.

Leah was wrong; I was as smart as a two-legged table.

She carried on, 'If you listened and concentrated you'd do really well.'

'What you doing?' I interrupted.

'Writing an essay. I have a deadline on Thursday. What you doing?'

'I'm in Cranston.'

She went quiet, then asked, 'Which part?'

'Not far from the prison, actually. Teachers make it sound like if I keep doing so well I'll end up here, so I thought I'd check it out.'

'You're mumbling,' she said. 'Your phone sounds far away.'

I turned my face back to my mobile. 'Sorry. I'm sorry, Leah.'

'Sorry for what?'

'Being shit at school.'

'Why you at the prison?'

'I'm not at it, I'm near it; there's this gaming shop I wanted to come to.'

'The lads with you?'

'Yes.'

'Let me speak to Jordan.'

'I'm joking, they're not. Hey, Leah, remember when we were kids and we had sparklers up Nan's that year?'

'Which year?'

'You know, that year. When she did hot dogs and all that, Betty was there. Rabbit was like a year old and was shivering.'

'Oh, yes.'

'I'm here to get sparklers, too.'

'Sure you couldn't have got them at Jonesies in Hilcombe?'

'I never thought of that.'

'Look, if I work on this assignment all of today and tomorrow ...'

I knew she'd offer to come see me. Her boyfriend was this old codger with an Audi, money and a face like an empty beef-and-onion crisp packet. He'd pay for her train.

'No, it's fine. I'm fine,' I said. An image flared in my head. That fucking dream, I squeezed my eyes shut, but couldn't see it. When I opened them I turned my back to the prison and started towards the bus stop out on the main road. 'I hope you get an A, sis.'

'You mean a first, bro,' she said. 'I wish I was that clever.'

CHAPTER 2

THEN

After school, Kai ran as fast as he could across the football field chasing Adam and Harry. Fast fast faster. Long grass brushed his calves as he whipped along.

Fast fast faster.

In the zip pocket of his blue shorts – blue was for boys – he carried fifty pence. It was a Thursday, 'dole day'. He didn't know what that meant, but was happy it brought him money for chocolate mice and strawberry laces from the fruit-and-veg man who had saucer eyes and trundled through the village on Mondays in a big white van.

Fast fast faster.

Green grass a blur under his Power Rangers trainers. He panted, the fastest runner in his primary school apart from his sister Crystal. Adam and Harry ahead of him kicked a football and shouted back, 'You can't catch us', but he was closing the gap.

'Oi, you little rascal!' Nanny Sheila bellowed. Over his shoulder, her flowery cotton dress rippled in the breeze around her giraffe body as she stood at the edge of the field with her daddy-long-legs fingers shielding the sun. He grinned, waved, tripped and fell. Daisies kissed his hot red cheeks.

'Kai,' she shouted, 'you all right?'

Kai roly-polied then crouched, hop, hop, hopped like Flopsy the school rabbit, before jumping up, smiling and breathless. 'Yeah.'

'Time to go home.'

For tea. He shouted goodbye to Adam and Harry. They lived next door to each other, in converted cottages on the main road. Plaques with 'Middledown Bakery 1845' were nailed above their front doors. When it rained their houses smelled of their Labrador dogs, Molly and Goldilocks. In the summer their houses smelled spicy and of pizza dough. Kai's house always smelled like fags and burnt toast.

He ran to the edge of the field, his reddish-brown curls catching the light, and threw his arms around Nanny Sheila, whose deep-set eyes and sharp cheekbones softened when she smiled. Her fingertips, always blue, were cold as she pinched his chin.

'See you soon, love.' They both grinned and he sped off past Saffie's house – her blue front door was open – towards Middledown main road. Kai ran everywhere he could because running was fun and the more he ran, the faster he'd become. When he was older he wanted to race like Linford Christie.

Hills rose high, separating the village from the outside world. His parents had moved to Middledown when he was a baby. Trees edged rolling fields, the sun lowered towards bedtime. Kai couldn't wait till he was twelve like Leah, who was allowed to stay up until half nine. She wasted it doing homework at the kitchen table. Boring.

On Middledown main road, he slowed to a walk as he passed The Station pub with its criss-cross leaded windows. A painting of a wagon hung above the door. Tucked inside, polishing beer taps, he saw Saffie's mum, who Mum had a fight with last Halloween. She lifted a palm and he waved back with both hands because she and Mum were friends again now.

Cracks and potholes in the pavement. Kai jumped hopped jumped around them, past cottages with moody black-framed doors. There was the Post Office, shut. He'd wait till Monday to spend his fifty pence with the fruit-and-veg man. Past East Road, Crook Street and Tyne Avenue, which stretched away from the main road. He balanced like a tightrope walker along the edge of the pavement, arms out. Best balancer about. Kai neared the yellow estate, Alfred Avenue, where he lived. Outside number 1 stood Mr Stokes with his shaggy white hair and slug eyebrows, talking over the low fence to leather-face Mr PeePee in his stained trousers.

'Blimey, air's thick in cow shit t'night, in't it?'

'Can't smell nothin'.'

Mr Stokes walked up the road on the opposite pavement to Kai, past more yellow houses where gardens were parcelled into squares. Outside Johnny the Prawn's, Johnny was crawling from a patch of mud on to the mattress left on his lawn, where his neighbour, the quiet lady, stood wearing pink flip-flops. Must be a diabetic fit, like always. He styled his hair like a Gallagher brother, Mum said, whoever that was, and wore blue, round sunglasses even in winter. He was grumbling. Mr Stokes, who drank at The Station every day and had skin redder than Santa's, stopped to pull Johnny up, but toppled over. The quiet lady, who lived the other side of Johnny, held out a pot of sugar, then spilt the whole lot over them and Johnny the Prawn got as red as Mr Stokes.

'Shall I get Kev?' Kai called.

The quiet lady grinned, must have forgotten to put in her false teeth. With a lisp she said, 'Yes.'

Kai lived at number 14 Alfred Avenue. He jogged next door to number 12, where his friends Jordan and Taylor lived. Their dog Kaos was barking round the back. Kai rang the bell and told Jordan and Taylor's dad Kev that Johnny needed him.

Kai stopped at his garden gate, black fingernails sliding the 'lock'. Behind the open window of the living room, the net curtain rippled. From upstairs music started – his sister Jade playing her second-hand Sony hi-fi.

Down the path, round the back, the garden stretched to a swing and a rotten shed. On the other side of the garden there was an apple tree. By the back window there was a drain that bubbled as water rushed into it from the sink inside. Kai pushed through the back door.

Three hours later, Dad and his mate Denner were playing cards at the kitchen table in front of the sink. Above them the lampshade looked like the moon. The kitchen and living room were open plan; at the other end were two settees. Kai sat on one of the settees and imagined polar bears, snow foxes and leopards dancing on the white planet as it swayed from music thudding through the floorboards. Jade and Crystal were playing The Fugees' 'Killing Me Softly' in the bedroom his three sisters shared. The moving shadows made Dad's freckles dance. Kai's sprinkling was identical. Dad's face had lost elasticity. The band snapped when Mum dealt the first hand three hours ago.

'Queen of hearts,' Dad had said when he slapped her ass as she bent over the table, shuffling a cream rainbow with her fast fingers – the only bit Mum was ever allowed to do during card games. Leah, her head in a book on a comfy chair opposite Kai, had wrinkled her nose and flicked one of her tree-trunk-colour waist-length plaits over her shoulder before sticking a thumb in her mouth, even though she was a big girl and should have known better. Jade and Crystal always told her she should stop because she was the oldest and was showing them up.

'If I'm the queen of hearts, what does that make you?' Mum had asked, her words as spiky as the holly in Middledown Woods. The hand was dealt. She left the table and crouched at the freezer, yanking at a drawer covered in ice. It squeaked as she pulled it free. She pulled out a tub and then a plate from the cupboard under the sink before she shunted the frozen mincemeat on to the table near the cards. The plate made a tiny crash.

'King of clubs.' Dad's throaty laugh was whiskery. He tap tap tapped ash from his smoke into the ashtray. Smoke thickened the air to white gravy.

It was hot. Mum had eaten an ice pole with so much tongue she looked like a dog, and when Denner sneezed – 'Pollen,' he said – Dad poked out his lips at her thinking no one had seen. Kai watched it all.

For three hours.

Card games were cool and that's what big men played.

Tonight felt funny. Always did when Dad had mates round because Mum said he acted a twat – twat meant idiot or like the big-I-am. Maybe Mum wished he had no friends, but that was mean because Kai couldn't imagine going to school without his best friend, Saffie, who made everything make sense. Things like the alphabet and why sharks could breathe in the sea – she said gills were doors into their tummies that stopped water but let in oxygen. They both believed the moon was made from silver and there were silver animals roaming it, which they had to protect from the furred hunters.

Least Mum never called Dad a pussy. Dad hated that. Weird because pussy cats purred and pounced and always landed on their feet and that was well cool, even though Nanny Sheila hated them for peeing on her marigolds. She threw a watering can at one once.

'Two days,' said Dad, lifting an eyebrow, keeping his eyes on the cards. Mum wanted to join in the game, Kai could tell. She kept butting in.

'What?' said Mum, who sat on the chair next to Leah, tapping her foot on the blue carpet.

'How long you lasted before you got a strop on because you want a drink.'

Mum was always trying to stop drinking. Over the top of her book, Leah watched too then looked at Kai. Would Mum drink? her look asked. Kai shrugged.

Dad said, 'You never last.'

'It's a Friday,' she said. 'Everyone drinks on a Friday.'

'Doesn't matter,' said Dad, pushing the plate of meat away with a fingertip because it was germy.

Mum got up and shoved Dad's ginger head, saying, 'Hush your gums, Jesse.' She looked at Kai, who sat on the arm of the settee, rolling a bogey. He froze until Mum looked away, then he flicked it.

'Why keep saying you're gonna quit?'

Leah read on, and when Mum sat down with her eyebrows looking glued together, Leah leaned away.

Kai moved further back on the arm of the settee. If Denner moved his head a centimetre, Kai would see his card and mime it to Dad. Jack of diamonds. He put his hands in a diamond shape, followed by a J with his finger to Dad, who scratched his nose before turning his attention to his treasure chest. A wooden box for grown-ups. It held ingredients for smokes on the top, but the stuff in the bottom drawer was hidden from Kai and his sisters. If Kai ever got to see the hidden bits he would keep the secret. After all, he knew about the gold chain, stuffed badger and sword that Dad brought home last week. The sword rested against the other settee; it was long, silver and well well heavy. The handle was patterned swirly as octopus legs. It was cool. The badger was best because it was macky; its eyes looked angry, and the black and white reminded him of skunks and zebras.

'You reckon Tyson will win?' said Denner, lifting a page of the *Sun* he'd brought round.

'He's the favourite,' said Dad.

'Course he will,' put in Mum. 'Real men always win.'

'A real man can take a beating,' said Dad.

How to win. Kai would learn that for when he was a big man.

It was fight night. Dad said playing cards set the right build-up to the first punch, due to start at eleven. Kai couldn't tell the time, but so what? He knew it was late because he could see the sky shutting its eyes through the yellow curtains. He wondered what it would be like in the woods.

'About Scottie.' Dad returned to Denner's question from before the game started. Scottie was Dad's mate from the pawn shop in town who even grinned when he lost money at the bookies and that was strange because Nanny Sheila said books were cheap if you knew where to go and Dad said Scottie had an eye for bargains and bargains meant cheap because Mum was always looking for them. 'He said to take the sword round his.'

'We'll stop in after the fight,' said Denner, swapping a card. That would be late. When he was fifteen Kai was definitely going to stay up all night, especially at Middledown Woods with Saffie so they could watch the moon.

The game was getting serious; it showed in Dad's jaw. The men wore their best tracksuit bottoms; Nike, Adidas with Ralph Lauren polos. If Steve had come, they'd be wearing shirts, skinny ties and heading up The Station and Mum would be wearing a skirt with no knickers because Kai heard Dad tell her not to sometimes. On the nights they went to The Station, Kai would wake to the sounds of them wrestling through his bedroom wall. It sounded weird. Puffing, panting and knocking.

When Kai was older he'd play poker too, win loads of money. Loads. Build Mum a house made from gold, because when her dad came to England from Guyana he was sad when he found out the pavements weren't made from it.

'How much longer you playing?' asked Mum. A pink bottle of Dark and Lovely hair cream rested by her feet. She picked it up and handed it to Leah, who straightened her back.

'Get the gaffer tape,' said Kai, and Dad and Leah laughed, Leah like a machine gun. It was Dad's joke that Mum was always banging on at the wrong time. Even Kai knew to hush his gums now; Mum didn't. She was pissed off.

'Watch your mouth.' Mum glared at Kai. He shrank into the settee and held his breath a beat, two beats, three, four. She looked away.

Dad stared at the cards. 'Put that in the fridge.' Mincemeat bled on to the plate next to his arm. 'It stinks.'

Mum pulled her thumbnail over her fingernail so that it made tiny snapping noises, ignoring Dad.

'Sherry!' he said.

The meat smelled sour, like the cold counters with the fish and beef at the supermarket.

'It's defrosting for your dinner tomorrow.' Mum pulled out two hairbands and her hair sprung out.

'You wanna drink?' Denner asked her.

Mum threw her head to the side like finally someone heard her and repeated, 'It's Friday.'

Kai bit his bottom lip. Leah squeezed the Dark and Lovely cream into her hand, rubbed her palms together and then started on Mum's hair.

Dad threw a card down. Denner chucked down his, laughing, and folded his arms behind his big square head. A sovereign shone from his pinkie. 'Thanks, Sherry.'

Mum kissed her teeth because she thought Denner was a good-for-nothing-piece-of-shit who always had twenties in his wallet. Kai thought he was cool. He'd already chucked Kai two quid for Pokémon cards. Mum flinched as Leah snagged a knot.

'Be careful,' she said.

Leah popped the lid closed on the cream. 'Finished.'

'You just lost me a oner,' said Dad. Mum rubbed the sides of her face before she jumped up and stretched; her grey hoody lifted and revealed an outie belly button above denim shorts.

'Good job I've put fifty on Tyson and he's gonna win. Go on, then.' Dad pushed a can forward and Mum grabbed it. As she cracked the ring pull, Dad weaved a hand between her legs, squeezing her calf, which was shiny from the shea butter she rubbed in every night.

'Mum,' said Leah. When Mum took a swig, Leah's soft face shrivelled before she turned her chocolate-drop eyes back to her book and tucked her feet and arms into her big, pale-blue T-shirt. Only her head and fingers stuck out, like a baby bird cracking out of a shell.

'What's it about?' Kai asked.

His sister's eyes got solid as she came back to the real world. 'A detective called Nancy Drew.'

'Cool,' he said. Reading made Leah happiest. Kai couldn't see the difference between Ds and Bs, Qs and Ps, probably because he was only five.

'Wanna do spellings?' she asked.

Kai pulled a Power Rangers sock off – the other was plain green and was Saffie's. He hated schoolwork. Dad flicked a lighter – tick, tick – it caught the end of his smoke, rings floated across the living room.

Kai looked at Leah. 'OK.'

'No you don't,' said Mum. 'Look how late it is. Bedtime.' She opened the door to the bottom of the stairs and yelled for the others to turn off the music before sitting next to Denner.

He asked Mum, 'You really trying to quit?'

'Don't even know why she says it,' Dad cut in. 'Every morning she says the same.'

'I quit smoking for five years,' said Denner; he flicked through the newspaper.

'How?'

'Why?' Dad's voice was high pitched as he held on to the smoke he'd sucked in. 'What made you start again?'

'There was this traffic jam.'

Leah rolled her eyes.

'You serious?' Mum asked.

Denner's eyes were liney at the sides and they folded as he said, 'I was on the A37 in 1993. It was Glastonbury weekend. Fucking forgot the traffic, didn't I?'

Kai listened to Denner talk about stoned hippies, a convoy the length of England, and hot weather so sticky car radiators exploded. He waited to be told again that it was time for bed.

Next morning, Kai woke to Mum thudding the wall between them. When he pushed through her door she was under two duvets and Dad's green sleeping bag; she hated the cold. The thin purple curtains were closed and light spread through the stuffy room on to a heap of clothes in front of the open wardrobe. A pint glass was empty on the bedside table next to the lamp, which was on. Miss

Butterworth said that was a waste of electric; he clicked it off.

'How's my favourite?' Mum croaked and stuck a hand out from the covers, searching. Her hand was soft and her nails were shaped like squares. 'Grab me some tablets, my prince.'

'Which ones?'

'The ones by the bathroom sink. And fill my cup up with water.'

After a slurp, head tilted back, pill swallowed, she sank into the bed burrow again. Dad's treasure chest, at the foot of the bed, was open. Kai moved towards it. There was a tray with sections that had been lifted out showing the space underneath. There were stinky green buds – Kai had seen those before for Mum and Dad's smokes, and also tiny plastic bags and something else, something white. He lifted a foot, the floor creaked.

'Oi.' Mum flicked back the covers so Kai climbed in, smelling her pickled breath. She folded around him like a sweet wrapper, and he lay cradled in her lap, feeling the rise and fall of her belly on his back. She whispered, 'This is where you were when you were in my tummy.'

'Was I blind then?' he asked because he couldn't remember seeing her belly button. Maybe it was an innie from the inside.

She grunted no before groaning. 'I'm not doing it any more. I mean it. It isn't right on your grandad's memory.'

Alcoholic. What Mum called her dad, who was dead. It meant drinking too much and never waking up. Kai closed his eyes, wondering what was in the bottom layer of the treasure chest.

'Did Mike Tyson win?' he asked.

'Dunno, love. I fell asleep.'

Along the landing the girls' bedroom door handle squeaked before someone, Crystal, the loudest, left the bathroom door open as she peed.

'Is Dad downstairs?' Mum asked, patting Kai's curls. 'Better get Crystal to plait your hair today.'

He hated having his hair done. It took too long and it hurt.

'I don't know where Dad is.'

'Must be at Scottie's,' she said. 'Hopefully. So long as he isn't at that good-for-nothing-piece-of-shit Denner's house.'

CHAPTER 3

5 November 2005

At home I'd gone straight upstairs for my toothbrush thinking about the last bus from Cranston, which had reversed into the bus behind and kept on moving as if it wasn't there. Some woman down the front had yelped like old Wheeler's Jack Russell and the bus driver had shouted 'Blood Claat', which made me laugh because no one else knew what it meant – just as well or he'd probably have lost his job. I managed to get the sparklers in Cranston because I looked quite old and the corner shop didn't bother ID'ing me. The whole way home I kept turning over the sparklers in my hands and wishing I was a kid again. By the time I got back I wanted to crawl into bed and sleep for a decade, except I had to get in and out the house without Mum knowing, so I used the front-door key. I'd got the key copied with my second wage packet from the paper round exactly for that reason. Mum never left the living room and sometimes I couldn't be bothered to talk. About school, friends, girls. Whatever. I wasn't interested.

The bathroom door was shut, locked when I tried the handle.

'Hang on,' shouted Crystal. The one up from me. Thought she was sophisticated now that she was eighteen. Always making her face look like a cinnamon bun.

I went into my room and grabbed my money box; it was old, made from china. I pulled out the black disc underneath and shook out two skinny red ribbons. Ten point two inches long. One was frayed at the end so I'd super-glued it to keep it from falling apart. Once they were shiny. Now they looked faded. They were good for the early hours when I couldn't sleep. I fiddled with them. I was good at making knots after Bob-Cycle showed me, so I made an overhand knot and lark's head knot; I left it in the last knot because it looked cool and shoved it back in the money box. Since working, I kept my actual money in a red metal tin under my bed, its key hidden.

Mum wanted me to cook with her that night, desperate to teach me curried goat, reckoned I wouldn't be good for any woman unless I could cook. Now and again we had fun stewing and frying. My favourite thing to make was cornmeal dumplings. Fried, obviously. It wasn't the day for it, though. There was this time I was in Nan's car – we were going for a day out at a lake in the Cotswolds with the girls – and we drove along twisty roads with steep inclines on one side and there was a sign saying 'Landslide' and I could see where rock and mud had slid off the cliffy bit. That was how I felt. Like something had slipped in me since the dream. That was the only way I could describe it. I wished I could remember it.

I went back to the bathroom. The door had a hole in from when I punched it after an argument with Yasmin. Staring at it, the plywood, the crinkled cardboard on the inside, made me feel like a right spud.

When I was older, I'd have a place made of oak. That's what I wanted, solid oak doors. My dream job was to be a tree house builder; I wanted to build loads, the houses would be clad with cedar and I'd only let homeless people live in them. Cedar smelled amazing, sweet and like pine trees. When I was about ten, Bob-Cycle over the road helped me make a cedar cigar box for Dad; he never smoked cigars, but I thought his fags could live in it. Bob moved out a couple of years back after meeting some woman. Actually, I missed him. Not as much as I missed Dad. His odd letter wasn't enough.

Why it bugged me that Crystal took so long in the bathroom or toilet was because it was like she was saying she was more important than everyone else on the planet. There was this time I needed a shit and she wouldn't hurry up and I had to go in the corn field up the top of the road. Gross because I didn't have tissue. I used a corn cob.

'What you even doing?' I asked.

'Getting ready?'

'For what? Christmas? You still got seven weeks.'

She hated Christmas. Never even went out any more. She used to, but stopped after breaking up with Taylor – he's a little prick. The clicking sound of small bottles and brushes carried on; I imagined her pulling stupid faces in the mirror and flicking her straightened dyed-black hair about like a right slut. I didn't like my sister looking like that. I whacked the door, went to shout, then remembered I didn't want Mum hearing me.

'Just pass my toothbrush,' I said quietly.

Crystal did my swede in, always ignoring me and wearing trampy clothes. I've hated the way she dresses ever since I caught Richie checking her out – he reckoned he didn't, but he's a bullshitter. Be much better if she dressed like Jade, who lived in trackies and dungarees, or Leah, who wore big, baggy shirts that looked like they came from some poor country. The pale colours made her face look yellowy. Not that she cared. Whenever Crystal asked to do a makeover on her Leah said she'd 'rather be favoured for her intellect than her body'. That cracked me up. Leah was definitely prettier because she wasn't a try-hard.

Finally I heard a zip – Crystal's suitcase full of make-up – and the door opened. It stank like marzipan. Sure enough, cinnamon bun. Her cheeks glittered.

'Your face looks sweaty,' I said.

She thumped into my shoulder to pass.

'That skirt makes you look like a slag, too.'

'You're boring, Kai. Maybe I'll put on a shorter one.'

After getting my toothbrush I crept down the stairs, a foot either side of the steps to avoid the creaky middle. It sounded like Mum was watching some trashy TV show; I snuck out the front door.

Outside it was freezing. Dark, too, because it was November. Everyone was celebrating Bonfire Night.

When I turned into Nan's estate a few kids were playing in the road on bikes. The street lamps were on and it was smoky from people starting a bonfire in the football field and there was a cold mist, too. The kids were little black shadows. If they were lucky, someone on the street would have thrown out a sofa and the little ones would have cut out the back of it to look for pennies before it went on the fire. I searched for Tyson.

'Kai!'

The kid was cute, I swear. The bike brakes squeaked when he stopped in front of me. His nose was runny under a black woollen hat. Because his dad wasn't on the scene I kicked a ball about with him sometimes; I've even taken him to the woods to watch the birds. The lad had a real thing about birds and was trying to learn all their names. Clever little shit. Like, by his age all I knew was a raven and an owl. He could name most things we spotted in Middledown.

'I saw a robin redbreast today.'

'Nice one, where?'

'On the bird table.'

It made me laugh, I was expecting him to tell me he'd been for a walk, and he smiled like he'd said something clever.

'I got you something,' I said, pulling out the sparklers and handing him one.

'Cool!'

'Hold that metal bit.' He was wearing gloves so I wasn't worried about him burning himself. I lit it. We watched as he swirled circles, and when his face turned into a massive grin it was the best feeling ever. When it flickered out I said bye and headed to Nan's to check on Rabbit.

Rabbit was old and I knew she'd die soon. Holding her in my arms, I felt her shiver like she knew the fireworks were about to start – she hated them and I wished she had a burrow in Nan's garden to hide in. I started telling Nan and Betty I'd stay to look after her, but they promised to keep her calm so I headed off. It was like they were trying to get rid of me. Sure they were a bit pissed, too.

I reached Yasmin's late. Earlier, I'd texted saying I'd be there by five and it was nine. Not that I cared. She'd be screwing, though, and the closer I got to her house the more I couldn't be assed to go in. Hopefully her mum would be in; she didn't try to be sexy then. That stuff freaked me out. The path by the side of the house was lit from the side window. I slowed my pace when I heard voices from the back garden: Yasmin and her mum.

It was obvious straight away that they were talking about something they shouldn't be. Their voices were lowered and now and again they whispered. My first thought was that they were bad-mouthing me. There was this nastiness to Yasmin when she told me something spiteful: I looked shit wearing orange, I snored like a pig with leprosy, and the one she kept repeating recently, I'd got too skinny – 'Way too skinny, Kai. What you wannabe like Victoria Beckham?' She was a proper bitch. The good, honest kind. There was a day at school when her year head pulled her into the office for bullying a girl called Louisa and when she was asked about it, Yasmin said, 'She annoys me so I say stuff.' No shame at all.

I didn't like that she was a bully. What could I do about it, though? She was her own person. Louisa was fit. A bookworm – at lunchtimes she read in the library. She had really long hair, a brace and eyelashes like dandelion wishes. Fluffy and white. Yasmin was jealous. Blatantly. Girls got mad like that.

'So anyway I told her,' Yasmin's Mum, 'I'm not having you parking outside mine. You've got the whole fucking street. Go park outside Denner's.'

'What did she say?' Yasmin. She had something in her mouth. Maybe a Chupa Chups, she ate them all the time. Kissing after she'd had one was nice. Actually, it was the only time it was nice. She always used too much tongue.

'Fucking cheek of it, mind; she said she'd listen to me once I got a car to park outside my own house rather than ten tonnes of negativity. Tell you what, it's a good job Denner was there. He pulled me back inside the house.'

I looked towards Denner's lawn down the rank. He had a pond now. Where his shed used to be. If fish weren't such miracles breathing under water and all I'd pour bleach in it.

'You know that Louisa girl, Mum?' Yasmin. Things must have started up between them again; well, Yasmin must have started on her again.

'Yeah.'

'I was in the library the other day –'

That was a lie. I felt myself frown.

'– during English.'

More believable; she wouldn't go in given a choice.

'And she kept looking at me. I kept catching her like, you know, looking me up and down.'

The bunch of people in the football field suddenly cheered. Her mum didn't respond.

'Like she was dogging me up.' Yasmin.

'Did you say anything?'

'No. Mr Lane told me I wasn't allowed to talk to her unless I could be nice or I'd start getting after-schools.'

Yasmin really fucked me off. I leaned my head against the wall of the house and looked at the stars.

The cheers erupted louder from the field; the bonfire must have been in full swing. The sound of a firework whizzed up and I heard a bang.

'Look.' Yasmin.

Their feet rustled about the floor. I wasn't worried because the field was the other direction to where I was stood. It should have been the time to join them, but I kept still, holding the packet of sparklers and remembering what was in my bag and that I had toothpaste in my den and a sleeping bag. I couldn't be assed. Whenever I went round, we'd end up in bed, her chatting shit through a film and me falling asleep before she'd get annoyed that I wasn't giving her enough attention or kissing her. She liked my eyes on her, she said. Those little things she said made her beautiful for split seconds. The other hours with her, her words were darts.

There was a break in the fireworks and Yasmin said, 'Where the fuck is he? I'd be worried about him if he wasn't such an unreliable prick.'

As another firework went up, I turned away and walked back towards the road, where I bumped into Denner.

'You all right, lad?' he said.

'Fucking great,' I said.

CHAPTER 4

THEN

Outside, Kaos, Jordan's dog next door, woke Kai up.

It wasn't morning, it was dark. Stars through the open curtain winked at the corner of his eyes. Green plastic stars glowed on the ceiling, too. Last weekend, Kai and the girls went to Nanny Sheila's for chicken roast. Yummy. After, on the football pitch as Farmer Reid ploughed the next field over, Kai and Leah laid on the grass rubbing bloated bellies. Leah said stars sat in the sky in the day and that the most powerful star, the sun, hid them. Crazy. That's why you could see the silver moon in the morning, especially in summer when the mornings were the same colour as Nanny Sheila's Sunday pearls.

Kaos growled. All gruff, gruff, like he had a croaky throat. Mad dog.

The sharpness of metal: the garden gate clanged. Dad? Footsteps, two pairs. Back door unlocked. Soon as Dad and

Denner were in, Kai felt warm. Nights like this brought gifts. Their voices grumbled and they laughed. Mum's bedroom door opened, then she was with them, oohing and aahing. A night hadn't passed like this for ages because Dad said he was sorting his shit out, keeping his head down.

Kai slid out of bed and crept to the girls' room, running his hand along the wardrobe then the chest of drawers, listening to the breaths of his three sisters, like little heart-beats of wind. It was magic that they all landed on earth at the same time. Leah said it blew her mind, because history was macky. He aimed for the bunk bed on the opposite side of the room, across from Leah's single, and whacked it with his hand, 'Ooosh.' Hard wood stung his knuckle.

'Get lost,' groaned Crystal, turning over to face the wall.

'Hush your gums,' he whispered, 'alien head.'

Leah wouldn't mind waking up, but Kai kept super quiet for her because she found sleep hard. Next to Crystal's head, he rested a foot on the second rung of the ladder and then felt around in the dark for Jade's warm foot; he squeezed it and she started, 'Yeah?'

'Shut up,' said Crystal.

'You shut up,' said Kai, then to Jade, 'Dad's been out.'

On the landing Kai pulled the toilet door shut quietly in case the toilet-flush monster watched, then lay on his tummy next to Jade, whose two round bubbles of hair like Minnie Mouse's ears were outlined by the moonlight that shone through the open door of the bathroom.

The men's voices sounded charged, 'Yeah, that fuck-off big house in town with the long drive. Fucking bushes. Buzzing.'

'Drink?' Dad's voice. 'Let's celebrate.'

'Jesse shouldn't drink in front of Mum,' said Jade.

'Shut up.' Kai bit. 'Least my dad loves her.'

'I'm glad mine and Crystal's pissed off or you wouldn't be here.' They bumped heads in the dark before she rested a hand on Kai's shoulder and carried on whispering, smelling of toothpaste and morning breath. Jade was ten, halfway between Leah and Crystal. His sisters didn't talk about dads much because Jade and Crystal's didn't stick around after they were born, and Leah's dad, who was called Nicholas, died in a motorbike accident. Nanny Sheila's eyes would go sad when his name was mentioned.

'I hope he got us something good this time,' said Jade.

Funny. Kai slapped hands over his mouth to keep his giggle in because Dad had given Jade a gollywog last time and she threw it out the back door and Dad said, 'Golly, how ungrateful.' It had mad big teeth. Dad said he thought she'd like it because it had lips like hers. Mum was pissed and wouldn't let him bring it back in the house. That night Dad slept on the settee in the sleeping bag and Jade slept with Mum. Gollywog was torn up outside the garden shed and when Nanny Sheila visited and saw it she said Dad was stupid.

The best thing about Dad's job was that when he gave Mum a bit of money she'd get better food.

'We'll get Nik Naks again,' said Jade.

'And chicken Kievs,' said Kai, bored of fried spam. 'Let's go to the bottom of the stairs. Stand on these bits so it isn't noisy.'

There was a banister each side of the stairwell and holding on, Kai led, with his feet balancing at the side of each stair to stop the creaking. At the bottom, they lay quietly, chins in hands. Dad's smoke tickled their noses from underneath the door.

'Now that's a nugget.' Mum's voice was full of breath.

The carpet scratched Kai's elbows and he remembered the woodlice with their hard grey shells and kicking legs when you flipped them upside down that sometimes got in by the front door and he hoped they wouldn't crawl on him. Gross.

'I wanna know what she's looking at,' said Jade.

'Bet it's a bracelet,' said Kai, because Mum had lost one and Dad said he'd get her a new one and Dad was good at keeping promises, like the time he said he'd get Kai an *X-Men* T-shirt and now he wore a Wolverine one. The best kept promise was his red cape from last Christmas.

'Might be a wedding ring,' said Jade, poking him in the ribs. 'You'd have to be a page boy then. Wear a stupid suit and—'

'Shh,' said Kai. 'Stop being annoying.'

'All right, freckle-breath.'

'You can't have freckles on your breath.'

'You do because—'

There was a gasp from Mum; Jade shut up.

'I love it, Jess.' Mum. Then they heard kissing and Denner telling them to get a room.

Jade coughed. Kai shoved her. 'You're ruining it.'

'They always catch us anyway.'

The door was flung open. Dad's Air Max trainers, always clean, were covered in mud. He wore his neon coat that had the letters **s e c u r i t y** on it.

'Quiet as two thieves in the night,' he said. They followed him into the living room, where Mum flicked the lid down on the treasure chest and shut a plate in the microwave. Kai knew what was on the plate because one time she walked out the room and he and Crystal looked at the plate and saw the tiny lines of white talcum powder. Even though Crystal said not to he rubbed one on his hand; it didn't smell sweet like the powder in Nanny's bathroom.

'All right, sonny,' said Denner, in a coat to match Dad's, rubbing a hand over Kai's nappy braids because he hated sleeping with Mum's tights on his head. Mum was shuffling through the hallway by the back door to the indoor shed where they kept old toys and garden rubbish.

A rucksack and black bin liner were sprawled over the carpet. There was an open jewellery box, chains, earrings, rings, two watches, red, green, blue, black Ray-Bans, a Kodak with a big lens that shot out when Dad picked it up, clothes and a pair of Clarks shoes.

Before he knelt, Kai grabbed his red cape off the settee and velcroed it round his neck. He picked up the green sunglasses.

Mum came back in rubbing her eye, talking to Dad, 'It's in the biggest saucepan.'

On the settee Dad rested a foot on his other knee and Kai jumped on his lap. 'Take what you want, Jade.' Dad tapped a magnifying glass against his leg. 'There's enough surprises for you kids.'

Laughing, Denner said, 'Fucking ought to be.'

'Got some making up to do for last time,' said Dad, 'haven't I?'

Jade stopped looking at the gold chain on Mum's wrist and knelt on the carpet, taking first dibs before Leah and Crystal got up. Not because she liked jewellery, but because usually Dad would bring her a souvenir mug. She had a collection at the bottom of her wardrobe; her favourite had a starfish on the front and she'd painted starfish for a week after. Starfish were crazy because they moved fast even though it was hard to see them moving. Tonight, Jade held up a mug with a blackbird on.

'I love it,' she said.

'We're lucky there wasn't a dog,' said Dad as Kai lay with his head on Dad's lap, closing eyes, feeling the red cape on his arms. Dad was the coolest.

'Dog?' Mum.

'I knew there wouldn't be.' Denner.

'How?' Mum's voice didn't believe him. She said the H extra hard and Kai knew she was making her eyes smaller like Miss Butterworth at school when he hid Saffie's twin sister's pen. 'How could you just know?'

'They're on holiday, Sherry.' Denner sounded bored.

Kai yawned and peered through squinted eyes at the blank TV, wishing it was on so it wasn't so quiet. Dad and Denner breathed like they had acorns up their noses. The bare bulb at this end of the room shone bright; the polar bears and snow foxes and leopards that lived on the white globe over the table were sleeping because that light was off.

Denner handed a smoke to Dad, who puffed and said, 'Ere.' Pulling Kai's arm and the jewellery box over, he stood Kai between his knees and draped him in chains, pushing a silver band on his thumb, far too big, still cool. 'Only the best for my boy.'

'I love it.' Kai ran two fingers around the chain. It felt cold and hard.

'About right,' Mum yawned, 'he'll come down to play with jewellery at five in the morning, but we can't get him to do his homework.'

'Are we rich now?' Kai asked.

Dad snorted before saying to Denner, 'Proper rush, though, wun't it, mate?'

Denner nodded, clearing his throat. 'I better be getting off.' He stood and bumped fists with Dad.

'See you, kids; bye, Sherry.'

'Still on for super cider Sunday?' Dad asked.

'Yeah,' said Denner. 'Pick you up at midday, princess.'

'I'll bring Kai, too,' said Dad.

At lunchtime in The Hilcombe Inn Dad and his mates were full of lager, laughter and the big-I-am talk. It was why Mum never came. Kai was allowed because he was one of the lads. Outside it was hot. Inside, they'd claimed the pool table. They stood around, slumped against the wall, the fruit machine and the small tables, checking out ladies. Kai wasn't allowed to tell Mum. The bar lady kept glancing at Scottie, and whenever the men sent him over for a round she flicked her hair and charged less.

'It's those sparkly eyes,' Dad said. It was obvious the lady, who had red lipstick and black hair, didn't know they were talking about her. She kept finding excuses to come over – dirty glasses, sticky tables, opening the windows. Each time she left, they said, 'Sexy bitch.'

Scottie aimed the cue in a lazy way, said he wasn't interested. 'I've got enough on my plate with Alice.'

There was cod caught in Kai's teeth from the fish and chips Dad bought when they first turned up. Half the food was left on the plate. The men hadn't eaten. The fish in his teeth felt like fabric from a cushion. He picked at it.

'Denner'll get more beak, mate,' Dad said, nudging Steve, who fiddled with the edge of his nose.

'What's beak?' asked Kai.

'Donald Duck's mouth,' said Dad.

'It's shit, mate,' Denner said, pint in hand, nodding along to the top-ten music chart on the TV next to the mirror. Around the corner a family cheered because a waitress in a black apron had brought out a birthday cake. The pub smelled of perfume and candles.

'I want a pint,' said Kai.

The bar lady across the room watched Scottie, who was leaning towards Dad and reminding him of the time they hunted for weed after a party at a local quarry and Dad fell off a ledge thirty feet through the air into the arms of a tree. Luckily. It placed Dad on the floor like he'd just been born.

'Mate,' said Dad, 'how could I forget? That was fucked. Still got the scar.' He was topless, skinny with muscles, and he turned, showing a pale white scar along his back that caught in the sunlight. 'What was your worst?'

'That one.' Scottie rubbed the thin white line that sliced his black eyebrow in half.

'Ere, Shorty,' said Steve, who had short grey hair and dull eyes. 'You wanted a pint.' He placed a half-pint glass on the beer-ringed wooden table, where Kai ran his finger over swirly tree lines.

Kai sipped. 'It's like fizzy apples.'

'No shit.'

'Go careful with that, son,' said Dad. 'I don't want to end up carrying you out like I do your mum.'

'Delicious,' said Kai. His glass was better because it was half the size and he was half the size of them.

Fifty-pence pieces lined the edge of the table. Scottie sat next to Kai and rolled another. The first smoke was forgotten behind his ear; tobacco bits landed in spilt lager.

'I've got this new machete,' said Scottie.

'What's a machete?' asked Kai.

'Watch your beak in front of him,' said Dad, scratching something on his arm. His trackies hung low, showing a Calvin Klein strip of boxers bought from the Sunday market. To Kai he said, 'A dinner knife. For prime steak.'

Across the room, the front door opened and Farmer Reid walked in with his Collie.

'Scottie's a collector,' said Dad, 'like you with those cards.'

Two boys played Pokémon at the next table. There was a chance they'd have a Charizard card. Exactly what he wanted. They were about his age; one was short, wearing a bright yellow cap.

Dad's shot. Three reds in.

'Take this,' said Denner to Kai. It was a pound. 'Get yourself some crisps.'

'Can I keep it for Pokémon cards?' Kai asked.

'No.' Dad shoved Kai's head. 'Go on.'

There were moments Dad made Kai go somewhere else so he could do man-talk; this was one of those times.

Cheese and onion. The bar lady was young, her black hair had curly bits and her painted lips were fat. She wore a nose ring like a pig and she was thin with a big bum in tight black jeans.

'What a cutie,' she shouted to Dad. 'He's got beautiful hair.'

'Takes after his dad,' he shouted back.

Kai passed the boys playing Pokémon. They had loads of cards. Kai plopped on the seat next to Steve, who looked down, flexing his biceps – they looked like the legs of lamb Nanny Sheila got at Christmas. The packet of crisps stank and sounded crunchy on the inside of his head. He could still taste fish and wasn't hungry.

Kai stood on the chair at the window to gaze outside. The sun beat down. People sat on pub benches and further on there was a small field next to Middle River, which whooshed out of the woods.

'Look, Dad,' said Kai, pointing at the splashes. 'The big kids are jumping in.'

'Wanna go in?' asked Scottie.

'Yeah.'

'Joker.' Dad started checking his back pockets. 'We'll go in if you want.'

Like the big kids diving and bombing. Swimming like a shark with the biggest fin. It would be better if Saffie was there.

'You got the stuff?' Dad asked. He picked up his Nike jacket and searched each pocket then cracked open his leather wallet. He looked inside a fag packet before he went around again, finding nothing. Back to his wallet and Kai spotted twenty-pound notes.

'Ere it is.' Scottie handed something to Dad. 'The last of it.'

'We'll river bomb after I've been for a piss,' said Dad.

'You're off your head,' said Denner.

'Nah, mate. It will be fun. Specially after this.' Dad winked before looking at Kai and raising his voice, 'And whatever my boy wants, he gets.' He headed to the loo.

Steve eyed his pint glass like he was doing a maths sum and Denner rubbed his head the way Mum did when she woke up after drinking too much.

'You hanging out your ass?' said Kai, and to his delight Denner, Steve and Scottie laughed.

'Who said that to you, sonny?' asked Denner.

'Mum gets it too,' he said. 'I can get you some water.'

Back at the bar, he asked for water and watched Dad strut back to the pool table. He heard Denner say his name and they all laughed and looked over. Dad's grin was so big he spotted the gap between his two front teeth. Kai glowed.

The kids playing Pokémon suddenly jumped up and ran through the back door that had a heavy black padlock – Kai desperately wanted a lock-picking kit for his birthday. He carried the glass of water for Denner and felt his heart speed up as he passed the table of cards. What would it feel like? He grabbed the nearest. Put it in his pocket under his red cape. Nanny Sheila said you shouldn't steal, but this was only practice. He'd put it back in a minute. When he reached Denner, the bar lady was nudging Dad's arm, saying, 'Your lad just took one of those kids' cards.'

Kai's tummy turned and he frowned at the woman as hard as Mum when she screamed at Dad like a howling wolf saying he was a useless junky-prick who had to clean up or clear off when he'd smoked the stinky stuff. That was ages ago.

'What you on about?' Dad said.

It was wrong to lie. Wrong. That's what Nanny Sheila said and she never told lies.

'I saw him.' The bar lady flicked her hair. 'He's cute, but he's naughty.' She pointed. 'Check his pocket.'

Dad smirked. 'Come here.' He grabbed his hand, lifted his cape and found the card. Pointing the card at Kai with each word he pretended to tell Kai off, 'You naughty little boy.'

Kai relaxed.

'You'll have to watch that one.' The lady took the card and collected the others, taking them to the bar.

'You rascal,' said Scottie.

CHAPTER 5

12 November 2005

I was avoiding Yasmin. At school we were in different year halves so we never shared lessons. At lunchtimes me and Jord would go for a smoke up the cycle path past the bike shed and most of that week I went to the den instead of class in the afternoon. It had pissed me off that Yasmin called me unreliable on Bonfire Night. Everyone knew I could be late. Unreliable didn't mean that. It was like she'd forgotten her quiet days, which used to happen a lot and always near Christmas and her birthday. Those days she'd text me saying she felt like she was floating or questioning her sanity, and when I went to her she'd be knelt next to the bed in the spare bedroom with her face pushed into the green blanket. Those days I'd lead her back to her room, make her a cup of tea, draw the curtains, put on Disney films and I'd lay behind her, holding her close as a parent does a child. Those days were king. Those days I really saw her.

Those days didn't often happen anymore; instead, she was moody, so I turned off my phone.

The weekend after Bonfire Night, I was tempted to go back to Cranston. But when I told Jord, he said, 'Mate, why?' And he was right, I could buy two bombs of mandy with the cost of three tickets, so me and the lads cycled to the posh stone house I'd found outside Vells. The sky was grim, but it wasn't cold. The house was four windows wide and each window had three or four panes. There was a chimney either end of the roof. Hedges surrounded it and on the gate there was a sign saying 'No Trespassing'. I liked the sign. It was like there was someone watching and I've always kind of felt like there was someone watching so it didn't bother me.

We scouted around the perimeter to check no one was in. No movement, no cars nearby, no lights shone. It had been abandoned for ages, but a while back someone started doing it up. Until a year ago. Since then, every time I cycled past it looked empty again. I stopped in front of the five-bar gate opposite the main door. The yard was massive, with an open barn on one side and overgrown grass leading down the other side of the house. Jord and Richie hopped over – Lynx Africa caught my nose in the breeze – their trainers crunching on gravel. The house looked miserable. One of the upstairs windows was smashed. The lads ran towards the barn and I jumped over and ran to catch up. There were holes in the roof of the barn and cosy spots behind the beams for birds. Rats would be stalking nearby.

Richie shot off across the yard. 'Let's go round the back.'

'No,' I shouted. 'The front door.' It would be lush to enter a place that big like I owned it. I imagined an entrance hall the same size as my house and wanted to peacock the fuck out of walking upstairs with a pumped-out chest. There was something special about the idea of walking through the front door of a place like that with your best mates. Excitement like winning Grand Theft Auto. I wanted to see what type of lock it was. There were two, a mortice deadlock and a night latch.

Richie turned the handle. Nothing. 'Round the back, then,' he said.

There was a short stone wall running along the front of the garden with three steps to walk up on to the lawn. Autumn had stripped the bushes and trees but I knew there'd be roses, and apples dropping to the ground in summer.

There was a rickety shed by the hedge halfway down the lawn. It made me think of Denner. That piece of shit.

'Come on,' I said, shoving through the shed door. It was full of debris and smelled the same as the wardrobe in Nan's small bedroom, which she wouldn't let us rummage through: like a million mothballs. 'Let's make a bonfire.'

I'd loved bonfires since Dad used to make them when we were kids. If I closed my eyes and tuned into the smoke and crackle, he could almost be there. I wanted Mum to want him back; I wanted him to come home. In his last letter, he promised he was doing squats, pull-ups and press-ups every day, taking care of himself, 'sorting his shit out', so that I'd go see him. So much was unsaid. It screwed with my head.

As if I could tell anyone that.

Jord picked up the leg of a chair. 'With this shit?'

Richie found a spoon and threw it over his shoulder. He was a short lad with a ratty face.

'Let's burn the whole thing,' I said.

'Walls and all?' Jord lifted both his eyebrows when he spoke. He wasn't surprised, just checking. His coat used to be his dad's; it was a size too big so the cuffs covered his fingers but they poked out like hermit crab legs when he started piling up stuff to set light to.

We left the shed once the fire caught and found a single-glazed back window to smash into the house with a stone from the little wall. We hopped over the windowsill. The kitchen was fancy as fuck. It had one of those cabinets that stand in the middle of the room with a sink in the middle and bar stools around. Above it hung a spatula, a hand whisk and a couple of big spoons. There was a cup on the side and a teabag dry as a crisp by the sink, like someone had meant to come back the same day, but that obviously hadn't happened. Mum would kill for a kitchen like that. The cooker was massive; it had a cream front with five little doors and silver plate things on top. The wall behind was stone but the rest of the kitchen was cream apart from the wooden beams. There was a table in front of sliding doors and even a sofa and TV. In the kitchen. Like it was a living room *and* a kitchen. Kind of like ours, but really not.

'Maaaate,' I said, tapping a potato masher above the sink as we passed, heading towards a door. 'Leah would love that.'

We entered the dining room. The walls had been plastered and pots of paint sat in a corner. A long table ran through the middle of the room – covered in clear plastic sheet to protect it; it was speckled in plaster. I would have turned it into a games room. Who needed another table? We found a newly wallpapered room overlooking a drained pond with a bookshelf and cardboard boxes filled with books. We thudded upstairs. In every other room, apart from the biggest bedroom, paint and wallpaper crumbled off the walls like peeling scabs. The rooms that needed decorating smelled mouldy. Richie pulled out his phone. The only sounds were our feet on the floorboards and Richie clicking photos. How quiet it was felt funny. I left the other two looking at marble sinks in a bathroom and returned to the bedrooms. In one of them there was a fireplace with a rocking horse in front of it. On a dressing table in the biggest bedroom I found a photo of a couple and a little girl; they squinted towards the sun. I picked up the photo. Someone had said something funny because they all looked as though they had just started laughing. This bedroom was nicely decorated. The bed was made and the duvet was folded back like someone had slept in it. A pair of black socks lay on the floor next to the bed. There was a glass with a bit of water in. I moved to the tall window to watch the shed burn. The gravel below the window looked damp. I opened the window. The fresh air touched me.

I wanted to jump.

'Oi!' Jord's voice sounded jumpy and he rushed in. He hooted when he saw the fire.

Then came Richie. We sat on the wide sill and the smoke filled our noses.

'I love the orange of fire,' Richie mumbled. 'What's your favourite colour?'

A landslide feeling filled my head. 'Orange too,' I said, 'like Nan's marigolds in spring.'

'I thought you'd say black,' said Jord, 'or grey.'

'That's depressing,' I said.

'Exactly,' snorted Richie, 'you sad bastard.'

Jord looked at me and nodded silently, asking if I was OK. I nodded yes before dropping my eyes to the stone we were sat on; the ledge outside was covered in bird shit, then there was a crash. The shed had caved in.

At the same time we heard sirens. Jord and Richie wanted to go to Jonesies and blag someone to get fags and I wanted to be on my own, so I went to the woods and thought about Saffie.

CHAPTER 6

THEN

Kai and Saffie ruled the silver moon. Their moon was in the secret garden at school, behind the two big buildings with the numbers **1 8 7 6** cut into the bricks above the tall doors and next to the small playground where everyone played bulldog. Crystal hung out round the front of the school buildings, where lanes were chalked on the grass, by the side of Middle River, which swished and plopped past on the other side of the wire fence that Kai could poke his fingers through. Sometimes he and Saffie spent lunch in the lanes when he felt like practising his running. With the fastest running feet Adam and Harry were always beat. Only Crystal he couldn't win, and that was OK because she was his sister. Mum said Kai should feel proud, and he did, but mainly because he knew he'd be faster than Crystal when he was older, because men were faster and stronger than girls.

Jade spent breaks and playtimes watering the plants in the beds at the side of the school buildings because she was on the 'Grow our Future' team. She made Kai touch the different leaves. Some were hard and scratchy and she'd say 'Rosemary' or 'Thyme' and some were soft and she'd say 'Sage'. They all smelled lush, sage like roast chicken. There were potatoes, onions and tall runner beans, and the beans felt rough and furry at the same time. Kai and Saffie's favourite plants were the sweet peas because they smelled like if sunshine had a smell. But usually Kai and Saffie hung out in the secret garden jumping stepping stones that led through the bushes, plants and flowers.

'That one's called a fern,' said Saffie, pointing with her asthma inhaler.

'There's lots,' said Kai, kneeling down among buttercups, crumpling his shorts, adding to the grass and mud stains. He ran a hand over a leaf. It felt almost wet and reminded him of Nanny Sheila's hair when she washed it on a Friday morning. Nanny Sheila wasn't actually Kai's real nan, she was only Leah's nan but the time Jade said that, Nanny Sheila's voice boomed loud saying she was grandmother to all of them and not to talk about it again because family was more than biology. Leah said biology was part of science. The same bit that taught about lungs, the heart and intestines. Kai didn't know what intestines were. It sounded like being inside a test, like a prison, the scariest place in England.

The secret garden was quiet. Adam and Harry sprinted past and then it was just Kai and Saffie in the fluttery shadows. Sun shone in slivers over leaves and bounced over their faces. Birds chirped. A motorbike growled past behind the conker and helicopter trees, then quiet again. The big trees were the greatest, so green in summer and full of gifts in autumn. Saffie liked the acorn tree outside the secret garden near the sandpit because she pulled the acorns apart and made finger hats with magic in them. Mum said they had the best playground she'd ever seen and that if Kai and the girls had grown up in town, then all they'd have would be a slab of concrete and a shitty hopscotch grid. Hopscotch was pooh.

'What animals need saving today?' asked Saffie. There was a tiny beauty spot under her eye that looked like an eyelash and her hair was macky red curls to her shoulders. It bounced when she ran, like Kai's did if his braids were out, which was never at school because Mum was scared he'd catch nits even though he didn't mind headlice because they made good pets and he really wanted a pet. More than anything. If he could have any pet, Kai would take Flopsy.

'The baby elephants,' said Kai. 'The big elephants were killed by the disease in the waterhole, remember? Because they couldn't stop drinking it, only the baby elephants could smell the danger.'

'Oh yeah, and the lady lions were coming to kill the elephants. Come on!' Saffie pulled Kai's hand, running further into the secret garden, past skinny silver birches to the pond where some days the frogs became dragons and the butterflies, eagles. Today they imagined elephants winning over lions. The real world fell away.

'I smell giant.' Code for teacher. They snuck behind the conker tree, where they bent their heads together and he smelled cherry shampoo like the colour of her hair. So similar to his, everyone said, which was why they were meant to be best friends because Kai looked more like

Saffie than her own twin, who was blonde. Saffie's twin always played by the sticky plants near the lanes. She liked tiaras and sparkly shoes. She was boring.

'Who was it?' Saffie asked.

'Hippie Mandy.'

That's what Mum called her. She lived up the road on Tyne Avenue and owned a van with a bed and miniature curtains that was parked outside her redbrick house. Saffie's shoulders hunched up and she threw a hand over her pale lips to keep laughter in because Hippie Mandy was the dinner lady and classroom assistant who, if she was having a moody day, was stricter than Miss Butterworth.

'There you both are,' said Hippie Mandy.

'Nooo,' Kai and Saffie whispered then shouted, 'Jinx.'

The long, layered skirt Hippie Mandy wore was pink and purple and orange, like a rainbow, and there were tiny tinkling bells along the bottom. Jangly bangles ran up each of her arms and her eyes had black lines all round like an Egyptian princess, except she looked more like a peanut with long black hair and black eyes.

'You two.'

'We know!' Kai jumped up, offering his hand to Saffie, who, once stood, played air violin – violin's what Hippie Mandy played – and Saffie squealed what Hippie Mandy always said, 'As perfect as a double stop.'

'Or night and day.' Hippie Mandy grinned and waved for them to follow her.

'I'll be the moon,' said Saffie, spraying her inhaler.

'You mustn't steal that from the teacher's table,' said Hippie Mandy, taking back the inhaler. Her skirt swished as they hopped stepping stones and swerved over ants.

Saffie carried on, 'Because it's made from silver water. And you be the sun because it's made of fire.'

When he thought of the moon, it was like Saffie, bright and shiny and a bit blue like her eyes. Kai's eyes were brown. It was their main difference.

'Dad called me fire,' said Kai, remembering a day he had a fight with Crystal. She was eight, but acted like she knew everything.

Out of the secret garden, the day was bright. Noise of the playground hit where kids screamed tag.

'The rest of Year One are having a monkey bar race,' said Hippie Mandy. They reached the back of the school building near the rabbit hutch; he peered in and smelled hay. No Flopsy. Must be at the bottom of the lanes by the sticky bushes where the Year Sixes took her. When he was in Year Six, he'd make sure he was in charge of Flopsy all the time.

'No one can beat us,' said Kai. 'Me and Saffie are the best in the school at monkey bars.'

'That's what I thought you two monkeys would say.'

'Kai!' Jade stood up from inspecting a little bush. Blue and purple paint covered her hands. She wanted to be an artist when she grew up. Around the top bunk at home her bright brushstrokes covered A4 paper on the wall. Crystal taped posters of boy bands to her wall and Leah's wall was naked apart from a page she'd ripped out of a poetry book, a poem called 'Chocolate Cake'. Now Leah was at senior school, the playground felt a bit empty because she had checked on Kai every playtime. Not that he needed it; she was just brilliant at being in charge. A teacher, that's what she wanted to be.

What would he be?

Someone who can get his hands on anything, like Dad.

'Come look at the tomatoes,' said Jade. Behind the rabbit hutch through the window Class Four grew green stems with red bulbs in black pots. Colours of Christmas, warmth of a greenhouse and the taste of pooh. Look at tomatoes? Not what he wanted to do. It was race time. Big sis gave him and his partner in crime a handful each of lemon balm for luck because Hippie Mandy said it was good for calming people, especially children. The lemony stink bashed their noses, yummy. They shoved the leaves into their blue and yellow socks – they'd swapped a sock that morning. It was the only item of clothes that didn't matter if you were boy or girl.

At the monkey bars, Year One lined up and Miss Butterworth tested a timer, holding a whistle in her mouth. Saffie's twin's hair was long and gold. She wore a yellow dress and kicked at the grass in shiny red shoes at the end of the line. Kai called her Boring Twin. She hummed before telling them she'd been playing fairies by the sticky plants. Kai spotted Crystal, pink-cheeked, and her friends sprawled by the lanes with her hair pulled back in a high blonde ponytail. She must have just raced, her tummy looked panty. Her hair was like Boring Twin's, which Leah and Jade, the two eldest, were jealous of because they both wanted straight hair. Their hair was brown, curly, and Jade's was always in buns, or plaited, to stop knots.

Year One chatted. Kai's belly turned. He had to win, be the fastest boy, like the Olympic champions who lived in the TV.

'I hate racing,' said Boring Twin.

'Wimp,' said Saffie.

'That's because you're rubbish,' said Kai. 'Obbiously.'

There were two lines for the two sets of monkey bars. Miss Butterworth gave a spare timer to Hippie Mandy. Kai swapped with Boring Twin so he was racing Tom B and Saffie could race her sister to make it fair. Tom B was the second fastest at running in Year One. Kai had never raced anyone on the monkey bars except for Saffie; what if he lost? Tom B's arms were long and he was tall. If Tom B won, Saffie might like him more. He looked at his best friend, who was tensing her arm muscle at her sister.

'Tie your hair up,' said Kai to Saffie; he knew the rules to be the best.

'I'll win you easy,' said Tom B.

'I'm the fastest in school.' He stuck out his chin like Dad did during poker.

'Bet you're not.'

'Wait and see.'

A whistle. Jordan and Danny were off. Swinging like Mowgli. Kai was Tarzan. The line grew smaller. Jordan had the best time so far: six seconds. Saffie beat Boring Twin easy, she did eight seconds and after puffing on her inhaler cheered Kai who had to win. Big men won.

'Go on, bro!' Crystal shouted from the lanes, punching a fist in the air. The metal steps in front were red, like his cape, like his and Saffie's hair, and he knew what they felt like, solid, like the bars above that he was about to swing from. The trick was to keep moving.

'On your marks,' shouted Miss Butterworth, 'get set . . .'

The whistle screeched; they leapt forward.

Cheers pounded his ears, his palms burned and legs swung too far. Vibrations teased his fingers as Tom B pulled ahead.

'Come on, Kai.' Saffie was petrol for muscles. Faster, faster, but Tom B swung on to the steps first. A moment later, Kai followed, Tom B jumped from the top rung of the ladder to the floor and the whistle sounded. Kai had lost.

He didn't hear how many seconds. All he saw was Tom B's shiny face, his V-shaped arms, shouting he was the best at Adam and Harry. At Jordan. At him.

'No worries, bro.' Crystal made Kai jump when she patted his back. 'We all lose sometimes.' She winked. 'Unless you're me.'

Tom B's tongue stuck out at him. Saffie's bottom lip poked out. With tingling hands, Kai thought of Mike Tyson, how big men fight and win, and ran at Tom B using both hands to push him so hard he thumped down on to the grass.

'Hey!' shouted Crystal, grabbing his shoulders. They lost their footing and toppled over. 'It doesn't matter,' she kept saying, rubbing his shoulder. He shoved Crystal's stupid hand off. The look on Miss Butterworth's face said he was in trouble; he scowled hard when she sat down beside him. A moment later, Saffie joined them and suddenly he heard what Miss Butterworth was saying.

'Life isn't about winning. It's about appreciating what you've got. There are lots of things you're good at. Aren't there, Saffie?'

Her blue eyes were opened big and she nodded. 'You're the best person in Middledown, no I mean England, or the world. The best in the world. You're the sun. Remember?'

Saffie's eyes stared like she was scared because she was his best friend, just like Dad and Denner.

*

After lunch, Year One played dead lions while Miss Butterworth read *Peter Pan*. Above the dark grey carpet with the white stain by Adam's table because he'd been sick – no one was allowed to stand on it or they'd get rabies – the classroom smelled of cheese sandwiches, pencil sharpenings and PVA glue. Kai and Saffie lay like starfish by the open window, enjoying the warm blanket of the sun, its heat on their black school trousers. At his fingertips, Kai felt Saffie's so that they were just touching, buzzing like silver moon bees in the hot hot room where the air was thick and stiff and the fan whirred gently. Tick tick ticking clock and Miss Butterworth telling the story of the boy in green who flew to Neverland, near their moon. There were sea creatures on their moon. He and Saffie would dive from the plank and swim with crocodiles because all animals would be nice in their world.

'Kai,' Miss Butterworth said. 'Mr T would like to see you.'

With a jump, he sat up. The headmaster?

'Go now.'

When he reached the headmaster's office, the door was open and another fan turned its head side to side from the top of the locked grey filing cabinet next to the big white clock, tick-tock, tick-tock. A computer took up most of the desk, with a chair either side. Next to Kai, there was a plastic chair like the ones in class that made his bum itchy, except this one was grown-up size. Headmaster T's chair was comfy cushion, like the one next to the window – probably for parents or teachers – which looked over the field. He could see the monkey bars, the lanes and the sticky plants. If only he was a moon bee so he could fly through the gap in the window.

A plant like what grew in the Amazon jungle where anacondas came from filled a corner with big palm leaves. He'd seen a programme about giant snakes. Kai took a deep breath, pressed his head on the door frame. What if he got told off? What would Saffie say? She was good at talking to teachers because she had what Nanny Sheila called confidence.

On the desk there was lots of paper, pens, a paperweight globe full of snow, a watch, glasses, a water bottle, a fluffy unicorn, a little dragon, Pogs, Nik Naks – Sir must have confiscated them. Not fair. Probably wanted to tell him off now about the fight with Tom B. This room was boring, except . . . Kai's eyes crossed the table, resting on the little dragon. It was metal with a spiky head, its tail wrapped round a tower, and there was a sparkling white stone on its chest by its heart that reminded him of the moon. Dragon would sit in his hand, grow real wings, lift off and fly over the garden, over Middledown Woods, heading towards their silver moon. Tick-tock, tick-tock, said the clock. Summer blew through the cracked window. Kai rested his buzzing fingertips on the desk in front of Dragon, which was hidden behind the computer like Sir must have forgotten it.

'Hello, Kai.' Headmaster T came from behind holding a clipboard, running a finger down the paper before sitting in front of the computer, pulling his black tie, undoing it, throwing it on the desk. As always his shirt was creased. Kai crunched his hands in his pockets; Dragon watched him.

'So,' said Headmaster T, dropping his clipboard and running a hand through his shaggy hair; it looked like it needed a wash. He sipped from the bottle of water and pointed at the window like he was telling the field off. 'I watched the monkey bar race.'

When it was hot Kai's hair itched, so he dug a finger beneath a plait. Dragon coughed smoke. Best not to say anything, even Dragon thought so. Headmaster T had the same eyes all teachers had, the ones that stare. Maybe Kai would grow a beard one day, he hoped not. Dad didn't have one and he wanted to look like Dad, who would laugh if he found out Kai had pushed Tom B, who was a wimp.

On one hand, Headmaster T's nails were long, the other had short nails and this one he used to rub his chin, which sounded like sandpaper; he must have been thinking hard about what to say.

'I saw your fight,' he said. A red light on the phone flashed and his eyes darted to it before returning to Kai. Who had left an answerphone message? Maybe a policeman. Kai stared at the grass stains on his knees and felt his face heat, hotter and hotter. Sir's staring eyes watched. He only pushed Tom B. It wasn't even bad.

Sir took a breath, leaned forward and took hold of the paperweight, shaking it; the snow scattered over the tiny mountain inside. 'Do you have anything to say?'

Kai shrugged. In his head felt like Nanny Sheila's knitting wool, all tangled.

'What happened, then?' The Head leaned back in his chair and twisted his tongue behind his lips in a way that meant he had bacon stuck in his teeth.

What to say? So angry his fists rolled up, it was Tom's fault and Kai might get told off. Not fair.

Sir started talking between sips of water about something called resolution and how to settle things. It wasn't even a fight. A fight was like Mike Tyson and Frank Bruno. He'd only pushed. At home, if he pushed one of the girls, they pushed back. So what? Mum and Dad fought, too.

Sir stopped talking, Kai said nothing, Sir talked again. On the office wall there were two paintings, one a guitar and the other a surfboard on a beach with small wooden shacks. They were done in red and blue paint and both had a white star in the sky.

If Kai painted a star, it would be silver like Dragon's heart stone, like the moon.

'Kai?'

'Yeah.'

With lifted eyebrows, Headmaster T said, 'It's not right to settle things through fighting, is it?'

Kai pursed his lips together and stared at Dragon. Dragon stared back, wanting to be his pet.

If only Dad was there. He'd pretend to tell him off like with the bar lady. None of this would matter. Dad said when someone pissed you off, you had it out. Had it out meant fight.

Sir made Kai say no, he stared at Dragon as Sir made him say sorry, so he decided he'd take Dragon, who blew smoke rings to try to calm his angry fists.

A repeated question. There were sweat patches in Sir's armpits. Gross.

Kai agreed, 'No, Mr T.'

There was a sound at the door, Tom B, so Kai sat straight and felt so angry being made to say sorry. Nanny Sheila said it was wrong to lie.

'You can go now,' said Headmaster T, keeping Tom B back.

When he left the room his small knuckles tingled with how much he wanted to whack Tom B.

In the middle of school, where the ceiling reached the sky outside of all the classes and where kids played hand bells on Fridays, Kai kicked the leg of a chair. Out through the back door with the big stone step wide enough to sleep on, he jumped, lifting his knees to his chest before stamping his frustration on to the floor of the playground opposite Jade's plants next to the rabbit hutch. Deep breath in, Tom B wasn't made to say sorry.

There was the rabbit hutch, a brown wooden rectangle at the side of school. Whack. Hard. Smack. The sting of the punch on the roof of the hutch cracked his knuckles. So angry he could roar like a dinosaur, until, no, the rabbit hutch door was closed. Flopsy would be locked in during lesson time.

Kai bent in front of the hutch; he grabbed his forehead when he saw Flopsy shivering inside.

He felt sick. This was the worst thing in history, even worse than the wicked king who chopped off people's heads. The latch slipped easy. Hay felt warm and crunchy on his hands as he delved in to hold Flopsy.

'Sorry. I'm so sorry,' Kai whispered into the ginger bunny's ear. 'I promise never to scare you again.'

On the school step where spiders scurried, he felt the hardness of the stone on his bum and rested the rabbit on his lap. Deep breaths. The rabbit was loving and kind. Her wriggling nose was funny and really cute.

Kai had to get a pet rabbit. With his red cape, he could get anything – that's what Dad said. Dragon would be his by the end of the week.

That would show Headmaster T.

After school, the house was quiet; Mum had shot off to Aunt Shad's earlier in the day.

They must have been fighting. Obvious from the way the wet washing was left half in, half out of the machine. His fight with Tom B might have happened at the same time. Headmaster T said he was going to call her and explain what had happened. Relieved Mum was out because he wouldn't get told off, Kai spent a couple of hours watching the slow-worms behind the garden shed. Maybe when school rang home about him, that made Mum leave. He rubbed a hand over the edge of the rough shed, left the slow-worms and scuffed down the garden path to where strawberries were growing, small, hard and green. They'd been planted by whoever lived there before.

Dad appeared between the gap of their house and next door. 'All right, lad?'

Later, Leah cooked cheese on toast and beans, not so good as Mum's stew; when Dad gave her his crumby plate he said it was the best he'd eaten.

'You're just saying that in case Mum isn't back tomorrow so you don't have to cook.' She squeezed a cloth over the washing-up bowl. 'I'm not stupid.'

Everyone knew Leah wasn't stupid. Crystal and Jade watched TV on the settee across from Dad, who bent his foot to his mouth to bite his toenails. For twenty-seven he was well bendy and could jump the garden fence that came up to Kai's shoulders without using his hands. Men had to be athletic if they did Dad's job, like Kai would. Dragon, once he got him, was going to live in his bedroom window to look out for burglars.

The living-room curtains flapped around the open windows and the sun shone whiteness through the room. *Fresh Prince of Bel-Air* started; Crystal and Jade rapped along, racing to see who knew the most words.

Last time Mum left, at Christmas, she'd screamed that Dad was a wasteman who wanted to try looking after five kids because he might as well have been one too, which was funny. Imagine Dad at school.

'There any pudding?' Dad winked at Kai, who pulled apart the Velcro on his red cape and re-stuck it so the black squares were perfect on top of each other, waiting for his sister's response. She closed her eyes hard for a second.

'Dunno, Jesse. Why don't you make something?'

Dad spoke around a toenail. 'Mardy pants.'

'You gonna tell Jesse what happened at school?' said Crystal. Such a dobber. If he could he'd kick her into Middle River for that because she was rubbish at swimming.

'Shut up,' Kai snapped. He stood up from the chair at the table with an empty plastic cup that Leah grabbed. It wasn't fair. He wouldn't have blabbed about Crystal.

'Oh ah,' said Dad. 'What was that?'

Kai climbed over the side of the chair, pushing open the door that led to the hallway by the back door, stamping over old daps, pulling on his trainers.

'Go on,' said Crystal, 'tell him.'

'Shut your fart mouth,' said Kai, opening the back door to run away. 'Just because you watch the boys on the lanes because you fancy them. No one even fancies you. You're alien head.'

Crystal lunged across the room, shoving him so he fell into the back door.

Kai threw Mum's brown sandal as he stood. He went to push her, but being bigger, Crystal pushed the top of his head down and he screamed as loud as he could, rolling his arms like aeroplane propellers.

Then Dad picked him up. 'Oi,' in his not-having-it voice, 'that's enough.'

He took Kai down the bottom of the garden under the apple tree in front of the blue flower bush. Leah followed. They sat on the grass.

'School rang,' Dad said. 'I know what happened.'

The grass felt cold. Kai drew his knees to his chest and rested his mouth on them, silent as a mouse. Why hadn't he said? Leah ran a hand through the grass like it was cat fur and Dad lay back, crossing one foot over the other and pulling a roll-up from behind his ear, click-click-clicking his Clipper lighter, the one with the spider on.

'I don't care about you having a scrap, son. I just care that you got caught. If you wanna fight, you gotta be clever,' Dad tapped his head, 'like Mike Tyson. You know that.' Then he used his fag-less hand to rub the small of Kai's back.

'It isn't right to fight, though,' said Leah, leaning to reach a black spotted apple and throwing it bouncing down the path. 'It's better to talk.'

What should he say? There were always two ways and what Dad said was always opposite to everyone else. Nanny Sheila would know; she was the oldest person Kai knew and told the truth because she went to church.

Drilling started somewhere out front, ruining the bird songs. Probably Bob-Cycle, who made and sold bikes and cars. Oh, how he wanted a bike; hopefully he'd get one on his birthday and a lock-picking kit. And a hammer, to make a den.

'So what happened?' his sister asked.

There was a wooden fence between his house and Jordan's and a tall green bush. Kaos's paws were tapping around next door. It was Tom B's face and the sound of Saffie's voice shouting his name during the race that made him do it. Saffie could have Dragon. Maybe. Dad's hand still gently stroked, up down up down; there was nothing to say because Dad wasn't angry. A shrill ring sounded from Dad's pocket and when he pulled his new Nokia out, the letters **b a b e** flashed.

When Dad answered, he said, 'Where's my baby gone? I'm sorry. I'll be better. Just come back. Baby, come on. I love you. You're the most important—'

Then he jumped to his feet and strolled towards the house, where he'd go upstairs and beg Mum to come back for the next hour because he loved her like a clown was a fool. That's what he always said.

'Will Mum come home?' Kai asked.

'Course,' said Leah. 'She always does.'

Against the tree trunk, Leah rested, putting an arm around him. Leah and Jade were his favourite sisters. Since Jade turned ten she'd been much more grown up; Leah was teaching her how to cook. Crystal was a pig show-off.

'Wanna know a secret?' Leah asked. Through the trees they could hear chickens clucking real crazy from the posh houses up behind their estate, and Kai wondered if a fox had found them, except foxes slept during the day.

'Yeah,' said Kai.

'Promise you won't tell anyone?'

'I'll tell you one back.'

'OK.' She picked at a splat of baked-bean juice on her jeans. 'I like it when Mum isn't here.'

It felt strange hearing her say that. He felt Mum missing like a macky hole; there was too much quiet because the washing machine stopped churning and the smell of brown chicken and plantain disappeared on Sundays.

'What's your secret?' Leah asked.

''Member when everyone said I had an imaginary friend and I said I didn't because the others laughed at me?'

'Yeah.'

'I did really.' It was a secret because everyone asked questions and Mum looked scared when Kai talked to his magic friend.

'What did he look like?'

'A rabbit made of silver, like the moon.'

Leah took a breath like she was going to say something, then stopped and lifted her eyes up at the house and he copied. The yellow paint looked dark round the windows. Sharon, Jordan's mum next door, kept ringing the council asking for a new coat of paint. Upstairs, Dad appeared in

Kai's bedroom window, still on the phone, watching them and resting a hand on the bedroom wall, frowning, grinning so it showed the gap in his teeth, frowning, resting a hand on his forehead, nodding like he was saying yes then no. Sorry. Kai saw Dad's mouth say sorry again and, I love you.

'Do you miss your dad?' asked Kai. Even though Leah was three when he died, there was a picture of him under her pillow. It was blotchy, like too much sun had faded it, and it was torn through the middle like one person was ripped away.

'Yeah, course.' She cleared her throat. 'And I don't miss Mum when she leaves.'

When men wanted big muscles they lifted heavy weights like Dad had in the shed; it felt like one had fallen on Kai's chest.

'I don't trust Mum,' said Leah.

'What's trust?'

'Like you can't trust someone if they tell lies.'

A funniness swamped his body. Mums were the best people, that's why they looked after children. 'Mum doesn't tell lies.'

'After my dad died, she pretended she loved him, but the day he drove off on his bike, she told him she never wanted to see him again. I remember it. I was little, but I remember. I'll never forget it.'

Kai folded his hands together like he did during assembly because he could feel her sadness and her anger like two cold bubbles and he didn't know what to say to pop them. A spider dangled from a branch and he followed its silk to its cobweb stretched between two branches. Spider spun lower and floated above his hand; he reached out and it raced over his skin.

He said, 'Mum tells Dad she never wants to see him again.'

'Let's hope it doesn't kill him.'

Sometimes Leah's words were like the sword Dad had taken to Scottie's. Kai shivered. Everything felt wrong, as though the sun had turned to a brown smudge, and he wished he could make his big sister feel better, but wished she wouldn't say horrible things and he wanted to explain this, but didn't know how and she might get angry because what she said was a secret nobody knew.

'Are you going to run away?'

'Ha!' she yelped. 'I have to stay here to make sure you're OK.'

He stood up and started shaking tree branches. Leah quickly lifted her hands to cover her head; one, two, three apples fell. He grabbed one, dropped it at the same time as swinging his foot and kicked it as hard as he could over the hedges towards the clucking chickens. They squawked louder and wings flapped as he spread out the edges of his red cape and whizzed off to the front garden.

That night Kai slept in with Dad on the musty-smelling pillows that told him of Mum and Dad's hair, and he wondered if they got sleep bogeys in their eyes that might stick in his curls.

'You're perfect,' Dad said. 'The best thing me and your mum ever did, you know that?' His breath smelled of Special Brew and he was talking like he had a million things to say, but halfway through he forgot what they were and started again.

The windows were open, no breeze cooled the heat. Inside Dad's treasure chest by the bed, its little shelf had been lifted out. Before they'd flicked off the lights Kai saw the little plastic bags of talcum powder; when he thought Kai wasn't watching, Dad put some in his mouth. It made him talk loads. The house got messy whenever Mum left; clothes and the duvets were kicked off the bed. Naked apart from boxers, they faced each other and Dad covered one of Kai's hands with his own.

'The day I met your mum she was the most beautiful piece I'd ever seen. You know that? Like when you see something really special, like, like, when you see the best thing and you know it's worth everything—'

'Like a dragon?' asked Kai.

'Exactly.' Dad squeezed his hand. 'You understand. She had this perfect stroppy face and round ass, and when she spoke to me like she could tear me apart I knew I loved her, and you know what she said?'

Kai knew because he heard the story every time Mum left and he slept on her side of the bed. He kept quiet, staring at the different shadows in the room, the TV, the wardrobe, the chest of the drawers, because Dad liked to tell the story. Thinking of her made Dad fall asleep when she wasn't there.

'She said, "You couldn't handle me freckles." Maybe she's right. Our dad used to say that every woman is beautiful if you polish her the right way and a man's job is to make her shine. That's what I've been forgetting to do and that's why she's gone.'

'Mum will be home.' Kai remembered what Leah said. 'She always comes back.'

'It doesn't matter what her baggage is, you know, son? I love your sisters like they're my own, you know that. When you meet the woman for you, you got to love her right. Give her what she wants and look after her, you know? Keep her safe.'

Whenever Dad felt sad because of Mum and talked like this, Kai never knew the best thing to say. All he knew was that they would be together for ever because they loved each other like the taste of lemonade at the football field on a sunny day. He had to make Dad think of something else.

'Can I have a bedtime story?'

Dad groaned. 'But I'm crap at them, lad.'

'No, you're the best, apart from Nanny Sheila. She's really good.'

'Course she is,' Dad huffed. 'OK.' He rolled on to his back and put a hand on Kai's knee.

'Back in the day, in old times, there was a grey tower where the pagans hid the sexiest woman in their tribe. Her name was Sue. They asked the king of the fire-breathing dragons to guard her so no man could take her, um, flower.'

'Flower?'

'Yeah, she had a beautiful red flower. Any man that saw it felt drunk and wanted to touch it, but the pagans weren't having it. Only the strongest man in the world could win her and her flower; he'd have to fight the fire-breathing dragon and the female's father, who was a big muscly cunt with freckles like you.' Dad pinched Kai's nose. 'He had so many freckles he even farted them.'

'No, he didn't.' Kai felt a tickle in his tummy.

'Son, I'm telling you, he did. So the freckly-bum dad –'

Kai burst out laughing and Dad's voice went up and down like he was blowing up a balloon.

'– well, he had a massive sword. One like we gave Scottie, except this one had a blue diamond on the handle. It was from the ancient pagans. Our kind, son, the Celts.' Dad fluffed Kai's hair. Dad's grandparents had been Scottish. 'They called the blue stone the eye of the sky and reckoned it kept away the storms and brought luck from the gods.'

'What gods?'

'Don't worry about what gods, you're your own god. So, they didn't think anyone would be able to beat freckle-bum –'

Kai tucked his feet to his chest when he started laughing again.

'– but they were wrong. One day, when the sun reached its highest point in the sky and all the pagans were pissed and dancing round a pole, they saw a big black horse carrying the biggest man they'd ever seen. From Africa he was and as black as your Mum's dad was, except this man's feet were like chicken feet, scarred from a fire because he'd fought dragons before. Course, the pagans were shit scared and ran round, spilling pints and hunting for their swords. Sue looked out the tower and saw the man on the big black horse and she felt a funny feeling down, um—'

'Down where?'

'In her flower. The flower shivered in a way that made her stomach kick and she knew the man was going to kill the dragon, her dad, and take the eye of the sky sword before throwing her on to the back of his horse.'

'Was she sad?'

'About what?'

'The man killing everyone.'

'Nah, she was chuffed to buggery. It was boring in the tower because her mobile phone ran out of battery.'

'What happened next?'

'Well, the man on the black horse got her and they ran off with the eye of the sky sword and lived in a castle made of gold.'

A castle made of gold, it would have towers at the four corners and a bridge he would pull up to stop any baddies getting in and there would be macky trees all around the castle and a gushing river. Each morning he and Saffie would eat bacon sandwiches and, yeah, his sisters would live there too so then they could do all the cooking and washing, and on the walls would be all of Jade's drawings.

'Sherry,' Dad croaked into the pillow, and Kai moved closer so they breathed on each other as they closed their eyes. Dad's breathing deepened and Kai thought of Saffie and Dragon at school because dragons protected princesses and even though Saffie hated tiaras and dresses she was the best girl in the world and didn't have a dad or brother to look after her and so it must be up to him to look after her like how Dad said. He'd take her away, to the best places in the world.

'Mum's right, you know?' Dad started. 'She's wanted a new kitchen since we met, that's all she's ever asked me for, and I haven't done it. Well, this time I'm gonna do it. You gonna help me, son? We'll fit her a brand spanking shiny new kitchen. She wants black worktops with gold handles on the drawers. Haven't done carpentry since our dad was alive, but it won't be hard, we'll do it together, ey, boy?'

'What's carpentry?' asked Kai.

'Using wood to make things.'

'From trees?'

'Yeah.'

Trees were the best thing in Middledown Woods and Kai wanted to learn how to make dens more than anything. 'I'll help. Can we build a den, too?'

Sleep caught Dad's voice and he answered slowly, 'Whatever you want, my boy.'

CHAPTER 7

12 November 2005

The night we set the shed on fire with the spider Clipper lighter it was too cold in the den and the landslide feeling filled my body to a point where I ended up pushing my bike (it was too dark to ride in the woods) to the Grey Tower and staring up at the boarded window. I couldn't see much so I gave up and went to Yasmin's. Because I'd avoided her most of the week, she was acting needy.

She threw her arms around me. 'Where have you been?'

'Las Vegas,' I said.

'Funny,' she said. The kitchen was smart, her mum was house-proud and everything was always polished. The walls were white. There was a red clock, canvases with red hearts on the wall, red table mats, red mugs; on a corner shelf there was a green and yellow picture of the zodiac sign Gemini. I sat at the table with my forehead resting on my hand. Yasmin plonked a cup of tea in front of me and I grabbed it so tight my hand started to burn. Her mum had quickly gone upstairs when I walked in. The bath taps were running.

I felt like I wanted my mum. Maybe I'd feel better if I hung out with her for a bit watching trash TV. Don't even know why, but there was this feeling of guilt and dread that had swamped the sky in my head and it wouldn't clear.

'I've been so worried. You disappear off the face of Middledown and I can't get hold of you because your phone's off.' Yasmin was stood next to me and placed fingers into my Afro – I couldn't be assed to have it braided – she called it her finger trap. I realised I couldn't remember when I last washed my hair. I pulled my head away.

'How could you do that to me?' she said. The chair next to me scraped when she pulled it out, then her hands were on mine. Her nails had sparkling chipped pink nail varnish on. It looked tacky. 'All I think about is you. I couldn't even sleep.'

As if. She slept like a hibernating hedgehog. This wasn't the first time we'd had the conversation and I felt like we both had lines to say, impossible when you hated bullshit.

'Look at me,' she said.

Yasmin. My girlfriend. Blonde hair cut short, face prettiest from the side. Always loved her nose the most. There was a look on her face like a thousand wasps buzzing. So desperate. The urge to laugh was massive.

'You knew I was OK,' I said. Course she did, I knew she'd spoken to Crystal who called me a cowardly cunt through my bedroom door in the week when I ignored her questions about why I wasn't talking to her. Yasmin even had the cheek to invite herself round Nan's. Actually, Nan was pretty good at pretending I wasn't there. I hid upstairs and listened to her honestly say, 'I saw him *yesterday*. You checked his mum's?'

'I do so much for you,' Yasmin said. Like I gave a shit about English homework and Marmite on toast. 'You should have texted. Do you even care about me? Have I done something?'

I sipped my tea. It needed more sugar.

'Where were you Bonfire Night?' She nudged my shoulder. 'Kai! Answer me. What's wrong with you? You don't talk any more.'

'Fuck!' I stood up.

She jumped back, surprised.

'I can't fucking deal with this.' I pulled my coat off the chair and she grabbed it too. I let go. Fuck the coat, she could have it.

'No, please,' she said, standing, eyes shiny with tears. 'Please, don't go. Have I done something wrong? Kai, I love you.'

I felt my head spin. Deep breath in like a pufferfish.

'How could you love an unreliable prick?' I asked. I pointed towards the side of the house where I'd stood. 'I was here Bonfire Night.'

Well, that started the fucking waterworks and I felt really bad because it hurt to see a girl cry. I told her, 'Fuck this, I don't want it,' and she begged and cried and begged, saying she was sorry, asking how she could make it up to me. She wiped her eyes and told me to go upstairs if I needed some time so I did and I slipped into the spare bedroom and picked up an ornament that was on the bedside table. A seahorse.

I felt so lonely. Being around my friends and family wasn't helping, though. In the dark, the colours of the seahorse were hidden. I must have been stood there a long time and didn't realise Yasmin was behind me; she cleared her throat and when I turned to her, she looked blurry.

I woke early. Heart chattering like teeth on a cold day. The same dream and I still couldn't see it. I was hot, sweaty, had fallen asleep in my clothes after a smoke. Yasmin snored. Through the curtains that I made her keep open the sky was navy blue. The morning world was one of the beautiful things. I pulled on my Reebok Classics silently, got my bag and slipped out, then I pushed my bike to Nan's and checked on Rabbit. She hardly moved. Could have been cold, could have been old, could have been closer to dying. I coughed. I felt choked. The hay was crunchy and smelled good when I rearranged her bed, and I took off one of my T-shirts so she would be extra warm, checked her food and water – Nan never let her down – and then I headed off for a walk through the football field, along the cycle path, back past the Grey Tower – I looked the opposite way – into the woods, down to the bridge above Middle River, where the paths split to the three villages, the water gushed on and on – it was the best place on earth. The birds started singing. Towards Jonesies for a ham and mustard sandwich, strawberry laces and a bottle of Sprite. I must have taken a few hours. By the time I walked along Brewer's Lane near Jonesies I could hear a few cars out in the village. A rich couple in tweed caps opened the iron gate of a massive house, a white and brown English Pointer followed. I imagined it was their only thing to do each morning. The sun was up. Their life looked bright.

Where Brewer's Lane met the road there was a tiny little sign stuck in the ground that always reminded me of Yasmin. It said, 'Hedgehogs crossing! Four hedgehogs killed here!' Someone had drawn a spiky ball and a pointy noise. I wondered if I stood next to the sign how long it would take to be killed there.

Fuck a ham sandwich, I wanted chicken.

CHAPTER 8

THEN

When Kai got home from school Dad was heading out. They got caught up in the hallway tiptoeing around shoes. A black PE dap caught under Kai's foot and his arms shot out to balance. Dad steadied him.

'Don't touch those,' he said, pointing at the table. There were brown crumbs by his mouth. 'Just going to Kev's. I won't be long.'

All the windows were open and the sweet smell of baking made Kai's mouth water as he chucked his school bag on the settee and pulled off his T-shirt, tossing it on top of his bag. So hot. So hot he couldn't finish his sandwiches at lunch and he was well hungry now. Leah must have gone to Nanny Sheila's, which she often did after school, and Jade and Crystal had stopped at the Post Office for bubble gum. He missed Mum, she should be there dishing up spicy mincemeat with gravy and rice and cornmeal dumplings.

Cooling on the kitchen table were chocolate cookies – the ones Dad said not to touch – and it felt weird because Dad never cooked. The washing-up bowl was filled with chocolaty bowls and spoons. Finger across the side of the bowl, Kai took a lump of sticky goo – licked, then frowned, remembering Dad had crumbs round his mouth, so why couldn't he have any? He picked up a cookie, bit, so chocolaty and strange, but one more bite. Not tasty. Lines crinkled Kai's nose as he put the cookie down, too gross for a third bite.

Back outside his Power Rangers trainers scuffed up the garden path; the shed window was broken from when he threw an apple at it. The apple tree was the best bit of the garden. It was next to the swing. In his pocket was an elastic band he'd taken from Miss Butterworth's desk that day – she had a whole macky ball of them. He crossed his legs under the shade of the tree and flicked the band, seeing how far it would fly; down past the swing, he ran to grab it and flicked it again, trying to beat the last go. Where the band stretched it looked whiter and if he pulled it hard enough it went past the swing almost to the back doorstep near the drain.

Kaos barked inside the house next door; Dad was probably wrestling a rope away from him. Jordan's dog had a tight jaw and muscly back legs because he was a Bull Lurcher. Not the sort of animal Kai liked, not because he was a dog, but because he always seemed angry and like he might bite your hand off, plus it was annoying when he barked through the night because Jordan's mum made him sleep in the kennel outside.

Deep breath in. So so hot. After a while, Kai's head felt a bit mixy. He lay down and enjoyed the warm sun on his chest. A bee buzzed over. On his and Saffie's silver moon, moon bees talked and the sea dripped watery metal from your skin when you splashed in it.

A little bird landed on a branch above Kai. The birds' voices were really sharp, pronouncing their Ts and yes-sir-thank-you-pleases, and the sky looked as blue as the eye of the sky diamond in the sword from the story Dad told him.

'Oi,' said Crystal's voice. Little bird flapped away, then Crystal's head blocked out the sky and the branches, she was a dark shadow chewing – she said snapping gum was satisfying. 'What's wrong with your face?'

'I feel all mixy.' Kai rubbed his hands to make a grass angel. It felt like marshmallows.

'What you on about?' She grabbed his hand, lifted it, and he felt it thud against the ground like a rabbit's thudding leg.

'The world is sparkly.'

'You're being weird,' she said, sitting next to him, and then he felt sprinkles on his face and Crystal was saying, 'You look even more like a girl with daisies in your hair.'

Crystal the crocodile. Gnash gnash gnashing teeth. Kai opened his mouth wide to tell her, but forgot his words, then he remembered his elastic band to flick in her face. He dipped his hand in a pocket, it was gone. Maybe swallowed by the drain.

Blink, blink, blink. Something in his tummy felt funny. Maybe he'd swallowed a moon bee. He heard his mouth say 'HA', really loud, because a moon bee was silver like Silver, his old imaginary friend the rabbit. Imagine having Silver's twitchy nose and thud thud thudding feet.

'Something's wrong with you,' Crystal said. 'Why you tapping your foot?' Then she shouted, 'Jesse!'

Dad's voice came from over the fence a moment later. 'What?'

'Something's wrong with Kai.' Crocodile-Crystal's hands shook his shoulders.

Jordan's voice came over the fence. 'What's happened?' And then Kaos barked. Crocodile-Crystal held Kai's hand and that's when the world stopped making sense because she was being cuddly and usually he annoyed her.

'Kai.' Dad pulled him up and darted his eyes side to side and Kai flopped against him. 'Get the kettle on, Crystal.'

A moment later Crystal shouted from the kitchen. 'Jesse.'

'What?'

Kai reached out, planting his hand on Dad's nose to see how far away he was, so close.

'Look.' Crystal fell to her knees next to them holding up a half-eaten cookie, and Kai pushed her hand so she dropped it. 'It's one of yours, I can tell from the smell.'

'I know,' said Dad.

'Tastes like bum hole,' Kai said.

Laughing, Dad made a big breath and picked him up. 'Teach you for being greedy,' he said. Dad sat against the apple tree, Kai between his legs. 'You'll be all right, my boy, just relax. It was only two bites, was it?'

Dad kissed the top of Kai's four chunky plaits, his ear, then his cheek, and wrapped him in a bear cuddle so his tummy flipped a little and Dad ordered Crystal to put four sugars in the cup of tea while Jordan's mum poked her nosy head over the fence like a gremlin and Dad said Kai was OK.

'Don't tell your mum,' Dad said to Crystal when she handed over the mug.

'What do I get out of it?' she asked.

'Con artist,' said Dad. 'A tenner.'

'OK.' She sang it as sharp as the screaming birds as she ran down the garden path back to the house, her wavy blonde ponytail swinging with each step.

'You didn't even make it upstairs before you ate that cookie, did you? There's a surprise up there for you.'

'I feel sick, Daddy,' said Kai.

'OK, son.' Dad helped him bend over by the tree trunk and rubbed his back when he dry-heaved.

Much later that evening, Kai and the girls crowded the table eating Smash and fried spam. The news droned in the background. Kai felt better and happy because he'd found the surprise Dad had left on his bed – a lock-picking set. While he picked at a baby padlock, Leah told them about *Stone Cold*, a book from book club at big school, and even though books were boring, Kai stopped himself butting in because they were her favourite thing and it turned her face smiley. If Leah could live in a book she would and that was sad because Kai would miss her. Now he knew her secret about Mum not loving her dad he understood why she might want to run away. If it was OK, Leah would probably live with Nanny Sheila, but Mum would kick right off. The secret pressed heavy in his head as he scooped in peppery Smash.

Imagine how much longer Mum would stay at Aunt Shad's if Leah moved to Nanny Sheila's. Whenever Mum walked out, it punished everyone and they all needed to figure out what they had done wrong and Kai had been trying to figure out his badness. He didn't know what he'd done, unless it was the fight at school, but no one really cared about that. Maybe it was because Dad had been hanging out with Steve recently – Kai overheard Dad talking on the phone to him, and Mum told Dad at Christmas, 'If you see that dealer c-word again, that will be the end of us. It's us or it.'

So maybe Dad chose Steve. Kai decided not to be worried because Mum and Dad argued the same stuff before and things always changed back to normal. It would be the same this time.

It had to be.

Hopefully Mum would be back soon. Dad got too chatty without her and he marched back and forth through the living room. The only thing he ate were those nasty chocolate cookies and chips and gravy. There were always three pots of gravy granules in the cupboard, two beef Bisto and the other was chicken, and they had chip-shop curry sauce granules too and that tasted lush with Smash, which Leah cooked because she couldn't get the lumps out of real potatoes, not like Mum could. Dad stopped marching and Kai heard his footsteps up the stairs; he sighed and mixed more gravy into his Smash.

'Is there dance lessons at secondary school?' Crystal asked, and the conversation swept off again while Kai cut black bits off his fried spam. Everything tasted better with Salad Cream, so he squirted as much of it over the meat, Smash and curry sauce as possible because Mum wasn't there to stop him. Overhead, his parents' bedroom floorboards creaked because Dad enjoyed his treasure chest more when Mum wasn't there. He needed smokes more and when Kai woke up for school that morning Dad sat on the edge of the bed hunched over the wooden chest and he jumped when Kai shouted 'Morning' before slamming the lid down. Dad was so excited and awake he cooked bacon sandwiches for breakfast and Leah smiled before twelve o'clock, which was Dad's joke to her, even though she didn't eat any – breakfast made her feel sick and Nanny Sheila said that was because she had teenager hormones. Must be what made teenagers moan, even though Leah never did.

In the handle of the back door there was a mouse that squeaked every time it opened.

'Mum!' squealed Crystal, the first to stand up for a hug, quickly followed by Kai.

'You missed me, then?' Mum asked. Everyone said yeah, even Leah because she hated cooking and Mum noticed because her eyes stopped on Leah a second and then she kissed Jade on the cheek, who smiled below her frizzy fringe, then Leah, who concentrated on her squealing knife and fork. Banging on the stairs, Dad burst in the room and he picked her up, swinging her round in the middle of the living room.

'My woo-man.' He put her down, kissed her and Mum laughed and he kissed her again with tongues – yuck – and ran his hands down her body, pinching her nipple – she yelped – then squeezing her bum. He told her, 'I'm gonna make your make-up run tonight, girl,' and she used her teeth on his bottom lip. Gross.

'Don't do that to me again.' Dad's voice had pleases in it and her face was full of pleases because they loved each other, always would, and now everything was sweet as Nanny Sheila's maple syrup. See? Kai knew they'd get back to normal.

'Me and Kai are gonna make you a new kitchen,' Dad said.

Crystal flicked the TV to MTV Base and turned the volume up because whenever Mum returned they danced; she grabbed Jade's hairbrush and sang. From the carrier bags, Mum pulled out potato waffles, fish fingers and chicken Kievs, which Leah put in the freezer because Mum also pulled out a bottle of Courvoisier for her and Dad to celebrate.

'It's from Shad,' she said.

'Nice,' said Dad.

'Sheila's gonna be around soon so not too much.'

'Nanny!' shouted Kai, smiling with Leah.

'She brought me home.'

'Where is she?' asked Leah.

'Gone to a meeting at the village hall with Betty.'

'Course she has,' said Dad. 'Queens of Lesbos be ruling Middledown.'

'Shut up,' said Leah, throwing plates into the sink, ramming the taps on at full speed.

'Oi,' said Mum to Dad. 'Be nice when she gets here. If it wasn't for her I wouldn't be back.'

'Well,' Dad grabbed her again, making a sucking sound on her neck, 'I'll kiss Queen of Lesbos's feet.'

'Jesse.' Mum slapped his arm and whispered because she thought the kids weren't listening. 'She isn't gay.'

'Could have fooled me.'

Gay meant being silly and that was one thing Dad was wrong about.

A ballerina, that was how Nanny Sheila moved about, because she reckoned she should have been one and that the world wouldn't have seen one like her before or after. Course, it never happened because in her day it was right for the ladies to get married. When Nanny Sheila arrived she dropped on to the settee and slid one leg over the other and Kai thought of the slow-worms behind the garden shed. He jumped on the settee next to her, placing a hand on her silky green dress – same colour as the ferns at school – that was square cut around her neck and short sleeved; the skirt bit was long and floaty and she wore a thick black belt around her skinny waist.

'All right, my love?' she said.

He nodded and reached for her necklace because her jewellery always matched her fancy clothes and the stone that rested on her chest was green. He poked it, thinking of Dragon's heart stone. If he could think of an excuse to get back into Headmaster T's office, he'd snatch it quicker than Jade nicked all the scampi-and-lemon Nik Naks from the multi-pack.

The girls moved around Nanny Sheila too, Leah on the other side, Jade next to him and Crystal cross-legged on the navy-blue carpet in front of her.

'Like Snow White,' snorted Dad.

'Get us a glass of water, please, pet.' Nanny's cheeks were red so Kai picked up the TV guide and fanned her; she closed her eyes and they listened to the chink of the ice cubes Leah spouted into a plastic cup. Through the back door, a lawnmower whirred in Jordan's garden and Kaos barked.

'Brandy?' Dad's eyes looked dark as he sipped, looking over with a smile round his mouth. But not in his eyes.

'No thanks.' Nanny Sheila kept her eyes closed. 'I don't drink around the kids.'

'Course you don't,' said Dad.

'Glad to have Sherry back?'

Their words felt like tennis balls being batted, and Kai wondered if Dad would be angry that he was sat on Nanny's side of the room. For the girls it didn't matter, for him it was different. A wriggling jaw showed Dad's serious face, he folded a leg on to the other and reached for the remote to flick channels. A glass ashtray was full by his feet and the room smelled like fags.

'Do you like my sunglasses, Nanny?' Kai pointed towards the gas fire across the room. 'Dad got them for me.'

'Super-duper.' She sipped the water. 'Very posh.' Clearing her throat. 'Where did you get them from, Jesse?'

Dad sipped. 'Specsavers.'

'But, Dad!' Kai knew Dad got them with Denner and he knew it wasn't from town. It could have been from stealing. 'They came in a black bag.'

Nanny Sheila's arm was around Kai and she used a finger to stroke his elbow. 'Thought so,' she said.

'Because you're a saint,' Dad said. 'I'm surprised they let your sort in church.'

Anger waved through Kai and he butted in before Leah could because if there was one good person he knew it was Nanny Sheila, who said prayers and looked after the butterflies with her flowers. 'Why you being horrible to Nanny? That's not fair.'

As Dad opened his mouth to speak, Mum pushed through the door with the wash basket, using the back of her hand to wipe her forehead. 'Christ, it's hot out there.

And you . . .' She pointed at Kai. 'I've never known anyone to have so many odd socks.'

The word batting stopped.

'Mate,' said Jordan's mum the next day, 'tell me about it, men don't have a clue what we do for them. It's not till we're gone they notice. Good for you.'

Why was she even there? Butting her nose in. Kai felt sorry for Jordan having a mum like her, with her black painted eyebrows, macky nose and the beetle mole on her arm. As if she knew anything except being nosy and noisy. Whenever he was outside her voice was screaming next door like a ship horn.

'But, you know what? When I came back? It was perfect again, like when we first met.' Eyes dreamy. They'd been wrestling all through the night. A bang on the wall woke Kai up.

'Did he tell you what happened with him?' Jordan's mum, Sharon, the snake, pointed at Kai, who was sat at the table munching and smudging Marmite on toast round his mouth next to both women as they drank tea and smoked. Kai gulped. Snaky-Sharon was fork-tongue, what Dad called Mum every time she promised to stop drinking. This was why Dad hated Sharon. Why Kai wanted to smash her pig-head. Had Dad been there, she wouldn't be opening her pig-mouth, but he'd shot off that morning to meet Denner because they were off on the hunt for black worktops for Mum's new kitchen.

Gaffer tape for her big fat mouth, that's what Kai needed.

With a long suck on her fag, Mum paused, turning her lips into an O to blow, squinting her eyes, waving a hand through the smoke away from Kai. She looked at him, then Sharon, and said, 'What d'you mean?'

'Well, I saw your Crystal saying Kai ate a chocolate cookie; reckon it was rammed with hash from the look of 'e.'

'You're butting in,' said Kai. He jumped up, fists rounded; there was no way he wanted Mum to leave again, she'd only just got back. 'Nothing, Mum—'

'Oi, choccie-orange.' Mum wound an arm round his waist. 'Go on, you tell me what happened.'

The lie hit his cheeks before his lips. 'I just felt sick, I didn't eat anything.'

Flicking ash into the glass ashtray that had diamond shapes carved into it, Mum nodded, blew smoke towards Sharon and said, 'Don't worry, love, I believe you.'

Moments like that was how Kai knew Mum and Dad loved each other so much.

CHAPTER 9

15 December 2005

I never brought Yasmin to the den. I never even told her about it. It's impossible to imagine her here. All she cares about is doing her hair and painting her nails. She'll only leave the house to go shopping. I've tried to get her to come for walks, but she thinks nature and wildlife is boring. How could anyone think that? When you look at the bark on the pine, it's like the skin between Mum's fingers when it goes dry and cracked.

Me and Yasmin only had sex three times. I never really wanted to. Something about the idea of it was gross. And I knew what it was, I knew. Sex was gross because it reminded me of hearing Mum and Dad at it after their car-crash arguments. Fucking was a blood-stained plaster. The relationship with Yasmin was difficult; I didn't want sex in case we ended up doing it for the same reasons. That was the worst thing I could imagine.

Each time we did it, Yasmin initiated it and I was fucked as in drunk. And then fucked as in fucked, too. The first time happened when her mum was in Swindon for a weekend on management training. It was on a low-backed sofa, the one in their living room, and if you didn't lie down on it you got neck ache, so we spooned watching *Kill Bill*. I like that film; it reminds me of the old Bruce Lee films Dad used to watch.

18 November 2005

'As if,' she said.

'As if, what?' I asked, wanting to move my tingling arm from under her.

'As if she could beat up all those men.'

'She was trained by the best,' I said. 'That Chinese dude in the shack.'

'I just can't believe it.'

'That a woman could beat up a man?' I asked.

'There are times I'd like to beat you up.' She took one of my fingers between her teeth and lightly bit, then she pushed her ass against my dick, trying to be all sexy. Luckily I was wearing jeans so didn't think much of it other than that the thought of fucking her from behind was disgusting. I remembered catching Mum and Dad at it when I was a kid. Nasty. The way Mum's hoop earring had swung, I could still see it if I thought about it.

'Get me another drink.' I tapped her hip. She liked being bossed around a bit.

We drank vodka. Yasmin's mum always had bottles hanging around from work. Half a bottle by the end of the film. My belly felt warm. I didn't think about contraception, she kissed me and had her hand on the zip of my jeans. Guess it was easy to get a boner when I was pissed and not thinking.

We did it again the night after; I drank half a bottle of vodka to myself. She'd had a couple of shots and disappeared into the bathroom. When she returned, I kept my eyes closed pretending to be asleep and she said my name louder and louder till I 'woke up'. Pink lace. What was it with girls? I'd much rather see her in one of my baggy T-shirts.

On *The Depths of Asia* one week, it was all about sea creatures and they'd shown this octopus crawling along, its legs and head rippling like waves and squeezing into any shape to move into any space. Gross and creepy. When she shimmied into the room wearing pink lace knickers and a matching vest, I remembered the octopus. I wondered how long the octopus had been wrapping around me.

I liked that she had determination, I did, I appreciated that she loved me, I did. Not wanting to fuck her, the look of that pink fucking lace, it made me feel like – it made me feel like I did the day Mum found out I'd stolen this little dragon toy thing from primary school. Ashamed. Guilty. I should have wanted to fuck her. I knew that. She *was* my girlfriend.

Anyway, I drank more and we did it and it felt amazing when I came, it really did. In that moment, I thought I loved her and said it for the first time.

'I want to marry you,' she said.

It made me feel sick. Then I choked on another shot of vodka, trying not to laugh the way Leah did, like she'd had a fucking lobotomy. Yasmin brought me in a pint of water.

Five minutes later, staring at the shadows and the boy band posters on the wall, I felt a bit sober and regretted the whole thing.

I didn't love her. Love felt different. Love was like if you had a star in the palm of your hand and stretched each point to make it as sharp and sparkly as possible. It made you laugh together, stand by each other, do the good and bad together, shine together. I'd felt it in the past. If life was the night sky, love was the North Star. Me and Yasmin were like the quicksand at Weston beach, stale and suffocating.

For the first time, laid next to her in bed in the dark listening to her snoring like a hedgehog, I felt the truth of being with someone and feeling alone. When we were kids, I'd wake Jade up in the middle of the night and we'd pick through Dad's stolen gifts on the carpet of the living room before getting sent back to bed, and those were the nights I'd sleep in the girls' room, waking up with Jade's toes in my face. I never felt alone then.

Pushing the bottle of vodka aside, I reached for the glass of water on the dressing table.

There had been arguments about me not doing homework, missing school; Mum was definitely setting her on my case too. I knew Yasmin cared about me and desperately wanted me to do well. My head wasn't in it. School wasn't for me. I was like Dad.

That vodka. Gross. Sour taste in the back of my mouth.

I listened to her breathing, regular and deep.

Truth was, I didn't want to be with her any more and that felt scary as fuck because without her so close recognising myself would be impossible.

I pressed a finger into her shoulder. 'Yaz.'

Nothing. And she thought I snored like a pig.

'Yaz.' I shook her shoulder.

She grunted, half-asleep. 'What?'

'Wake up.'

'What?' She cleared her throat. 'What for?'

Careful not to knock the glass of water or vodka bottle, I clicked on the purple lampshade.

'What, Kai?' She tilted her head away from me. 'Why you always waking me up when I'm trying to sleep?'

The room felt spinny. I stuck my leg out from under the duvet, planting a foot on the floor to ground me.

'I'm sorry,' I said.

'Sorry for what?' she asked.

I took a deep breath.

The bed hardly moved when she sat up. Her short hair flat on one side, and like a splat of paint on the other, her mouth was the perfect hole to put my finger in. I was still laid down, foot reassuringly on the carpet.

'For fuck sake, Kai!' she shouted, shoving my finger away from her face. 'I'm trying to sleep.'

'The pill,' I said.

She scowled, leaning towards my face. 'If you're gonna wake me up, talk normally.'

'The pill!'

'Don't shout.' She sniffed and it reminded me of Mum, how she used to suck up lines of coke. 'What pill?'

'Are you on the pill?'

'What d'you mean, am I on the pill?'

'The pill. Are you on it?'

'You're a fucking prick,' she said, lying back down, turning away from me. 'Waking me up to ask that.'

I knew I was a prick, she told me all the time, but she was avoiding the question; that was what she did.

'We just fucked!' I said.

'Don't shout at me.' She pulled a pillow over her head.

Both of us were being loud but I couldn't give a shit. Her mum wasn't in.

It was a simple question, with a simple answer, and I was pissed she was ignoring me so I yanked the pillow off her and threw it across the room. She sat up, yelled I was a cunt, and I told her she looked like a slut wearing pink lace before I tried to stand up to put my hoody on to leave. It was on the floor and when I bent for it, I thumped my forehead on the wardrobe handle.

'Don't go.' Her voice was small. 'Please.'

I asked her the question again.

'Yes,' she said. 'Yeah, I'm on it.'

She pulled back the duvet and I crawled in and while I waited for her to fall back to sleep, I finished the glass of water and sobered up a bit.

The heat between Yasmin's body and mine burned.

I had to get out of bed, the house. The relationship. I dressed. The next day I'd tell her, I thought, I'd definitely tell her. The bedroom door clicked shut and I stopped, resting my head and a hand on the door of the spare room for a moment before taking a deep breath. I'd tell her it was over.

CHAPTER 10

THEN

It was the end of a hot, muggy week. The sky was plastered white, a bonfire and barbecue spat and sizzled while Jade's hi-fi blasted from Kai's bedroom window, beat beat beating over Mum and Crystal dancing, Dad and Denner laughing, Leah and Jade talking about colour wheels and how secondary colours were made from primary ones under the apple tree. Kai danced in front of flames that burned the stuff from Dad's bin liner they didn't want. Kai waved his hands, feeling the heat, the music, loving the smell of burning meat.

Ding-a-ling-ling. An ice-cream van crawled along the road out front.

'Mum, please!' They shouted.

'Didn't you know?' said Mum. 'It means the ice cream's run out when the man plays the music.'

'Yeah, right,' said Kai to Mum, looking at Leah. 'You're bum-lying.'

With shut eyes, Mum blanked him out; lifting a hand to the sky, she tapped her feet.

Out the front Kai rushed to the van and asked, 'D'you have ice creams?'

'Course, sonny, what d'you want?'

Kai gasped – Leah was right, Mum lied – and ran back to Dad for money. Denner waved a tenner and so they all got double Mr Whippys and flakes, apart from Kai who had apple cider to be like Dad, who was nailing a three-litre carton of Cheddar Scrumpy.

His sisters wore white, green, pink bikinis, and after Mum refilled her Courvoisier and Coke, she pulled at her tight see-through T-shirt that showed off her black bikini underneath; it stuck on her nose and that was the moment, there, before it popped off, where she could have been better, but now Mum had her black bikini out in front of Denner.

What was she thinking? That's not the sort of thing Dad put up with. Getting her boobies out for the boys when she was his piece and the thing he loved more than anything in the world, apart from Kai, who was the best thing he'd made, and that felt better than the smell of Flopsy.

'What you doing?' Dad, whose face was getting redder and redder from the sun, held a skewer and pierced a sausage, tossing it on a plate on top of the orange blanket spread over the grass that Mum and Crystal wriggled about and sang on, pretending to dance like in a music video, all bums and hips, and Kai didn't like how Mum looked the same age as eight-year-old Crystal, except her feet were wobbly, words were slurry and when she twirled her drink sloshed on to the grass. She moved to Dad.

'Oh, babe.' Running a hand from Dad's shoulder down his burning-from-sun chest, resting on the seam of his jeans, sliding a finger lower than the waistband. Mum said, 'Relax.'

Bonfire roared. Kai jumped up and down, lifting his red cape like wings, the heat burned like he was on fire. He wore shorts and his feet were black on the bottom from a day playing outside pretending the grass was head-height – apparently there was a secret meadow in Middledown Woods with grass that high.

'Go easy.' Dad turned to Denner, and Kai joined them and he was handed a beef burger; charcoal powdered the bun and Kai squirted ketchup on top. The red sauce dripped on to his hands and when he bit, down his chin. It tasted smoky, beefy, tasty. Mum grabbed sausages and burgers and bread, taking the lot to the girls under the tree and as the girls circled her like lion cubs fanning themselves and munching, Mum lay on her back, a calf resting on a knee turning her toe in a circle over and over. Since the barbecue had sizzled, she'd been running upstairs a lot.

Kai knelt on the fluffy blanket. He noticed Dad's darting chin and Denner's wide-open eyes, which always happened after they smoked from Dad's pipe, which came out on special occasions and was only smoked upstairs in the bedroom. Mum and Dad thought Kai didn't know; he did because he'd crept up and watched Mum, who never knew he was great at spying. They did it at Christmas, birthdays, and on bonfire days.

'I want a smoke.' Kai spoke between mouthfuls.

Dad flipped a burger and pointed the tongs. 'Well, you ain't allowed, son, it's no good for you.'

'You all smoke.'

Denner raised his eyebrows; his macky chest was out, and his arm looked like a robot when he glugged beer. When he was older Kai was going to do pull-ups and press-ups and weights every day.

'We're grown-ups.'

'So I can smoke when I grow up?'

'If you want, but you shouldn't.'

'Why not?'

'Because it can give you cancer.'

Not so big as Denner, Dad was skinny, except he had much more mouth – that's what Mum said when she wasn't stupid under the apple tree. 'What's that?'

'An illness that can kill you.' Dad switched the tongs for a sausage and when he bit in, grease spurted and he flinched his body away, still munching. 'So you aren't allowed.'

Kai placed half his burger back on the plate, no longer hungry because kill meant dead, like what happened to Leah's dad. 'I don't want you to smoke any more.'

Now Dad was rubbing his hand over his eye and scratching his armpit, which he did when he was thinking seriously. 'Story of my life.' He grabbed the carton of cider, slurped, burped and added, 'Guess I better give up, then?'

Daisies spotted the grass and Kai thought how they would look in Saffie's hair even though she would hate them. This afternoon she was playing in the football field and he wished there was time to meet her and to tell her that all the grown-ups they knew apart from Nanny Sheila smoked even though it could kill them. What would she think?

Boxing rattled the TV in the living room and Dad and Denner leapt from their chairs and roared, they sparred with Kai, showing him how to punch, making sure his thumb wasn't tucked in or it would break and how to jab jab jab, where to crack ribs and catch someone under the chin. Such fun. Now he was growing into a big man. Panting, he lay on the settee.

The girls were upstairs when Mum placed a hand on Denner's muscly arm, asking, 'Another drink?'

At the table she swayed, chin shuddering more than Dad's, clenching and unclenching a hand, taking a deep breath before giving out more drinks, but not to Kai, who was thirsty – he rose to pour cherryade and enjoyed the fizz, watching Mum over the rim of his cup. She was still wearing her bikini top and acting like one of the women that Dad called sluts who posed in the ring before the men fought. Bum-lady. Why did she have to keep wriggling it?

'I'm better than them, aren't I, babe?'

Obviously Denner didn't know where to put his eyes. Kai felt shame – what Dad felt, too, when her mouth grew too big for her pea head.

'Sit your ass down,' said Dad, and Kai was glad because she was drunk and embarrassing them.

'What's wrong with you?' She raised her voice – uh-oh – if only Kai had Gaffer tape, he'd wrap it round her mouth eleven times for how many drinks she'd downed, because now Dad's face looked like a stone and he jumped up, tilting his face down to hers.

'Sit the fuck down, woman.'

'Or what?' Face so close they must have smelled each other's beer breaths. Their sweaty skin shone like two hissing cobras. 'You don't realise how fucking lucky you are.'

Pushing it. Dad only wanted to calm her down and she was kicking off like she did on the special occasions she drank too much and smoked on the smelly pipes. Why in the mornings she groaned she needed to give up the drink. If Kai could dig the ugliness of the drink out of Mum, he would, and he'd put it in a shark's mouth on his and Saffie's silver moon so they would never see it again.

Closed eyes, Kai wished he was with Silver, his old imaginary friend, but he was pretend. Silver made things happier when arguments erupted. An eruption came from volcanoes and they bubbled like his tummy at times of stress – when Miss Butterworth said it was important to take deep breaths, when his heart felt too fast.

It stopped working.

Stopped working because Dad said again, 'Woman, sit your fucking ass down.'

And Kai moved closer, but stopped when Mum thudded Dad with two hands on the chest; he pushed her on the chair, she was back up again, he slapped her.

Hard. Across the face.

Even though Mum deserved it Kai was scared because men were stronger so he ran forwards holding up his hands, pushing Dad's hips away from Mum. 'Daddy, stop!'

Denner pulled Dad out into the hallway towards the front door.

Mum shouted behind Kai as he followed the men to the front door, 'You woman-beating bastard. You fucking evil cunt. Rot in hell, you cunt bastard. Don't think you're coming back here.'

Kai's fingers were in his ears, blocking out the c-words, and Mum was trying to block out Dad from ever coming back. That's what she'd said to Leah's dad, and tears burned Kai's eyes as he watched Dad whining into Denner's neck as they stumbled through the gate. They'd go to Denner's house, along from Nanny Sheila's. Mum smashed something in the living room and swore. Crystal rumbled down the stairs.

A light flicked on over the road in Bob-Cycle's house, a curtain twitched. The air smelled of warm grass and a bit smoky. Under the dark blue night, Kai ran to the gate, resting a hand on the metal clasp, listening to Dad howl, 'Sherry, I'm sorry, Sherry.'

Johnny the Prawn opened his door holding a crutch and limped on his small patio in front of his garden to a plastic chair and sparked up. The tiny light of the fag was like a firefly.

Tears fell down Kai's cheeks and when he heard a knock on a window, he turned to the house and saw Leah and Jade curling their fingers for him to come in.

'See what he's like?' said Mum when Kai closed the door and looked at her. 'That's the sort of man your father is.'

The problem with Mum and Dad wrestling was they loved it and panted and creaked the bed louder after they argued, so Kai had to shove his head under the pillow because it sounded disgusting. It was early. Breath was hot. At least they loved each other today and the fight last night was over.

Whack whack whack on the wall.

'Kai,' Dad shouted.

'What?'

'Get dressed; we're going to Steve's to pick up your mum's kitchen tops.'

Brilliantness. It was time to learn about building – soon he'd be able to build a den.

They stopped in town first, Dad wanted a double McMuffin and a strawberry milkshake and Kai copied. He couldn't eat it all so wrapped the burger up and put it in his rucksack. Kai, draped in his red cape, slurping milkshake, followed Dad through the aisles of Marks and Spencer to a different part of town.

Up the high street they passed shops and women in sexy clothes, who Dad grinned at. The women all looked the other way.

'Slag,' laughed Dad. 'Let's look in here.' He pointed at the sportswear shop. The air was stuffy and the lights headachy. Trainers in rows from ceiling to floor, everything they could ever wish for: Adidas, Puma, Reebok. As they passed a shelf in the boys' section, Dad grabbed the coolest black flat peak, Nike, and plonked it on Kai's head.

'Keep that on,' he said.

Kai's tummy flipped. Dad was teaching him. This must be how Dad filled the black bags, thieving like Robin Hood. Kai put on a boxer face as they walked towards the door. His ears burned. Hand in hand they strolled down the road, turning on to a cobbled side street; Kai grinned from ear to ear and Dad planted a kiss on the back of his hand.

'What else can we get?'

'Anything you want, my boy.'

'What if something bad happens?'

'Like what?'

'The police.'

They stopped at a fountain and under the trickling water there were pennies. Wishes.

'No one can get you in that cape,' Dad said, pulling out coppers from his wallet, handing them over then rolling tobacco and Rizla. 'Make sure it's a good one.'

With his eyes closed, Kai blew on the pennies, thinking as hard as he could, hearing a busker singing somewhere; the voice echoed around the walls. As he tossed the coins, he wished for Mum and Dad to stop smoking, but as he realised he didn't know who he was wishing to the words in his head melted away before they were strong. The coins plopped one, two, three into the water. Sunlight made shimmery lines. He delved a hand into the rushing water and drew his fingers through the coins then whooshed water at Dad.

'Oi!' He splashed back with a floppy roll-up hanging from his mouth.

'Mate.' Dad nodded now to a man with a grubby coat who was carrying a rucksack, sleeping bag and being followed by a beige dog with black fur round dark eyes, not on a lead. The dog was calm, the opposite of Kaos.

'Long time,' said Dad.

'I know, man.' The man's voice was croaky and yuck, his black teeth looked like the top of the old wall in Middledown Woods, and he had crazy spiky hair. He bumped fists with Dad, and even Kai! Yuck – Kai strained to see the man, who hid the dirty hands in his pockets. 'What you been up to? All right, young'un? Nice hat.'

Kai tilted it to the side to look cooler. 'It's new. What kind of dog is he?'

'She's a mongrel,' he said. His hands looked like they hadn't been washed for weeks when he ruffled her. 'Called Elf. She won't bite.'

Kai stroked her, then remembered Jordan saying that Kaos liked getting little squeezes because it reminded him of being a puppy in his mum's teeth, and when Kai did this Elf lifted her head up and made slitty eyes. She loved it. During the conversation Dad said how much he missed the old days, said he was settled now and keeping his head down, having the right woman sorts a man out, not that he wouldn't like a proper smoke sometimes, know what he meant? But she wouldn't have it. What she did do was give him a kid like him, pointing at Kai, so it was all worth it.

'He's just like you,' said dog man and Kai felt pumped up.

Dad grinned too because most people said he looked like Mum, but that was a bum-lie because her head was too skinny. 'Yeah, but darker.' Dad pressed his sunburned nose. 'Thank God.'

'Couldn't ask what he'd been up to, could I?' said Dad when they made their goodbyes and walked through a narrow alley that opened on to a cobbled square with grass in the middle and black benches around. There was a macky tree in the middle. A helicopter tree that Miss Butterworth called Sickmore, gross.

'Why not?'

'Nothing, my boy, just some people don't have strong minds and get trapped and before you know it they're on the streets.'

Kai betted living outside was cold and he felt bad for the man with the dirty hands. There should be taps outside for washing hands and drinking and where did he wee?

Bushes, probably. That felt nice, getting cocky out for a free-wee. Kai asked, 'What's a mongrel?'

'When it's a mixture of breeds.' Dad squeezed his shoulder, left his hand there. 'Bit like you.'

Kai frowned. Sometimes Dad talked silly on purpose to wind people up so now must be one of them times. If a mongrel was two things, it must be what mermaids and half-man-half-horse men were and they weren't even real so it couldn't be for people, just animals.

Behind the big tree a man was painted gold and stood like a statue; people threw change in a hat in front of him.

'Dare?' Dad said.

Best game ever. 'Yeah.'

'Go and poke him in the tummy.'

First Kai laughed, then put on a serious face, his heart beat beat beat fast as he moved to the gold statue man. Dad watched from the corner of the square near a road leading back to the shops, like Kai was Robin Hood and this time he was Little John.

The paint on the man's face was cracked on his forehead and by his eyes. Poke.

Gold man flinched. 'Oi!'

Kai ran with his fastest running feet to Dad and they laughed back towards the shops. Spotting a jeweller's, they stopped and Kai placed his hands on the stone sill, gazing at rings, watches and chains. So sparkly.

'I want to be a thief like you, Dad,' he said.

Dad kept quiet a moment. 'What makes you think I'm a thief?'

Carefully, he put his knowings together. 'Because you go in the night, and the bonfires and black bags.' Kai rubbed a finger on the window near a ring with a blue stone. 'You have a baccylava. It's obbious.'

Dad crouched to his height. 'If anyone asks, that isn't my job, Kai. If anyone asks, I don't have one.'

Anger pressed his tummy. 'I'm not stupid.'

'I know, but this is important, lad. If the police or any grown-ups that you don't know ever talk to you, you must deny everything, OK? Say you don't know nothing. Even if they said I'd confessed everything, OK?'

'What's confessed?'

'Admitted, told the truth.'

'I'm not stupid.'

'No. You're not.' Dad tilted his head to the side; his freckles were faded from where the sun had burned his skin at the barbecue and his eyelashes were white, Mum's favourites in the world. 'I'm not a proper thief, though, boy. I just take what I can get my hands on to help Mum out.'

Dad stood, they held hands. With a deep breath, he said, 'A thief.'

With eyes fixed on the ring in front of him, Kai asked, 'Could we buy that ring?'

'Not a chance. That's a lot of money. Two years of dole money.'

'Then, yes.' Kai nodded. 'I want to be a thief so I can have anything.'

From Kai's bag, Dad pulled out his tobacco and started rolling again. 'So long as you don't want to smoke, lad, you'll be fine.'

At Steve's, they sat around a big wooden table waiting for Denner to finish work. He was a roofer and only worked when he wanted to. Denner would drive Mum's new worktops home in the van. Beers were out and for Kai a cold can of Coke.

The house was big with four bedrooms, Dad said when they walked up the path, and Steve had stuck an extension on round the back where he'd built a home gym. Maybe Steve was always miserable because he was lonely. There was a photo of a woman and a little boy, both with black hair, in the hallway when they walked in. Surprised, Kai pointed it out to Dad, who put a sovereign-ringed finger to his lips to shush.

How Kai realised the lady and boy didn't live there was that there were no toys or girl stuff like hairbrushes, knickers on the radiators or nail varnish – Crystal left stuff everywhere – and it looked like a shit-hole with no carpets. The floorboards had dried drips of paint on, the wallpaper flaked in certain areas. But there were expensive things, like the music system and flat TV on the wall in the living room and there was a dead brown plant in the corner. No ornaments like at Nanny's. The house felt dead. What would it be like upstairs?

'Saw Tone in town looking like he crawled out someone's ass,' said Dad.

'Tone?'

'Tone, you remember Tone, with the teeth.'

'Tony-teeth?'

'Yeah.'

'I saw him two weeks ago round Al's. Never changes.'

'Tell you what, though, mate, put me in the mind of getting a proper smoke.'

Steve sipped from the green beer bottle; water dribbles ran down the glass. How was it possible for a man to be so red? His ears had ripples on the top edges, like thin leaves he saw the light through. Ugliest ears ever after Harry at school, whose ears stuck out like an elephant's. Kai's toes felt squat in his trainers; he kicked them off.

'Is there any about?'

'You sure? It's been, what,' looking at Kai, Steve said, 'six months? Didn't Sherry go ape-shit last time?'

Dad leaned back in the chair and stared at the ceiling, filling up his chest. He scratched his hair, eyed Kai. 'You're right.'

'I need a wee.' Kai jumped up.

'Upstairs, turn left, at the end.' Steve grabbed Dad's hand and pressed something small into it. 'Call it twenty. Same stuff you had at the week—'

Their voices went quiet when Kai shut the kitchen door. The floorboards snagged at his odd-socked feet; he was still wearing Saffie's from school on Friday. At the top of the stairs he went right. Not nervous because Steve was Dad's friend, even though Mum called him a good-for-nothing-dealer-c-word.

In the first room there was a double bed without any sheets. The second room was medium size and around a settee were open boxes of fans and black pots for plants and funnels like they had at school for the water pit and triangle paper that spelled **f i l t e r** on the box. Room three, as tiny as Kai's, was empty apart from a drawn blind and a ladder where leads were plugged in running to the attic. Tiptoe tiptoe back past the stairs. The fourth room was the biggest. Dark red paint covered the walls. It made him think of the vampire book Leah had read. There were posts round the bed and a mirror on the ceiling. Nothing else. Pants, socks, vests and long johns like what Dad wore filled the chest of drawers and in the bottom drawer – Kai's mouth opened big; he saw his reflection out the corner of his eye in the other mirror to the side of him – there were horse whips. Steve placed bets on horses, Dad went with him sometimes. Did he have a horse, too?

Laughter erupted from the kitchen. Kai quickly threw a whip inside the drawer and closed it.

The final door had a key left in the lock, he twisted it and pushed into a study with a black computer and maps over the walls, with red, black and yellow pins in. Above the computer was a map that was different to the others. Kai spotted Middledown. This map was bare apart from a single blue pin pushed in near the Grey Tower, which overlooked the valley next to Middledown Woods. It looked as though the pin had been stabbed in a few times around the spot because of the tiny little dots surrounding it. Kai hadn't been to the tower or the woods for ages. Soon as the holidays came, he'd go with Saffie and maybe Jordan, who would want Saffie's Boring Twin to come because he thought she was pretty. So, no, actually, maybe just him and Saffie. Closer. The computer chair swung a little when he climbed on to it and he used both hands to balance. Map paper pressed against his nose and his eyes crossed. Fuzzy.

There was a drawer in the desk and inside a red money tin with another key in the lock. When he opened it there were tiny bags of white talcum powder in little sections like he'd seen in Dad's treasure chest, but this one had little bags of brown powder in too. He took one, popped it in his pocket. There was a drawer that he pulled out and underneath was, he held his breath, nothing. Just lots of the brown and white powders and crystals and blue and orange tablets.

'Kai!' Dad's voice yelled and Kai jumped so hard he fell off the chair. By the time Dad was at the top of the stairs holding out his Power Rangers trainers, Kai was on the landing.

'Why you taking so long? Denner's here. Time to go.'

'I needed a poo.' Keeping his eyes on his laces before Kai pushed past him. It was the second lie he'd told. It was easy.

CHAPTER 11

22 November 2005

When I got home from school the grass squelched under my trainers as I walked up the garden to sit on the swing over from the apple tree for a roll-up. The apple tree was bare, its branches gnarly as Jord's dog Kaos used to be. A shadow moved behind the textured window of the back door so I pulled my earphones out. The squeak went in the handle and Mum came out holding an envelope. I felt nervous.

'It's from your dad,' she said. She handed it over, unopened. It was his handwriting: small square capitals. He'd addressed the front, 'MY BOY, KA1'. Guess he thought the number was clever.

Mum took baccy and Rizla from her pocket and started rolling.

'Gotta light?'

The sky was darkening. Heavy clouds were ready to chuck it down. The lights in all the yellow houses in the rank were stuttering on. Mum waited for me to open the envelope. I wouldn't give that to her.

'How was school?' she asked.

'Boring.'

Our smoke tangled together. I really loved Mum, but he'd sent the letter to me. Not her. She grabbed the chain of the swing, then dropped her hand to run over my hair.

'How are things with Yasmin?'

Probably Yaz had texted her saying stuff. Hopefully not confessing we'd done it.

'All right.' I shrugged, checking the back door to Jord's house was shut. His mum was a nosy wench. 'Yasmin's Yaz, isn't she?'

'Are you happy with her, Kai?'

I blew air, making my lips vibrate. Through the kitchen window I saw Jade grab an onion and a moment later a knife. She was a carer at the old people's home in Vells. On her days off, she'd cook us curried goat if she'd managed to get over to Cranston for the meat, or shepherd's pie, and if it was one of our birthdays she'd make hash cookies. We ate them when Leah wasn't around, she 'didn't approve'.

'When's Leah back from uni?' I asked.

'She's staying at Dean's a couple of weeks before coming back for Christmas.'

'Dean,' I said. 'Wet blanket.'

'You'll never think anyone's good enough for your sisters.'

'They aren't.' But I turned my nose up thinking of Crystal.

Mum's hoody pulled around her pot belly, her jeans were tight and her hips bulged from the top of them. Roll-ups and a cup of tea were her go-to breakfast, but she spent every evening eating like a pig, telling us all how the low-carb diet would start tomorrow.

'Seriously,' she said between puffs, 'you don't have to stay with her, you know? Just because you've been together so long.'

It surprised me. That she knew, that she could always guess how I was feeling, and it pissed me off a bit. I pushed back on the seat and lifted my legs so I swung a few times.

'Where's your school bag?' she asked.

'At school.' I never brought it home, dunno why she was suddenly asking; it had all my books in so I never had to unpack or repack. It lived on top of the lockers in which-ever block I'd had last lesson. Some days I'd get to school and not know where it was. I'd have to try to remember which exit I'd left from the last time I'd gone in.

Mum never asked about homework. I think Leah did so much without having to be told she just assumed the rest of us would do the same and, lucky for me, Jade did enough to study art at college. Not that it got her anywhere. Crystal was lazy, she worked as a nursery assistant the days she didn't phone in sick.

'But yeah, about Yasmin—'

'Mum!' I threw the end of the roll-up. 'Stop talking about it.'

'Don't get stuck with someone who isn't good for you.'

I stood up to walk away. 'I don't chuck people away.'

She snorted. 'All right, Kai.' As I walked towards the door, she added, 'Pick up that roll-up.'

You do it, I thought. The chain creaked on the swing as she sat on it and I went in the house.

Onions and garlic being fried in the kitchen. Jade looking at the envelope. 'All right?' I nodded. Past Crystal sprawled on the sofa; she'd taken up reading when Harry Potter came out, *The Half-Blood Prince*.

In my bedroom, the corners of the envelope were sharp. I laid back and closed my eyes; there was enough sleep built up in me to comatose an army.

Sleep.

I woke to Jade giving my forehead a kiss. She pulled the earphones out; dinner was ready.

'I'll be down in a bit.'

The letter was a grenade and I was about to pull its pin.

Jade said, 'Yeah, read that first.'

Last time Dad had wanted me to go see him. It felt weird, though. And I tried. I really did. It just wasn't easy. After Jade left, I gently tore open the envelope, holding it above my face because my pillow was a good spot to stay laid on if it spun me out.

MY BOY

I CANT WAIT TO SEE YOU. I HAVEN'T SEEN YOU IN TO LONG. ARE YOU LOOKING AFTER UR MUM? I KNOW YOU ARE. I NEED TO SEE HER SO BADLY. I WONT TO SAY SORRY. I DIDN'T MEAN WOT I SAID TO HER BEFORE. TELL HER I LOVE HER. I LOVE YOU TO. MORE THAN ANYFING. THERE'S SOMFING I NEED TO TALK TO YOU BOTH ABOUT. THE DOCTOR SAID I'M ILL. SO WHEN I COME TO SEE YOU BE READY. I FINK ABOUT YOU EVERYDAY. UR MY BOY. UR MUM WILL ALWAYS BE MY WOMAN. NOFING IS MORE IMPORTENT THAN MY

FAMILY. YOU KNOW IT. I HOPE UR BEING GOOD AT SHCOOL. SEE YOU SOON.

I LOVE YOU MY BOY.

DAD XXX

Ill? What stopped him spelling it out? The landslide slipped from my head to my chest to the point behind my belly button. It had to be bad.

Why I felt nervous getting post from Dad was because it was pathetic to cry. He sent me letters a couple of times a year. It was hard to reply because what was in my head never came out how it was meant to and Leah or Nan could help me, but I didn't want them to know that I missed him so much it stopped me sleeping.

I was scared to see him. Like he said, my job was to look after Mum, that meant being on her side. He was the one who'd fucked it.

I couldn't eat now. I wasn't hungry.

At the bottom of my wardrobe, in a pair of old odd socks, I found the key to my red tin and locked the letter away, then I climbed into bed and put my earphones back in. There was no way I was going to school the next day. I'd go to the den.

CHAPTER 12

THEN

Mum had a look on her like she was angry, but she liked Nanny Sheila and whenever she came round Mum was usually in a good mood. They sat together on the settee. Now Kai knew Mum didn't love Leah's dad when he died when everyone thought she had, he thought Mum owed Nanny for the rest of her life because Leah's dad was Nanny Sheila's son and if she knew the truth, well, life would be terrible if Nanny wasn't there. Must be why Mum made Dad be nice to Nanny Sheila even though he always moaned about her.

When they got back from Steve's, Dad and Denner hammered, banged and whacked the old worktops out – great because Kai got to smash cupboard doors out on the lawn – promising to fit the black worktop and cupboard doors the day after. They needed screws so shot off, leaving Mum and Nanny Sheila chatting.

Leah poured a glass of orange squash then sat with lots of books and pressed a pen against her head at the kitchen table. Must be maths, otherwise the pen would be like a wriggling, dotting magic wand because she scored best in class for English and French. Even with her cleverness she wasn't Mum's favourite. Kai was. He frowned. There shouldn't be favourites, not when he'd done nothing to deserve it.

'He's no good for you.' Nanny Sheila raised her voice, checked her hair was in place and tucked her hand between the cross of her legs. 'A leopard can't change its spots and he's been, he's been, different recently. I've seen him at The Hilcombe Inn.'

'Sheila.' Mum's voice was flat, like she was trying hard to keep it as still as possible so it wouldn't smash. 'What you heard was a long time ago. He always puts food on the table, and look . . .' Mum flicked her hand towards the cupboards under the sink – the old doors were tossed outside on top of the burnt grass where the bonfire had been; the new black doors messed the floor and were splashed in soapy water from Jade's rubbish washing-up. 'Everything I ever want he sorts out. He's a good man.'

'What's that mark on your face?'

Where Dad slapped Mum there was a little cut on her cheekbone from his ring. The need to stick up for Dad grew in Kai's tummy like apple seeds would if you ate them.

'Me,' Kai jumped in, unsure the lie would come out until he was saying it. 'That was me.' Pointing at the living room. 'I pushed that door into Mum.'

A clatter happened at the table. Leah jumped up. 'Damn it.' Squash drenched her yellow dress.

'Oh, right.' As she stood Nanny Sheila looked at Mum, who quickly changed her surprised round eyes to a smile face, then she grabbed a tea towel from under the sink and handed it to Leah.

'Yeah.' Mum lied with Kai and now they had a secret, which he felt bad about. It was the right thing to do, though. Mum added, 'Stupid me, stood right in front of it.'

From the swing in the garden, Crystal could be heard squealing as Jade pushed her higher and higher, a game they always played: see who could be pushed the highest without getting scared. Both girls were brave as dragons and when the swing ropes went soft at the top they cried out because of the waves in their tummies.

Sitting back down Nanny Sheila crossed her legs and threw her chin in the air. She rolled her fingers on the edge of the settee. The slosh slosh slosh of the washing machine churned, and people on *Jerry Springer*, Mum's favourite show, shouted and pulled each other's hair in the background. On a plate next to Nanny there was a bite taken out of cheese on toast. 'All I'm saying is be careful.'

'I know.' Mum made a big breath and built a roll-up. 'I know you're looking out for me and I appreciate everything you do for us, I really do. Without you being about all these years I don't know where we'd be.'

It was true. Nanny Sheila brought round shopping bags when Mum moaned about money and took Kai or one or two of the girls to stay at her house after big arguments. When he was older if he had to have a girlfriend, Kai would never argue. It was the horriblest thing in the world.

A horn beeped.

'Denner!' Kai ran out the back door, glad to be away from poky talk, past the girls screaming at the swing and when Denner turned the car at the top of the street and drove back down, Kai waved to Dad before Denner drove off.

Course, Nanny Sheila left as soon as Dad turned up and when they passed each other at the gate, she said, 'Nasty bruise on Sherry's cheek.'

Dad's face wobbled, Kai threw his arms around him and he crouched to Kai's height, ignoring Nanny Sheila as she click-clocked down the road in blue heels.

Inside the house, Dad grabbed Kai's rucksack; dipping his hand in the unzipped front pocket he pulled out a gold necklace with a dangly on and threw it on Mum's lap.

'Keep it coming,' Mum said.

Dad fell on to the settee next to her, gripping her in a headlock and making her laugh with whispers.

'Where's that from?' asked Kai.

'That,' Dad winked, 'is a fancy necklace; it's a Marks and Spencer necklace.'

Must have took it when they walked through the shops and Kai had helped without even knowing. So cool. It was time for Kai to take Dragon. On Monday.

The warmth of summer glowed in the living room and Mum and Dad got out their special pipe for a cheeky smoke. Tonight was OK, they were happy and had lots to say, then they cracked open beer cans and laughed about the time they'd first met at Scottie's shitty old flat.

It wasn't a word he understood, blacky, but from the poison sound of Tom B's voice when he said it – saying the L extra loud – it was obvious he was being nasty. He'd watched Kai win a race against Jordan.

'Good for a blacky.'

They stood five feet from each other at the bottom of the lanes. Saffie was about to race two of the girls and Kai really should have been cheering her. He stopped a moment. 'What?'

Tom B's gaze dropped to the grass. The school gardens were freshly cut and above an aeroplane left white lines – a noughts and crosses board – on the blue sky. Braver, Kai thought. Tom B's braver today because his sisters were on a school trip and wouldn't take over like they always did, so now he wanted a fight.

'I'm faster,' Tom B said, 'but you're OK for a blacky.'

For a week Dad had sparred with Kai, showing him the best moves. He was ready, jab jab in the ribcage like Mike Tyson. Keep calm, Dad said, keep calm when you want to win. That's what he'd do, show Tom B that he was the strongest in school and he couldn't be messed with.

When Kai walked over, not understanding the word Tom B had said, although his breath was quick he felt relaxed, and the moment before it happened Tom B's smile disappeared.

With a pounding heart, Kai stood in front of Tom B and said, 'You're a pussy,' punching him quick – one side, then the other, jab jab in the ribcage – and Tom B bent over, clutching his sides, with his stupid face crumbling, and Kai leaned down, saying, 'Punch like a blacky too.'

Hippie Mandy ran over, lifting her long tie-dye skirt so she wouldn't trip, shouting, 'That's enough.'

Kai stepped away, watching Tom B cry, and it felt good. Two hands clamped, one to each of his shoulders. Saffie was in front of him before Hippie Mandy arrived and Kai's gaze rested on her pale lips, the same colour as Nanny Sheila's marigolds, except lighter, and they were a perfect heart shape.

'What's wrong?' asked Saffie. 'You're going to get in trouble, they might kick you out of school, or even worstest, call your mum and dad to get you.'

'I don't care.' He yanked himself away. She grabbed his arm and he pushed her to the ground. As soon as he saw her push a red curl from her shocked face and sprawled next to the boy he hated more than anyone, his tummy turned, then Hippie Mandy was there, guiding him towards the plants where Jade should be, past Flopsy's hutch, leaving Miss Butterworth to question the others.

Outside Headmaster T's office were two plastic chairs where Hippie Mandy asked him what happened and he couldn't speak because he felt sick and angry. Saffie shouldn't have tried to help him. It was none of her business.

'Try this breathing.' Hippie Mandy changed her voice when he didn't respond. 'You take a long, deep deep breath in, like a pufferfish, make your chest big. Yeah, that's right, well done. Now, once the air is in you hold it a few seconds and then slowly slowly let it out. Well done, a bit slower. Try it again.'

She'd shown him the breathing before, stupid woman. How could she have forgotten?

The sky could be seen through the high windows and the white lines from the aeroplane were spreading thick.

On his silver moon, there would be no Tom Bs, no teachers, no one, just him. So so angry at Saffie, who should have kept her stupid face out of it.

'Stop!' she'd yelled; he remembered hearing her now as she ran over from the lanes.

Funny how there was no sign of the punches on his knuckles. Maybe Tom B would have some, though. He deserved it. Tom B's dad was grey-haired and had a small chin, he wore glasses. At sports day, he and Tom B ran the three-legged race. Dad hadn't been to sports day last summer so Kai couldn't run in the parents' race. He won everything else, though, unless he was up against Crystal – he came second to her in the whole school cross-country round the field twice. Dad would beat up Tom B's dad if they ever met.

'Oh,' said Hippie Mandy, who had pushed open Headmaster T's office door. 'He's not in. Stay here.'

Like he could go anywhere else. Except, he could – and Dragon was in the office waiting to come home with him. The trousers Kai had on had deep pockets with cool zips – he chose the trousers on purpose and was going to wear them all week, until he placed Dragon into them.

In Headmaster T's office, the clock tick-tock tick-tocked on the wall. The blinds were pulled down, but he could see everyone playing by the lanes and the sticky bushes through the slips of white plastic. Saffie wasn't by the lanes any more. She might be in class or gone to the secret garden without him. Or, worse still, she might be playing with Tom B. He made a deep breath. No, that wasn't allowed. She might not want to be his friend. What had he done? She was his best friend in the whole world. Orange lips like Nanny's flowers. Confusing, like when Dad hit Mum and the next day they were tongue-kissing. Was that how to make up with girls, with tongue-kisses? Yuck.

Head all mixy, Kai made another big breath, turned back to the room, listening for noise outside – he couldn't be caught by Headmaster T creeping up – and noticed one of the drawers opened in the filing cabinet. Boring grown-up stuff like all the papers on the table. There, half-hidden behind the computer screen, was Dragon. The tiny grey ornament felt heavy and cold, pointy and hard, as he pushed his fingers over the spikes across his head. Kai's heart pumped fast. When he and Dad left the sports shop and he was wearing the cap they acted as though everything was normal. He returned to the chair outside the office before he heard the whistling that told him Headmaster T was walking down the corridor.

This time the Head rubbed his hands together like he was having a great idea; his floppy blond hair slid back when he looked up to the ceiling.

'What are we going to do with you?'

Should he answer? Unsure, Kai kept a hand on Dragon in his pocket. Rubbing his head meant he and Dragon could mind-read and Dragon was excited to go to the silver moon. Who's Saffie? Dragon wanted to know. Kai didn't know if she was his best friend any more.

'What happened out there?'

The problem with people like police and teachers was that you couldn't really trust them. All they liked were grasses and Dad said a grass was the worst excuse of a man in the world. He wasn't sure how much to say and squeezed Dragon as hard as he could, like he might kill him – but it was OK, Dragon was hard, brave and didn't mind. The spikes dug into the fold of his skin. A nice feeling.

One of the hand bells – there were seven of different notes low to high – was being rung by Hippie Mandy outside. It was the end of lunch and school became louder as Kai's school mates stormed the halls for class.

'He called me a name,' said Kai.

'What did he say?'

'I can't remember.' Kai wanted to know what the word meant before he told anyone what Tom B had said, so he didn't look stupid.

'It must have made you very angry if you hit him.'

Last time, Headmaster T admitted that he'd seen the fight, this time he didn't, so Kai thought he could say anything and get away with it. He hadn't felt angry, not until Saffie touched him. He said, 'He made me really angry and I lost my temper.'

When Dad shouted at Mum, he always said sorry, even when Kai thought Dad wasn't wrong, so maybe that meant that it was important to say sorry just to make things calm. Saying sorry now would get him out of trouble and out of the office.

'Sorry,' he said quietly.

'What are you sorry for?'

For getting caught. 'Making Tom B cry.' Now he was a real liar. Nanny Sheila better not hear about this.

'Miss Butterworth saw you from her classroom window and said that someone might have shown you how to fight?'

Headmaster T leaned back in his chair and rubbed his chin, staring at Kai with poking eyes that made Kai want to say lots of things even if they weren't true just because he felt like he should be talking.

'I watch Mike Tyson and Dad shows me jabs.'

Headmaster T's hand stopped rubbing his chin and both hands rested on his desk. Kai made himself not look at the back of the computer in case Sir looked there and found Dragon gone.

'How are things at home?'

The question made his head dizzy. It made no sense to ask about home when the fight was with someone at school. He shrugged.

'Both your mum and dad are at home, aren't they?'

Kai nodded. 'Unless it's a time when Mum leaves.'

'She leaves?'

It wasn't wrong that Mum left sometimes to clear her head because every mum must need that and anyway it was good because when she came back things got brilliant. Until the next time. The picture of the surfboard on Sir's wall looked brighter today, maybe because it was sunnier.

'Where does she go?'

'Aunt Shad's.'

'Why does she go there?'

'When they're shouting.'

'Who shouts?'

Too many questions. Deep pufferfish breath.

'Mum and Dad shout sometimes. It's OK because they make up and kiss with tongues and Dad gives her jewellery because he'll get her anything she wants and then they're OK.'

'Is Mum at home at the moment?'

Kai nodded. 'Yeah, she came back ages ago.'

*

After school, the family waited for plantain to fry to go with the chicken and gravy. Leah poked rice as she tested Jade on her times tables. Jade was drawing a face in charcoal at the table next to Kai as she gave her answers. Mum and Dad were huddled over a blue tablecloth, on top of which were dry, green leaves. Piles and piles of them from Steve, who would only throw them away. They picked out the dead ones, drinking tea. Mum made hash with leaves, ice, a glass vase and a ton of patience, which Dad didn't have. In the background *Wish You Were Here* played on TV. Greek beaches looked pretty.

'Nice cup of tea, that is, Leah,' said Dad.

'What's that?' asked Mum, pointing at the table between Dad's hands.

'Where?'

'That's all the bullshit falling out your mouth.'

They each used one hand to pick and drop dead leaves into the other pile. They wore reading glasses from Poundland.

'Can I help?' asked Kai.

'Yeah,' said Mum. 'Put the yellow ones over here.'

Mum rested her head on her thin fingers and asked Leah how her English homework was going.

'Excruciating,' she answered. 'Because I can't control Mrs Toghill's responses.'

'All you can do is give it your best shot,' said Dad.

'You wanna practise what you preach,' said Mum, who started moaning about Saffie's mum, who had been round next door with Sharon – the council had been on the phone.

'Who else would have reported us for changing the kitchen? She's a jealous fat pig. Who does she think she is?'

Being angry at her mum made Kai more annoyed at Saffie. Crystal started singing a TLC song from the settee, her voice so whiny it sounded like a hedge strimmer.

'Shut up, blacky,' he said.

Not seeing the colour of Mum's skin. Not noticing that he and the girls had caramel-coloured skin rather than peachy like his dad's or Nanny Sheila's. Not thinking of his aunty, uncles or the amount of times Mum had said her dad's skin had been the colour of dark rum. Everyone froze, apart from Crystal, whose mouth dropped open – her eyes darted to Mum, whose face twisted up. He felt terrible. How could a word be so bad? Kai watched Mum's chest to see if she was holding her breath. She tilted her head and stared at the leaves, then looked at Dad.

'Where did you hear that word, Kai?' he asked.

Never heard Dad's voice so gentle. He answered, carefully, 'School.'

'We don't talk like that, all right? It's racist. Blacky is a nasty word because you're calling someone a name because of the colour of their skin. Do you think skin colour makes people different?' Dad leaned over and tapped Kai's temple, then his chest where his heart was, before he added, 'On the inside?'

Kai shook his head. Questions from grown-ups were often hard to answer. This time it wasn't.

'No.'

Next to the leaves was a pile of Jade's drawings. An image of a girl's face was distorted, pulled apart, stretched. She'd repeated the same image in pencil, paint, charcoal, chalk and collage. Creepy things looked beautiful when she drew them. Next to the pictures was a cola can that was Mum and Dad's new pipe. They'd been smoking in the living room since Mum got back.

Dad took Mum's hand, laced it with his thick sovereign-ringed knuckles. He pulled their hands across the table to Kai.

'Look,' he said.

Mum's brown fingers and Dad's so pale and freckly.

Kai felt something new, it was horrible and he didn't know what it meant. It was very big and he felt guilty at hurting Mum's feelings. He hated Tom B.

'You're quarter-caste, my boy.' Dad pinched his nose and Kai relaxed, looking at his tiny pale brown hand as though it was the first time he'd ever seen it before. He unzipped a pocket and pulled out Dragon to change the subject, to make the room go happy again.

'Look.' He held it up to show Dad.

'What?' He grabbed it, turning it over. 'New toy? What's he called?'

'Moon Dragon,' said Kai. 'Look, there's a diamond for a heart.'

'What's that?' said Dad. 'That's as useless as the tack Crystal wears.'

Crystal shouted, 'Get lost, you stinky B.'

Embarrassed, Kai bit his lip as Dad stopped sticking his finger up to Crystal. He wanted to impress so said, 'It was my first steal, like when we got the hat.'

Dad cleared his throat and started to ask Mum what she was doing the next day – did she want to visit Scottie? – but she took Dragon, asking, 'What d'you mean your first steal?'

'It's from Headmaster T's office.'

For the second time that evening Mum pulled a strange face, but this time she stared at him. 'Did you steal it, Kai?' She placed a finger on the cola-can pipe. There were bags under her eyes and she hadn't painted her eyelashes.

Dad fiddled in his pockets, looking for something, pulling out his wallet, not there. Finding a tobacco pouch he dropped it on the table like he'd just won at cards, nudged it towards Mum and told her there was a surprise inside and when she looked, still asking Kai, 'Did you steal it?', the crinkle between her eyebrows disappeared.

'Dragon wanted to be mine. Sir didn't even know it was there and now I'm like Dad.'

'Like that's a good thing,' said Leah.

Dad rolled his eyes. 'All right, beak.' Then he told Mum, 'I need to go to town.'

'Why?'

'To see Tone.'

'Who's Tone?'

'A good friend. You met him and his dog the other day, didn't you?'

Kai nodded.

'He was nice, wasn't he?'

Dragon told him to keep quiet.

Mum pinged the ring-pull of the can, over and over. 'You know what you're gonna do?' Pinching two fingers, she pulled a ball of tin foil from the tobacco pouch as she talked. 'You're gonna go to church with Nan so she can teach you right from wrong. I think there's a lot that goes on that's confusing you.'

'He don't need to go—' Dad said.

'You've done enough.' Mum coughed, stood up and grabbed the can, heading to the other side of the room to go upstairs. 'Yeah, you can tell Nan what you did, see what she thinks of it, and on Sunday you'll go to church with her.'

'And me,' said Leah.

Cool. Kai always wondered what it was like in church because Nanny Sheila, who went every Sunday with her best friend Betty, loved it and her best stories were about baby Jesus and the Easter bunny, who came from the Bible.

CHAPTER 13

24 November 2005

Because Mum was constantly getting letters from school, it made her aggy as fuck. The child-missing-from-school person had been round the day before – when I was at the den – holding a folder and threatening 'court action' because my attendance was thirty-two per cent. I really tried to go. In the mornings, after I'd heard enough of Mum banging on, I'd get up, put on the stiff shirt, and cycle there. Sometimes if it didn't make me feel dizzy, I even made it through the main entrance, so long as a teacher didn't put a spanner in the works by the coach-turning circle where I passed them first.

The day after the child-missing-from-school person came to our house, a new girl started at school. Her name was Ammi. I liked it because it meant there was someone else in school who was 'black' – in fact, she *was* black; I imagined when people saw us together they realised how light

I was. We had I.T. together. And when she walked in, she smiled – I'd shown her to tutor that morning. It was her first day. The Head had pulled me for a chat – about my attendance – and when we were done told me to take the new girl to G12. In I.T. she ignored everyone watching her and sat next to me. Thank fuck Yasmin wasn't there. Ammi smelled like sherbet lemons. We didn't talk much and I was so aware of how massive my chunky thumbs looked on the keyboard next to her butterfly hands that all I did for half an hour was title columns with one finger in an Excel spreadsheet. Anyway, this weird thing happened. Mr Bishop had been called into the next room for some reason – he was as useful as a blunt chainsaw – and had been gone ages. I checked my phone, forgot it was in my left hand then went to pick up hers with my right hand at the same time she reached for it. I jumped out my skin – I swear, my heart splattered faster than the sleet against the windows outside – then I dropped my phone on the floor and stammered when I apologised. She laughed.

She had dimples.

Just before spring, starlings danced over the valley. A black flock twisted and turned in the air and I liked to watch them from the big branch of the Great Oak. Hopefully little Tyson would see them one day. Watching them made me feel like I could fly too.

That moment with Ammi reminded me of the starlings. It felt strange. I couldn't look at her after. I googled 'marigolds' because I'd forgotten the colour of them.

Instead of going to next lesson, I threw my school bag on top of the lockers in the I.T. block and went to the bike shed. Lock picking wasn't something I did any more, but after setting the shed on fire at the abandoned manor house I'd been thinking a lot about Dad and started carrying my lock-picking set in the inside pocket of my coat. It had been years, and as I stood looking through the windows at the rows of bikes, I thought, Who cares? I got the tiny wrench and snake out – I'd had to order a new set because Saffie had the original – and was inside so quickly it surprised me. The room felt still despite the rows of fast tyres, and I sat between my bike and another with my knees bent and my forehead on them, until I got bored and stared at the scar on the palm of my hand – it was smaller since I got old, a tiny dash – then I got out a spliff I'd made for school. It was a bit bent. I had two puffs.

Guess I must have been there half an hour before I heard a noise at the door and saw the caretaker and Mr Wright. The caretaker had the keys to everything and Mr Wright was the deputy head. My joint was safely in my pocket.

'How did you get in here?' Mr Wright asked.

'I'm good with a lock, Sir.'

The caretaker had the backbone of a slug; Richie kicked a football at him once, right in the ass, and he didn't even turn round. That day, he mooched off with a leaf blower so we were alone.

'Do you have a key?' Mr Wright asked. The suit jacket he had on was so ironed its edges looked like a cocaine wrap.

'Where would I get one of them from?'

'How did you get in?' Mr Wright was usually chilled, trying to do chit-chat and keep me 'on side'; that day someone had put fifty pence in the dickhead and he'd turned into a right jobsworth.

'I teleported.' I stood up.

'Have you been smoking weed, Kai?'

'No,' I said. 'That shit gives people psychosis. You think I'm stupid?'

'You'd be stupid to smoke here.'

We faced each other like cowboys. Suddenly I felt savage.

'Can you empty your pockets?' he asked.

I wanted to laugh. I could have KO'd him.

'No,' I said. I looked past him through the open door. The cycle path was just outside. I'd have to leave my bike, but could easily break in and get it that night when he was tucked up in bed next to his fat wife.

'Let's go to my office,' he said.

I didn't reply. He stopped to shut the shed door behind me, the padlock clicked, and before he'd turned round I'd started running up the cycle path to Middledown Woods. I jumped over dog shit, spat, punched a drooping tree branch.

I heard him shout, 'You'll regret this one day, Kai.'

'Yeah right, Mr Wright,' I shouted over my shoulder.

The whole way to the bridge I laughed manic like Leah used to.

CHAPTER 14

THEN

Church was freezing, Kai wrapped his arms over his chest. People said Nanny Sheila was a hard woman, a cold woman – weak people, Leah said, people like Johnny the Prawn. Unbelievable. Nanny Sheila was the best grown-up on the planet. Dad was the coolest. Saffie was the best girl. It made no sense what people thought of Nanny, though, because she loved them. Betty was another story.

Betty was hard and cold like the walls of the church when they walked in, and she stood up in a macky furry coat and a flash of sun struck her face, showing its frown-lines, thin red lips and square chin; her wiry hair was striped like a badger. Badgers were vicious. For a second she dropped her gaze to Kai, raising a black triangle eyebrow.

'So this is your thief?' she said.

He was sure the hairs on the back of his neck stood up. Leah took his hand and said, 'I like your earrings, Betty.'

Macky diamonds that pulled her earlobes down so that the pierced holes looked like slits, and when she touched one, saying, 'These old things?' her fingers dripped with sparkling rings. Her perfume was thick, heavy, and it made Kai's throat want to shut. Nanny Sheila followed Betty into the pew, then Kai, then Leah sat down on skinny embroidered cushions. Well uncomfortable.

The vicar cleared his throat and started and Betty leaned over to Nanny Sheila and whispered very very quietly, 'Ever green, the fairy queen.'

Why Nanny liked such a strange friend was a mystery. She had a small smile under a green floppy hat and was wearing her favourite green dress, the lower half crinkled like a fan. When he was a big man and had loads of money Kai would take her to the shop Dad got Mum's necklace in, in town, and spend a hundred pounds on a dress for her. Nanny even had grass-coloured lace gloves – they were placed on her lap so she could flick through the thin pages of the Bible that she kept showing Kai, running her finger down the page to follow as the vicar read. He had macky eyebrows and wobbles in his voice. The white and purple robes he wore were the same as Johnny the Prawn's at Halloween, except Johnny's had puke stains down his because he was a drunk sicko.

Arches ran along the sides of the room. Stained-glass windows of Jesus were bright above the vicar, who talked about something called temptation. Nanny Sheila nodded her head with her eyes closed. Deep breath in like a pufferfish. Why did Mum make Leah tell her about Dragon? Nanny had gone mad and that was scarier than Mum and Dad because she never went shouty, she went dead still and her eyes turned dark to match her voice and it was like all the shadows at night were strangling him. She'd said, shaking a bunch of rosemary in front of his nose, 'Stealing is a sin of the devil.' It made him feel something called shame – that's what Nanny called it – even though he wasn't sure how much he believed her because Mum proved that grown-ups lied, and also because Dad said stealing was a good job if you did it without being caught. Maybe it was only a sin to get caught. It made his head want to pop.

Betty's real name was Elizabeth. Both her and Nanny's nails were short and painted red. Betty's fingers were knobbly knuckled and she had big freckles on the back of her hands. The smell of her perfume and the sound of the vicar rambling were ingredients to make Kai sleep. Never would he come here again. Never ever. Copying Nanny, he shut his eyes. After this boringness, he and Leah would help her cook a roast and Jade and Crystal would eat it too and probably stinky Betty, who, when she and Nanny ate together on Sundays, laughed like how deer bark. It was fun cooking roast, especially cleaning the mud from potatoes, the black swishing down the plug-hole when he stood on a kitchen chair at the sink, magicking out their yellow-spotted skins. Peeling them was best, trying to make one macky curl. Nanny Sheila said ages ago she'd give him a pound if he could do it in one, but it was impossible. On the silver moon, all the food was silver, maybe it would turn their skin silver when they ate it; he would have to ask Saffie about that.

Saffie. It was wrong that he pushed her and he was going to say sorry because saying sorry was how to make things right when mistakes happened. Dad always said sorry, even when it was Mum's fault. When he'd pushed Saffie it was his fault. Maybe he could do something special to prove how sorry he was. Dragon. He'd forgotten – Dragon was for Saffie because there weren't any boys in her family to look after her. Soon as they got to Nanny's he would call for her and they would be friends again.

Kai rubbed Nanny's leg and she opened the eye nearest him. 'How much longer?'

She put a finger to her lips.

Deep deep breath in like a pufferfish.

On the silver moon, there were no churches and no places where they had to go to be told right and wrong because he and Saffie made the rules.

Outside, there was a graveyard with stones so old the names were invisible. Did people really turn to ghosts when they died? No way. Leah's dad wasn't or he would talk to her. Church was even more boring than assembly at school.

The pews were made from wood, what Kai wanted to learn so he could make a den. Dad still hadn't finished Mum's cabinets and he'd been gone for days. The new doors were piled on the floor by the kitchen table. How long would it take before they could make a den together? In Middledown Woods there was a macky acorn tree and today, if Saffie wanted to play, they'd climb it. One side was thicker, with swoopy branches overlooking the valley; on the shaded side facing the woods there were fewer branches. At school, Kai had seen a picture of the roots of a tree on the computer. The picture made the roots look exactly the same as the branches above ground, but roots must be much bigger. With a tree that big, he could build his own wooden castle, and it would have a log fire with a furry rug like Nanny had in front of her fireplace. Mum and Dad could live in a building he made outside so he couldn't hear them shouting or smell their disgusting can pipe.

Suddenly, Nanny squeezed the sensitive bit of Kai's leg above his knee and he squealed, opening his eyes.

'Shh,' she whispered when everyone turned to look at him. She winked and he held his hands to cover his mouth to hide the giggles.

The carpet in the woods was green, blue, white and yellow from ferns and flowers. Stinky garlic crunched their noses as they snapped sticks underfoot. They ran side by side. The red cape he wore rippling behind him.

'I want a cape,' Saffie yelled.

On the mud path next to the higgledy-piggledy wall in Middledown Woods they jump jump jumped over twisty tree roots.

'This is my favourite place,' Kai said.

They stopped by the Great Acorn, panting, resting hands on the trunk. To see the furthest dancing leaves he leaned his head back. So tall, the top so far away. Behind, the sky looked like a dream.

'Come on.' She reached for his hand and pulled him towards the lowest branch. When he'd knocked at her door, she'd shouted his name and hugged him because she knew they'd make up when he felt better. 'Thank you for saying sorry,' she'd said, and he thought those words were the nicest ever.

Bark felt crusty under his filthy fingers and scratched as Kai and Saffie pulled each other up. All grazed knees and rosy cheeks. Twigs decorated his reddish-brown curls and hers, a shade lighter with blonde lightning bits, shuddered like Dragon's breath around her circle face. Finally they sat on a branch high enough to see across Middledown valley, where the sun left a bright dot in their eyes when they looked away to watch a raven lift from the top of the Grey Tower half a mile away – the same tower from Dad's story. He told it to Saffie. A tractor rolled across a hill on the other side, turning it into brown stripes.

'I have a secret,' Kai said.

'What?'

'If I tell you, you must promise it's for us, no one else.'

'I only want me and you to know our secrets. I promise.'

'I'm gonna be a thief.' Again, he saw her pale lips and that made him feel a bit mixy. His neck got hot. Deep pufferfish breath.

'Cool. Can I be one too?' she asked.

'Yeah, but if you're going to be one it has to be a secret that nobody knows, not even the police or teachers or the vicar.'

She nodded. 'I hate the vicar. Mum said they're all pervs.'

'What's that?'

'I dunno. She said not to go near them.'

So why did Nanny? 'There's something else I need to tell you if you're going to be my partner.'

'What?'

He told her about Dragon.

'You stole from Headmaster T?'

'Dragon wanted to come with me. He's for our silver moon to fight baddies.'

Her bottom lip stuck forward.

'Do you still like me?'

'Yeah.'

'So we can be partners like Robin Hood and Little John? They always work together and you're my best friend so no one else can do it.' Without her, everything felt impossible.

The tractor on the hill stopped at a gate and they watched the farmer open it before rolling through. The Great Acorn they sat on was in a spot that hid some of the valley. If they went to the Grey Tower they'd be able to see Hilcombe one way and Vells the other. Taylor, Jordan's big brother, had told them about it, but the doors were locked – Taylor had broken in with older boys from the village. The Grey Tower's rectangle window was big and as black as tar. Kai had walked by there with Dad once on the way to Jonesies in Hilcombe.

Saffie placed a hand on Kai's shoulder and said, 'I'll do it, but only if you do something for me.'

His heart sped up. For the first time he spotted freckles across her nose, matching his.

She pointed her inhaler at the tower and sprayed. 'You'll go there with me.'

'Easy! We can go now.'

'No,' she said. 'At school, Taylor said you have to break in; we need him to come too.'

'You want to go inside?'

Nodding, she grinned and he felt as excited as he did when twizzling sparklers on Bonfire Night.

'Deal,' he said, leaning back against the trunk. 'We're the same. Everyone says it. Our ideas are the best.'

'Hippie Mandy says we're soulmates.'

'What's that?'

'I don't know.' Their legs swung from the branch in time with each other. 'When two people are the bestest mates that could ever be.'

'They talked about soul at church today.'

'What did they say?'

'Some go to heaven. If we're soulmates we must be going to heaven together.'

'Cool.'

'Dad and Jade don't believe in heaven.'

'Do you?'

He shrugged, gazing at the smashed window of the Grey Tower, wondering how to get Taylor to take them there. He didn't really like Taylor – he was a pig show-off – but if it was the only way to make Saffie happy he would ask him.

'Look.' Kai pointed to the hedge in the field below them. Three grey rabbits hopped along, stopping to eat dandelions. Saffie moved closer to him. 'They're like Flopsy at school; even better because they're wild and you know the best thing about rabbits?'

'What?' she asked.

'They live in big families underground in warrens. I watched about it on TV. They have real feelings and look after each other.'

'I don't know about rabbits.'

'I'll teach you everything, if you want?'

'OK.'

He felt as fizzy as cherryade because Saffie was really interested and put a hand on his knee then pressed the side of her head against his.

'Let's follow them,' he said, 'but we have to be really quiet.'

After that he went to the woods all the time to watch the rabbits. If he stayed out late enough and kept quiet they came and scurried about right next to him. At the start he followed them, but was too loud, so he learned to watch from a distance. Then he brought carrots, cauliflower and basil from Nanny Sheila's. Papa Grey was the largest buck, the leader, and protected the others even though they moved away when he hopped near and it made Kai think Papa Grey was king of the woods. They were his pets.

One afternoon he told Nanny Sheila all he knew about rabbits as they drank tea and squash in her back garden waiting for rock cakes to cook.

'There are sometimes two or three bucks in a warren,' said Kai, 'if it's a big warren. The female rabbits are called does. They like eating fruit and vegetables, but not apple pips – they're poisonous.'

'How do you know about rabbits?' Nanny Sheila asked as he bounded across her garden in cartwheels and roly-polies. Stopping suddenly, realising he couldn't flip on hard ground.

'They're in the woods and I look at the picture books at school,' he called over his shoulder. He crouched on the grass, turned to her and tapped the lawn with his back leg.

'You're king of rabbits, Kai,' Nanny Sheila said.

'Yeah!' He jumped up, clapping his hands because she'd reminded him of Papa Grey, and he ran back to Nanny Sheila, who licked her thumb and rubbed his cheek with her cold daddy-long-leg fingers.

'My little king of rabbits,' she said.

CHAPTER 15

25 November 2005

That Friday, after I got suspended from school for running away – apparently 'I was a danger to myself and contravening health and safety regulations' – me and the lads went to town to play pool. I'd told them how fucked I felt about Rabbit being about to die, I'd had her since I could remember, so we agreed to get some mandy from Taylor, who gave us three bombs for fifteen quid. The pool hall was dead. I'd forgotten the smell of the place: musty, a hint of hairspray and piss. The walls were burgundy and the wooden floorboards scuffed. We decided to wait till we left to swallow the bombs in case the bar girls noticed us buzzing. Brightly lit fridges brimmed with alcopops, beers and ciders, and the sliding drawer of the till rang with each bought drink. The two bar girls – one skinny, flicking a ponytail around a face of rainbow make-up, the other chubby with an undercut and not wearing a scrap of make-up – poured drinks and wiped tables slowly.

Jord was the best at pool. He won all the time because he played with his dad every other weekend. Every time me and Richie played him, he tried to rinse us for cash. When he first made us go there, we must have both lost thirty quid – Jade had been pissed because it was pocket money she'd given me – till we cottoned on; after that we only bet a quid a game. There were TV screens showing a cricket game. I leaned on the next table as they took shots, eating dry-roasted peanuts and thumbing through the messages on my phone, wondering if Dad would ever play pool with me, he used to be good at it. Maybe I'd never see him again; I was choosing Mum. I put my phone down and watched three lads over the room playing with a girl wearing a sequined jacket and a beanie hat.

The lonely feeling was back. In the past I would have spoken to Saffie. Life changed the older you got. It got harder. And then you died.

' . . . don't you reckon, Kai?' asked Jord.

'What was that?' I asked.

'Mate, wake up, you've been away with the fairies all night,' he said.

'Probably thinking about Rabbit,' said Richie, chalking a cue.

The low-hanging lights they had above the pool tables were good because it meant I didn't have to look at them. I said, 'Actually, I was wondering what the point of it all is.'

'Of what?' asked Richie.

'Life, mate.'

Bent over the table, Jord pointed a cue in one direction then another. Before he hit the white, he said, 'Deep shit.'

'Deep as your mum,' said Richie.

'Just like you,' said Jord, missing a red ball, 'to have nothing deep to say.'

'Well, I don't know,' Richie snorted. 'I don't give a fuck.' He took a shot and potted a yellow. 'The purpose of life is to not get old. To never be that old codger wearing socks in sandals, I'd rather die.'

'What d'you think?' Jord asked, putting his drink down next to me.

'Not much.' I gulped Jord's pint. 'We're just dust floating round in a galaxy. We mean fuck all.'

'You think too much,' said Richie, sipping his lemonade.

'Maybe you don't think enough,' jumped in Jord.

'There's no point to anything,' said Richie.

Thinking of Nan, I said, 'I don't believe in God.'

'Nor me.' Jord whacked a ball in. He looked at Richie. 'But if there was no point in anything, old people wouldn't ever do anything.'

We watched Jord pot the black.

'What d'you think?' I asked him.

'I'm gonna save the world, mate.'

That started Richie off laughing. He asked, 'How's that?'

'I'll spike everyone's water with hallucinogenics.'

'We're a shower of fucking pillocks,' I said, thinking about the galaxies, 'not stardust.'

After we left the pub we went to a local park, sat in one of the tunnels and took the mandy; it wasn't much, but enough to make our eyes shake. We were walking through a field just out of town when we started coming up. It was dark. The full moon shone on the icy mud so it looked like silk, or the sea at Weymouth when it shimmers in summer. Richie walked ahead of us and me and Jord watched him jump on to the wooden fence between ours and the next field. He lifted his head to the moon and howled. My head slipped. Richie howled again and I cupped my hands around my mouth, sucked in a wedge of air and copied. What would Saffie be up to? No moments in my life had been better than the ones with her. They felt holy.

'Come on,' I said to Jord, pulling his arm, and he howled.

We ran to Richie, jumped up and balanced with a leg each side of the fence, howling at the moon. I imagined all the other cunts who had ever done it. I loved that shit. It was like you were connected to every other person who'd ever been on the dangling planet before you, and those who would come after and would howl at the fucking beautiful moon. Forever was in those moments.

An hour later, closer to Middledown, the buzz started wearing off. I began feeling guilty and like, because I was using drugs, I'd probably be a crackhead gauging out on a sofa by the time I was twenty. Worse than Mum and Dad. The next day, on my paper round, I'd have a comedown and hate myself even more. Every time I did it, I wound up knowing what a piece of shit I was. Least I'd forgotten about Rabbit for an hour, though.

CHAPTER 16

THEN

Kai had got Jordan and Taylor to bring Kaos for a walk with Saffie and Boring Twin. In Middledown Woods, they picked cowslips and threw sticks for the woofing Kaos, who bounced backwards and forwards chasing after every dash of squirrel, barking at trees long after they'd passed so that Taylor had to do his angry voice to call the dog back.

The day felt golden. The woodland floor lifted and dipped as they dodged between spindly old roots of helicopter trees and the holly bushes, which looked too spiky and Christmassy outside of winter.

Fern, Saffie's favourite. They ran hands over leaves, seeing tiny balls on the underside – seeds? The ferns looked like baby palm trees from far away and wild garlic was green tongues. They found a metal graveyard of rusty bike frames, fan-shaped iron, a microwave – horrible – as they hurdled across mud still gooey from spring, following the footpath running alongside the brown river, skimming pebbles. They hopped over a stile into a small meadow – it had to be the secret one! – where the grass shuffled, sounding like rice against their trainers and sandals. Kaos trotted at Kai's side, being cute for once, rubbing his head into Kai's hip, wagging his tail when Kai gently squeezed the muscle on his back. Ahead, Saffie asked Taylor questions about tractors and cars because he knew all about them.

'Saffie,' Kai called, and she slowed to wait for him. 'This is Middledown Woods' secret.'

'I've been to the meadow before.'

'But it looks like a secret, doesn't it?'

'Because the trees are thicker at the sides.'

Through grass and buttercups up to their knees, the wind shuddered. They threw off their rucksacks and flopped to the ground, pulling out plastic bottles with frozen black-currant squash inside, enjoying the freezing-cold sweetness splash their mouths as the sun felt rich on their arms. An invisible chicken squawked.

'Here.' Saffie pulled out strawberry laces from her bag.

The last two weeks there had been no pocket money to buy sweets, probably because he'd stolen Dragon. So sweet, so tasty, Kai's mouth watered as he chewed.

'If you could go anywhere in the world, where would you go?' asked Jordan, through mouthfuls of sausage rolls he started to share out.

'Disneyland,' said Boring Twin, who always wanted to play mummies and daddies with Jordan, though he preferred pirates. They had the same bright lemon-coloured hair; Nanny Sheila called them cherubs.

'America,' said Taylor. 'To Las Vegas to win loads of money.'

'Is there loads of money there?' asked Kai.

'Duh, it's a gambling city.'

Pig show-off. At least Crystal wasn't there – Taylor acted the big-man around her. Today, the main thing was to climb the Grey Tower. It hit him how to get them there.

'Where would you go, Saffie?'

'The Grey Tower.'

Taylor snorted. 'That's stupid.'

'No it isn't,' Kai snapped.

'But why there? It's too close.'

For a moment she thought about the question, cross-legged next to her boring sister. She looked like a rainbow next to a grey sky. 'So I could see everywhere we go at the same time from up high, like the sun and moon when they watch us.'

'You need a ladder to get into there, unless you can pick a lock.'

'What type of lock is it?' Kai asked, and he felt like a crow hunting a mouse.

'What d'you mean "what kind of lock"? A lock.'

'There are lots of types,' said Kai. He wanted to call Taylor a durr-brain, but it was more important to find out the answer. 'You get locks like deadlocks and padlocks.' There were more; these were the only two Dad had told him about when he'd given him the lock-picking kit and Kai had only practised on the padlocks of their and Nanny's sheds, oh and Leah's diary.

'It's padlocked. You'll never get in. There's like ten on there or something stupid; that's why we smashed the window.'

Leah's diary padlock didn't really count. Kai lay back, crossing his arms behind his head. As soon as he and Saffie ran away from the others they could go to the tower. He had his lock-picking set in his rucksack. Grass tickled his neck. He imagined the ants and worms underneath. A bumblebee buzzed over; it hovered above the grass like a black blob of chocolate. The plane he'd spotted earlier disappeared behind clouds, grumbling goodbye.

Kai asked, 'Where's the worst place you've been?'

Saffie snapped off a buttercup. A butterfly twisted past, flashing red and black. 'Your house when your mum and dad argue.'

Kai froze, and everyone went quiet. Saffie kept snapping bits of grass.

'Everyone's parents fight,' he said.

'No they don't.'

'Your dad doesn't even live with you.'

'So?' Boring Twin said.

'So, what do you know?'

'Ours don't shout,' Jordan said, raising a hand to shield his eyes from the sun.

What to say? Kai knew his parents loved each other and would always be together. How could he say that, in case everyone said the opposite?

A duck batted its wings in front of clouds that looked like steam, its long neck thick, naked, and its mouth open. Dogs barked from the woods and Kaos growled.

'Come on.' Taylor pulled out Kaos's lead. 'Don't want him starting.'

*

Kai and Saffie said they wanted to stay in the woods. Jordan and Taylor were only too happy to have Boring Twin to themselves. As soon as they disappeared Kai pulled Saffie by the hand to the cycle path that led through thousands of gnats to the tower. There was a plaque, 'Grey Tower built in 1768 by Harry Grey'. There was more writing. Kai pulled Saffie away. She was wearing red gloves with snowflakes on and a red jumper with a fluffy white snowman printed on it, the best red clothes to match his red cape, even though she was so hot.

At the huge door, 'Oak,' said Saffie, 'it said on the sign, from Middledown Woods. Oh, no.'

'What?'

'It's properly locked. Taylor was right.'

Excited, Kai pulled the black leather pouch from his rucksack. It was a special thing he could do and he was going to take Saffie where she really wanted to go. 'I can get in to any building.'

'How?'

He stopped to watch her. 'I'm a lock picker.'

She clapped her hands, keeping her eyes on the closed pouch. 'Like a real thief?'

'All the best thieves know how.'

She dropped her hands, her bottom lip pinker where she'd pursed them together, and she unzipped the pouch in his hands before touching the tools – the worm, the snake, the hook, the diamond. She whispered, 'You're brilliant. Can you really?'

Pride felt like the red and black butterfly he'd seen earlier in the meadow flying through his insides. 'Hopefully, soon, I'll be able to do every lock on our street.'

'How?'

'I'm going to practise.'

There were three old padlocks. Dad said the modern ones were much harder to get into so he felt like he could do it.

'Look,' he took out the first piece of metal, 'this is the wrench.'

He was slow and steady. Saffie watched closely.

It was meant to be. Kai was brilliant at opening padlocks. They pushed open the creaky door. An old settee with ripped embroidered fabric like the cushions in church had dark varnished lion's feet, one broken. Light from small windows leading to the big window shone over a winding staircase. There was hay on the floor and sheets of paper. He stood closer, muddy footprints covered the papers, the floorboards. Even smashed eggshells. There must be a nest.

Saffie picked up two sheets; reading without her purple glasses screwed her nose up. She tossed it and the paper spun like giant leaves, making dust dance in the sunlight.

It smelled old. The wooden floorboards were dull under their feet and echoed slightly at the bottom of the steps. Dried bird poo dripped down the black staircase, gross, and the metal clanged as Kai climbed. He felt the best. Breaking into the tower.

At the top of the stairs was a trapdoor with a handle and a clip at the top big enough for a thumb. He pressed down and pushed. The heavy door lifted and Kai pushed hard and it clattered open. He poked his head through.

Raven watched from the windowsill.

'Hello, Raven,' he said.

Feathers so dark they shimmered purple. Eyes two small buttons. Sharp wings.

There was a macky furry cream-coloured rug with purple stains on, a smashed bottle and other bottles with melted candles in. On a wall, a painting of a man in a large hat stared. He had white wispy hair, a big belly and pink cheeks and a look on his face like he would break you in half if he caught you in his tower.

'That's Mr Grey,' said Kai.

'And that one,' said Saffie, pointing to the opposite side of the room at another painting, 'is his wife.'

The woman wore purple velvet and small birds in her high curly hair. Her face looked cruel and it reminded Kai of somebody. Nanny's friend, Betty.

'Saffie, is there ... is there anything special you can do? Like, that nobody knows about, not even me?'

Raven watched from the windowsill.

'There is one thing, yeah.'

'What?' Kai felt jealousy ping from the secret she hid from him.

Her chin jutted out.

'What?' he asked.

The snowflakes on her gloves flashed when she put her hands over her eyes. Raven flew off.

'I'm sorry.' He touched her arm. 'Don't cry.'

When she lowered her hands her face had the same wildness like when they ran on the lanes or played on their silver moon and beat the furred hunters.

'No,' she was fierce, 'I'm not a baby. I don't cry. It's real, Kai.'

'What is it?'

'I can fly.'

Impossible. Like Peter Pan? No one could, and he was about to say this, then remembered everyone laughing when he told them about Silver his rabbit who they said was imaginary, so he thought, Why not? Maybe Saffie could fly.

'Cool,' he said. 'You can teach me.'

And she clapped. It was always great to say the right thing.

Opposite the window was an old desk with a green leather top and a green leather chair to match. The leather felt soft, the shiny scratched wood was grimy. On top was a lamp shaped like a flower, plugged in. It didn't turn on when he flicked the switch. There were drawers, which were stiff to open without the metal bits that made them slide easy like he had in his drawers at home. The top drawer had a bronze lock. He'd not tried anything except padlocks. Maybe he could open it. He pulled out the little wrench and snake pick and started to rake the pins, enjoying the zippy sounds, fast then slow – click click click click click – five pins.

Click. Nervous, Kai swallowed, pulling the handle. The drawer slid forward. Nothing. What if he found something really amazing and Saffie wanted it? They were partners now, weren't they? He'd whizzed his part of the deal and broken into her tower, quickly too. Among the shadows at the back of the drawers he saw something.

'Look.' He held up a large copper coin. The mackiest coin he'd ever seen, with a man with curly hair on it. And there was a compass, like Leah used for Maths homework, and a map, the sort a pirate would have. He looked back at the painting on the wall, wondering how far they were from the sea. It took hours and hours to get to Weymouth in Nanny Sheila's red Fiesta.

'Come here.' Saffie waved at him and they sat on the sun-warmed stone windowsill inspecting each item. The map had countries and oceans on; Middledown was nowhere to be seen. The compass was sharp as his diamond pick.

'So,' said Kai, 'are you my partner now?'

With a sigh that lifted her chest she said, 'Obbiously.'

He placed the coin in his bag and remembered Dragon. 'This is for you.'

'From Headmaster T's office?'

'It's yours because dragons are for protection.'

'But I'm not scared.'

He shrugged. 'Your dad isn't around to save you if anything happens.'

'What could happen?'

When Dad told him the story of Princess Sue in the tower the baddies turned out to be her own family. It made his mind mixy to think about it.

'You're around if anything happened, anyway.'

Squeezing Dragon's sharp tail, he watched his finger turn yellowy. 'His breath's the same colour as your hair, he lives on our silver moon and when I'm not near you he'll be there instead. He knows what I think.'

'I know what you think, too.' She took Dragon, placing him on her knee, and Dragon yawned happily.

'Me you, too.'

Outside they could see Vells and Hilcombe. They were the wrong side of the woods to see Middledown.

'Look,' said Kai. They watched three rabbits hop along the wall below them out across the cycle path into the woods, one of them big and brave. He was the leader. 'I bet it's Papa Grey.'

Kai twiddled the compass round and round then placed the sharp tip on the stone they sat on. He scratched his initials and handed it to Saffie who scratched hers.

'We could live here,' she said. 'It's our world,' she pointed at the sky, 'and we're being watched.'

The curved white of the moon was high in the sky, which was slowly turning to dark oranges and pinks, and the sun slid lower to the valley walls. 'But we couldn't because this tower has an owner.'

Saffie jumped up suddenly, making Kai's heart quicken. Keeping one hand on the window frame, she leaned forward; her hair whipped about and suddenly she howled.

'I'm a wolf!' She howled again, too close to the window ledge.

'No,' Kai shouted. He grabbed her free hand, pulling her back, and she fell into him, laughing. 'That's dangerous.'

They lay on the rug, staring at thick black cobwebs in the domed ceiling, their hands close to each other's. Kai told Saffie things he didn't even realise he'd thought. When Saffie had said that his parents were scary to be around when they argued, she was right. He knew that. He also recognised the bottles that were placed around the tower were the same as the ones in Nanny Sheila's bin.

'I want you to be with me always,' he said.

'I will,' she said. 'We could be blood brother and sister then we'll be stuck together for ever.'

The compass was on the windowsill; when he grabbed it he heard crows cawing like crying witches. He took the compass to Saffie and they sat cross-legged in front of each other. Digging the spike into his palm he clenched his teeth. He was a big strong boy so kept pressing in the spike, wriggling it, like his skin was a lock to be picked, revealing treasure. It hurt. Blood poked through, a blob on his skin. 'Shall I do you?'

She snatched the compass. 'You need to make it bleed more.'

She stabbed him quick, sharply, pressed hard and he yelped; her eyes were wide open. She then worked hard to dig the sharp metal tip into her own hand.

'Ow!' she yelled. 'Ow!' Stabbing again, blood appeared and she laughed, holding her hand up high before yanking it down and stabbing again. 'Ow! Quick.'

They rubbed their palms together and he felt like he'd just done the most important thing of his life.

CHAPTER 17

26 November 2005

The Saturday after we played pool, one of the kids called in sick. I felt like shit – twisted up in the comedown – but I had to deliver Middledown's papers as well as Hilcombe's. Why it annoyed me was because I could end up bumping into Yasmin and I was still trying to decide how to dump her. Bad enough to think about on a normal day, let alone with a hangover.

Less people had a paper in Middledown and the ones who did read the *Sun*, not the *Independent*. I'd just reached Nan's estate. It was a crisp morning, where the sky was white and blue and the world felt like ice.

Because I did Hilcombe first, some old codger moaned her paper was late – in return for me pushing it through her letter box, she flung the door open, frowning. It was 11 a.m. It pissed me off, but I kept my mouth shut because I needed the money. Soon as I was old enough I'd got this job. Kids were shouting in the football field down the other end of the street. Little Tyson would be there.

My bell rang a bit as I stopped outside number 1, the last delivery; I knew old Wheeler would have a paper. His Jack Russell, called Badger, started barking. The dog was nine. Old Wheeler had been wearing the same blue dickie bow, embroidered waistcoat and monocle for almost a decade. Nan said he was mad as a hatter. Couldn't stand him. During the 1940s he lived in America. Everyone knew it because he ran the village leaflet about events and local news, basically none, so he filled it with his stories of America. Nan hasn't spoken to him since he refused to print something Leah wrote about St John's Church when she was my age. Leah was over it, but Nan wasn't.

Old Wheeler was all right – I didn't have any beef with him – but he might tell Yasmin he'd seen me. From my pocket, I pulled the scrap of paper that my manager gave me with the newspapers and matching addresses. I guessed old Wheeler was a *Daily Mail* kind of bloke. To stop the words jumping, I ran my finger down the page till I found his name. I was right: The *Mail*. I hopped off my bike, leaned it against the perfectly trimmed hedge and walked up the path. He had the most boring garden in Middledown: one square of short grass with six curled dog shits on. I preferred gardens with bird baths, kids' bikes and saws.

Old Wheeler opened the door, Badger ran towards me, jumping and wagging his tail. Another way I earned money was by walking him on Sundays. When I dropped to my knees he licked my face. Badger was funny. Wasn't scared of anything. If a dog twice his size came to sniff him, he'd want to fight. Earlier, in the paper shop, I'd bought a couple of dog treats, three bone-shaped biscuits. Badger was well chuffed.

'Not your walk day today, mate, sorry.'

'Where's the usual lad?' asked old Wheeler. Because his nose was long and he was tall, he looked like a snob the way he looked down at you. Probably another reason Nan hated him.

'Pulled a sickie.' I stood to give him the paper.

'Can't get the staff.' He twisted one side of his curly moustache. 'What you doing Thursday night, sonny Jim?'

I shrugged. 'Nothing. Probably be seeing Yasmin.'

'One of our skittles players is on holiday. Would you like to step in?'

'Step in where?'

'Skittles, boy; would you like to play on Middledown's team, help us out?'

No I fucking would not. 'Oh, right,' I said.

What excuse could I use? As if hanging out with a bunch of old fogeys would be any fun. Breaking up with my girlfriend almost seemed the better option. 'Well, I said I'd see Yasmin.'

'Don't worry about her,' he said. 'Just tell her I arranged it. She'll be fine.'

The thing is, I knew she would be. Yasmin loved old Wheeler and visited him Mondays after school to play Othello. Badger started sniffing round the fence to number 12. I felt sorry for him, trapped in the garden.

'OK.' I said. 'Where is it?'

'The Station at seven thirty.'

*

I pedalled to Nan's – risky when I was avoiding Yasmin, but I had to. Dolly Parton was playing through the crack in the small front window; Nan would be in the kitchen with an apron on. Instead of going through the front door, I went straight round the back to Rabbit's hutch; the door to the hutch was open. Not unusual. Most days she hopped round the house, so I went inside.

'Oh, love,' said Nan, holding the phone. 'I was just calling you.'

My heart rocketed to outer space. 'What?'

'It's Rabbit. She's ready to go heavenwards.'

Nan followed me into the lounge, where I found Rabbit. My baby. My best friend. She was on a 'powder-blue' cushion in the middle of the room; the coffee table was pushed in front of the pale yellow display cabinet to give her space. She hardly moved. It made my heart hurt. I dropped beside her and drew the cushion close, resting my hand on her yellow and white fur. The old-fashioned gramophone sounded too loud.

'Can you turn that off?' I asked.

The track scratched to a stop.

'Here.' Nan popped a spare cushion under my head, placed a box of tissues next to me and left the room, quietly shutting the door.

I stayed with Rabbit till her breathing stopped.

CHAPTER 18

THEN

Dad had been away for ages. Where could he have gone all this time? To Tony-teeth from town? The time they'd seen Steve, Dad had said he wanted to smoke with his old mate. It didn't make sense because he smoked at home anyway. But Kai really wanted Dad back because Mum drank less when he was home. She'd drunk two cans in the last hour since she'd got up.

When Denner turned up in a black vest showing off his big muscles, slick black hair parted on the side, he walked in like he owned the place, swinging the door open without knocking, sitting on Dad's dented cushion on the settee, spreading his legs wide, one hand opening a newspaper he'd brought with him, the other flung along the back of the settee, saying to Mum, 'Get the kettle on, lovely.'

Strangest thing, she did.

Usually Mum snapped at Denner. Usually, unless she was drunk, she looked like she'd eaten a mouthful of Nanny's un-sugared rhubarb when he visited.

'He's still not back, then?'

The denim skirt she wore was so short it showed the bottom of her bum cheeks when she bent over the sink to open the window. Denner watched and Kai imagined sticking his baby wrench in his ear.

Denner stood, 'Here.' He threw two twenty-pound notes on the kitchen table before moving back to sit down.

Mum clattered the spoon in Dad's Bruce Lee mug. No one used Dad's mug. There were other clean ones. Kai stood, walked to Mum and standing on the black cupboard doors, which were still piled on the floor in front of the sink, tipped the tea away.

'What you doing?' Her voice raised.

'Why you using Dad's cup? It's not for him.' He put the cup under his *X-Men* T-shirt and sat on the chair opposite Denner, holding the cup as tight as possible so Mum couldn't take it back. If she tried he'd throw it hard at the wall and smash it. She didn't. Instead, she poured water into his favourite teacup with the rabbit on. Kai ground his teeth.

'Thanks, lovely.' Denner's big-man hand patted the seat next to him like Mum would sit next to him.

She did. Why was she acting like this? Kai pressed a finger on the volume button on the remote so the wildlife programme got louder and the clash of the sea filled the room. Mum's voice dropped and Denner's finger touched her knee briefly.

'Like I always say,' Mum said, 'he'll be back, he always is. I'm not sure when. He admitted to me he's smoking it again.'

'Fucking idiot.'

Dad wasn't an idiot. He was the coolest grown-up in the world and better than fathead Denner. Even though it was healed, Kai felt his heart beat in the scratch on the palm of his hand from being Saffie's blood twin.

'And I'm worried, you know? I'm worried. Smoking, it's like one step away from—' She lowered her voice.

'What started it?'

'The cheek of it, Den, he only blamed me, said he didn't think I was coming back last time I was at our Shad's. As if. As if I'd ever leave my kids. They're my kids. More than his. I do everything around here.'

That was a lie. Leah and Jade did loads and were doing more and more since Mum hid in her stinky bedroom all the time making her eyebags darker.

'You do,' he said, finger higher than her knee. 'You always were the best girlfriend.'

From the corner of his eye Kai knew Mum was looking at him. He stared at the TV, feeling strange because it sounded like Denner used to be Mum's boyfriend. He wanted to run away. It was time to build a den. What would he need? A hammer? He didn't have one. He jumped up.

In his bedroom he grabbed his rucksack, shoving in the lock-picking pouch, then he crept downstairs quietly to sneak out the front door. He didn't want Mum to hear. The living-room door was open a crack and he could hear Denner's grumbly voice so he pressed his eye to the gap of the living-room door, flinching as he thumbed the end of the banister and picked up a splinter.

Mum's face was screwed up, biting her bottom lip. Denner sat sideways with his big robot arm resting on her leg. His hand was up her skirt and his elbow wriggled.

A wave swept through Kai. Paint looked flaky around the door frame that he pressed his knuckles against before he opened the front door. He slammed it as hard as he could – so what if they heard? He ran. As fast as he could, fast fast faster, with his fastest running feet, to the other end of Middledown village, past Nanny's house, past pig-face Denner's house, through the football field, along the cycle path; he didn't stop running until he reached the entrance of Middledown Woods.

He sat down, watching leaf shadows on the floor. The sun started to cool on his arms and the mud felt warm on his hands. It was time to build the den, with or without Dad, and if Dad came home and didn't want to live with Mum they could move to his house in the woods.

A scratching noise caught his attention. Papa Grey watched him from the bottom of a silver-trunked tree, his ears stood up pointy and his eyes were black. A rabbit who wasn't scared. Best rabbit ever.

Now it was just him in a house of women. Kai wanted Dad. He missed watching TV together and listening to him talk about Mike Tyson and Frank Bruno fights. Kai thought about Dad at school, at home, at Nanny Sheila's, before he fell to sleep and then he'd dream about him.

Would he remember him? Come back?

Needing Dad was a heat behind his eyes and in his chest. No smiles, no running like Linford Christie or bouncing like bunnies with Saffie. Sadness was as normal as Adam and Harry's silly jokes because they were always happy, probably because they had their daddies.

Dad, who was big, strong and funny, had crinkly eyes when he smiled, a lumpy sunburned nose and stinky hair.

Big hands with wormy veins and short fingernails. Kai started to bite his fingernails. It got him in trouble with Mum, so what? Mum was a pig-face who let Denner put his hand up her skirt. If Dad came back, did Kai have to tell him? He might leave for ever like Jade and Crystal's dad.

Kai missed Dad's hand that held his in bed when he'd said that Kai was the best thing he and Mum had ever done. It didn't feel like it. Everything was wrong.

'Kai!'

Miss Butterworth stood at the front of the class with her hands on her hips. Must have asked a question. Saffie, on the opposite side of the table, held up her hands under her chin.

'What?'

'We don't say "what", we say "pardon",' Miss Butterworth said. 'What's the answer?'

Kai looked at Saffie, who held up fingers.

'Six,' he said.

Miss Butterworth crossed her arms over her waist, cleared her throat and went on doing sums. Kai couldn't look at Saffie to say thanks, he felt too embarrassed. Men shouldn't need to ask girls. Not when they did things like Mum did.

At afternoon break Saffie followed Kai to Flopsy's hutch. She knew Dad still wasn't home because Jordan knew because he lived next door and he told her sister who told Saffie. If it was up to Kai it would be a secret.

'I wish your dad was back,' she said.

With his hands resting on the hutch, he stared down at Flopsy. He loved the smell of rabbits, the hay and how it reminded him of fields in the valley. Saffie placed a hand on his shoulder and his tummy went bubbly; she leaned forward and kissed his cheek. He felt all hot, like he did when he saw Mum's stupid face through the door when Denner's arm looked like a robot.

'Why have you followed me?' he asked.

'What do you mean?'

'You're always following me.'

'But we always play together.'

'Maybe we shouldn't.' Kai sat in front of Flopsy's hutch.

'What have I done?'

Flopsy was settled in the corner. Kai liked how rabbits moved – their back legs kicking up, their wriggling noses, floppy ears that bolted upright when they listened, how Flopsy's fur went spiky on the top of her head when it rained, their different coloured fur and big black eyes, how they flicked their paws, how sometimes they looked like squirrels and gerbils and rats, but they were bouncing bunnies. And there were so many different types – they talked about it on TV– all over the world in lots of different shapes, sizes and colours. They were different to hares because they hung out in families.

When Flopsy's hutch appeared at school Kai was in Reception class. During assembly Headmaster T read *Peter Rabbit*. He told the children about their new pet and how the children would take it in turns to look after her, how it was important to be calm and quiet near her. The children voted on a name.

The first time Kai saw Flopsy, he stopped thinking.

'Kai's mesmerised,' smiled Miss Quiller, the Reception-class teacher.

Kai was allowed to hold Flopsy and feed her. Unclicking the latch on the hutch, he slipped in hay and celery. The rabbit was soft, furry and cuddly. Flopsy guzzled milk so quick her ears and fur twitched. The teachers said he was brilliant, the best rabbit-looker-after in his class. It was the best thing he'd ever done at school. When it was his class's turn to look after Flopsy, Kai tried to get as many gold stars as possible so that he could feed Flopsy carrots during break times.

He grabbed some cold lettuce. When he squeezed it, it crunched; he started breaking it apart.

Why was he being mean to Saffie? He didn't know and he didn't know how to stop.

'Why are you being mean?' she asked because she could read his mind. 'We're meant to be blood twins.'

And best friends and partners.

Kai carefully placed lettuce into Flopsy's hutch. Before he could shut the door, Saffie grabbed his hand, found the cut on the palm that had a yellow bruise around it and pressed hard.

Jordan was cool to hang out with. Not as fun as Saffie because he wasn't good at seeing things that weren't there, but he played pirates and Pokémon cards. On the school coach they sat on top of the wheel and led the kids in the coach song that had been passed on year after year.

Daisy, Daisy, gimme your tits to chew
I'm half crazy my balls are going blue
I can't afford a condom
A plastic bag will do, so
Lie on your back
And open your crack
And I'll make love to you.

Everyone laughed. Kai knew it was rude because it said tits and balls and told the woman to lie down and not many girls sang along apart from Crystal, who loved singing. It was the funniest saying naughty things where none of the teachers or grown-ups heard except the coach driver, who stared at the road, driving as fast as he could through the country lanes where trees made a tunnel either side and they bumped up and down over the lumps – it was why over-the-wheel seats were best. When they finished that song they started on 'The Wheels on the Bus'.

The zip on Jordan's school bag always tugged; he yanked at the front of it, pulling out his Pokémon cards, sorting through them.

'Charizard!' Kai poked the one at the top, the one he wanted, a golden dragon with one hundred and twenty HP points. There was no way he'd be able to get it, though; he had no savings because pocket money had stopped. 'You wanna come to my nanny's house? She's got cars to play with and she'll have cakes we can eat.'

When they arrived Nanny Sheila was in the front garden wearing garden mitts.

'Take those trowels,' she said, pointing at two small spades. They picked them up and she pointed at five brown pots of mud. 'Use them to make the soil crumbly. I need it crumbly as the top of a raw apple crumble after you've put the sugar in. OK? You hungry, boys?'

'Yes!'

She disappeared through the front door, her flowery dress touched by a breeze, and they dug in among old roots, bulbs, centipedes and green spiders, stabbing hard bits to make the earth loose. Saffie walked past; she'd got off the coach after them and when she neared the garden gate, she kicked it. He pretended not to hear. After a while, Kai lifted his head; Saffie was stood by the side of her house – the dirty peach walls needed new paint like his house – and when their eyes met she stuck out her tongue and ran down the path to her back garden.

A whistle pierced the air, 'Singing in the Rain'. Stupid because it hadn't rained in ages; it must be Mr Wheeler, who Nanny hated. The moustached man trotted round like he was on a film, his monocle swinging down his black spotted shirt as he passed the garden. Nanny Sheila's flip-flops slopped against the front doorstep. She made her eyes slitty when she saw him.

'Bloody man,' she grumbled under her breath as he disappeared down the road.

'What you planting?' Kai asked when she handed out blueberry muffins. They were warm and the blueberries had burst, seeping over the cake like vampire blood. Yummy.

'Wild flowers, like poppies. You know the red ones like we wear to remember the men who died in the wars?' Then she went back in and when she returned she brought out three glasses – Nanny didn't like plastic – of purple lemonade made from honey, lavender, lemons and fizzy water.

Ice clinked. Kai had only broken three of Nanny's glasses. She didn't care, so long as he froze like an iceberg when it happened so she could sweep it up; Crystal had broken four. When Jordan put it to his nose, he frowned. 'It smells funny.'

'It's good for you and very tasty,' Nanny said. 'All the pixies and trolls drink it because it comes from the meadows.'

So they drank. Perfumey as Nan's bedroom and very tasty because of the bees' honey.

Nanny picked up a large bag and sliced it open with one side of a pair of scissors. It was filled with new black earth. 'This is to mix in.' She scooped handfuls out and plopped it into the pots and they started mixing it with the old mud. 'Your dad home yet?'

'No.' Kai felt the muscles in his arms tighten as he stirred the fresh and old soil and he wondered if the insects in it felt happy that their home was getting new walls and carpets, if they liked the dampness on their shells from the new stuff.

'You know where he is?' Nanny's voice sounded like Hippie Mandy's when she'd asked him lots of questions and he'd decided not to say much, just that Dad had gone to his friend's, but Nanny knew Mum and Dad shouted sometimes so it didn't matter what he told her.

'In town. I think he's with Tone, his mate he likes to smoke with. It's stupid because he smokes at home, even the smelly pipes.'

'Smelly pipes?'

'Yeah.' At the sound of her question, Kai felt an invisible wall close around him because he remembered those pipes were Mum and Dad's secret, which is why they usually only smoked them in the bedroom where he wasn't meant to see.

'What pipes are they?'

Kai shrugged. 'All the smoking smells. What's next?'

'Here.' Nanny Sheila tore off the top of a packet of seeds. 'Hold your hands out, both of you, yes. Sprinkle them on top of the mud and then we're going to cover them with more soil. Spread them out, well done.'

The soil from the bag was full of special nutrients to help the seeds grow. After they topped up the pots, Nanny gave them watering cans to sprinkle. Finally they moved the pots round the edges of the lawn until Nanny was happy they would get lots of sun.

'Shall we play Pokémon?' asked Kai, wanting to see Charizard again.

'Yeah,' said Jordan.

They flopped on to the grass next to the bird bath that had a tiny gurgling fountain and pulled out the cards and Kai knew before they left Nanny Sheila's that he was going to take Charizard because it was a special test to practise if he could get his hands on anything.

It had taken days and days to build the den under the needle tree. What Kai loved most about his den was nobody knowing where he was. As he finished preparing the walls, snapping off branches from the inside of the bush, he knew Mum would be worried at home, imagining him lost and lonely, like she did the night Denner had been there and he'd said he'd been in the football field and she'd said he should be careful and to stay at Nanny's. She was wrong, so wrong, and this was now his special place. Maybe the girls had secret places, but he doubted it because all Leah cared about was books, Jade her sketchbooks and Crystal her nail varnish. Except Leah said each book held another world for the mind. Strange; he believed her, though, because Leah didn't tell lies, she was a child and the last few weeks showed him the difference between children and grown-ups was that the big ones lied and that could only mean one thing: he was a bit of a grown-up too because he was a professional now.

Beneath the back of his knees, where his skin was soft like a leg-armpit, the floor was covered in moss, so the sounds of the woods were muffled and when he lay down to look at the sky through the knobbly branches it felt soft on his arms and calf muscles. Finally, he had built three rooms in the den and there was no denying that there was a small one for Saffie where she could do her girly things, a room for him to do his manly things like practising poker, picking locks and spying on the rabbit hole, and the big room, which was next to the tallest needle tree in Middledown Woods. The big room was where he and Saffie would be able to eat strawberry laces, Chupa Chups and plan their missions because all good thieves needed a secret place to plan.

Kai thumped the moss, hating that Dad was friends with Denner. At least because Saffie was a child she would never do something so bad he felt it in his bones – only grown-ups did that. Oh, he missed her. There was no one to talk to about the silver moon.

A cloud through the branches looked like a cat; it started to stretch as it moved and he wondered if God chased them out of heaven like Nanny Sheila did in her garden.

Denner's robot arm, so disgusting, kept getting in his head. Mum had done wrong, too, to let him do that. Except Kai had, come to think of it, seen her hand pushing his arm away, trying to pull her skirt down, saying, 'No, Denner, stop.' That was what happened, Kai was sure; he'd felt so dizzy he'd run instead of helping. Maybe it was his fault. Now his head felt like a river about to burst its banks. He shook it.

Hippie Mandy said to listen to the birds and wind and to take pufferfish breaths. The teaching assistant was nice; she helped him read when the letters crawled up the page like ants. He held a hand up where an ant tickled across, he turned it and watched it crawl along the scar he had made with Saffie. How he wanted her to be in the den now so they could name the trees and birds. There was another tree with caterpillar bits that he thought should be called caterpillar tree. How could he decide without Saffie, who always made his ideas better?

If winter came and he hadn't built a roof then he would get wet. They needed something, him and Dad and Saffie, so they'd be protected from the wind. On his own he just couldn't think and his tummy bubbled. He needed Saffie. She was his best friend and he'd been nasty when all she did was try to make him feel better. Being nasty was being like Denner. No. No way. It was time to do the right thing and say sorry. Again.

Back at home, there was an incoming-call-only phone in the living room with big black buttons. After he got in and Mum questioned where he'd been and he said the football field, she told him Dad was on his way home, he'd called. So exciting! Where best to sit so he could see Dad as soon as he showed up? In the girls' bedroom looking out of the window so he could see down the road? Or on the settee so he'd be closer when Dad walked in the room? Or by the living-room window so he could see him walk up the garden path? The garden path?

Outside, Kai sat on the yellow toy tractor at the garden gate looking down the road. Over the road, Bob-Cycle was fixing a mountain bike in his shed, playing the radio, singing along.

Kai waited quietly; he'd got in two hours ago.

Remembering how tall Dad was, how strong. The smell of his hair, his short fingernails. He could throw Kai over his shoulder. Dad would be so happy to see him, hug and play. Dad would say sorry for being gone so long. Ages had passed since he'd disappeared. His sisters didn't care; Kai did. The evening smelled spicy, and Kai imagined Mum's jerk spices landing on his tongue when he stuck it out.

'Having fun, young'un?' called Bob. The vest he wore had sweat patches under the arms and pulled around his beer belly. Bob had stopped mending the bike to sprinkle breadcrumbs in his bird house, surrounded by orange roses, in the middle of the garden. Kai liked Bob, who had shown him how to fix tyres and reattach bike chains. Again he wished to the silver moon for a bike on his birthday. It was really soon.

'Yeah,' said Kai, his voice high. 'Just waiting for my dad.'

He moved and leaned over the fence. Inside his Power Rangers trainer; he wiggled toes. Two whole weeks was ages. He couldn't wait for a cuddle and to be held up in the air. Kai ran back down the path to his tractor.

Suddenly Dad was by the garden fence and Kai jumped up with a foot each side of the tractor. Dad's face looked blank and a little bit strange, a bit wonky. He strolled with his shoulders back, a rucksack hanging from one, and a smoke in his hand, his red nose pointed up. The other hand he kept in his tracksuit pocket. Man with swag, that's what Mum called him, in Adidas trackies. Bright red curls, much brighter red than his. Daddy was home!

He walked slowly. Bob stood by the roses, watching. Dad rested a hand on the gate, looked at the house, took a last puff, threw the butt on the floor and crushed it with his Air Max. Usually his trainers were crisp, today they were filthy. The gate creaked as he unlocked it. He strolled up the path, past Kai and round the back.

Kai felt his eyes burn. Did he do something wrong? Inside his chest something twisted. The garden held him, birds chirped. He studied the steering wheel of his tractor: it had a Pikachu Pokémon sticker on it.

'You all right, cocker?' called Bob.

Kai lifted his head and nodded then followed Dad inside. Maybe he'd get a cuddle now?

He didn't. Until Dad drank four cans of Special Brew and made the room smell gross from smoking the cola can at the kitchen table, and suddenly he grabbed Kai, kissed him, told him to sit on the chair by him and Kai felt puffed up when Dad pulled a special knife from his rucksack to show him, holding the brown leather handle in one hand and resting the spike on a finger of the other. He twisted it forward and back, catching the dull light from the white lampshade above the table.

'It's a special one this, son. Can cut through anything.'

Must be to add to Dad's special tools, Kai thought, holding his hands out to take it.

'No,' said Mum, grumpy. 'It's too sharp.'

'I've got something too,' said Kai, pulling Jordan's Charizard card from his pocket. Dad knew Kai had lots of Pokémon cards and didn't look impressed. 'It's a special one and, and—'

Mum grabbed the cola can and sparked the lighter.

'I got it from Jordan,' Kai finished. 'Right in front of him.'

There were different types of smoking Mum and Dad did and it got confusing. There were the ones when they went sleepy and the ones when they went really chatty and Kai wasn't sure which one it was today because Dad was sleepy but he talked quite a bit. What Kai didn't think about was that the puff Mum had just taken was her first that night and she'd not drunk that day because she didn't have money till dole day. She'd spent the money Denner gave her on drink – that ran out yesterday. When her eyes squinted at him he realised the smoke was the chatty one where they listened to everything and he'd been confused because Dad wasn't acting normal. Everything felt blurry. Like the time the sun had felt like a brown smudge when Leah had told him her secret.

'You did what?' asked Mum. 'You took that off Jordan?'

'It was just practice.'

'Leave the boy alone,' said Dad.

'You can shut the fuck up, too,' said Mum.

Jade and Crystal jumped off the settees and ran upstairs and Leah stared at her book. She wasn't reading, Kai could tell because her eyes were looking near the floor by Dad's feet. Dad didn't say anything; he carried on twisting the knife round in his hand, poking his tongue in the gap between his front two teeth.

Embarrassed, Kai lowered his eyes to the card; he didn't want to make them fall out as soon as Dad was back. 'Sorry, Mum.'

'You're taking that back.' Mum stood up, lifted her shoulders up and down like bouncing beans had taken over her. 'Come on. Now.'

On TV, the ITV news reporter said that Labour was gaining popularity and Mum mumbled, 'As if those rasses know what real life's like.' She often swore at the TV. She turned and clapped her hands at him. 'Come on, then.'

'Let Kai go on his own,' said Leah. She crossed the room and sat at the table, which was strange. On his own? At least that way he could speak to Jordan without Mum and Sharon going on about how naughty he was. Leah looked at the cola can as if it was a cowpat before she carried on, 'We need to talk about what we're doing for Kai's birthday tomorrow.'

Tomorrow? Not even Kai had known! Suddenly, Mum looked like a statue. Dad winked at Kai, saying, 'I've got you a present, lad, you're gonna love it.'

CHAPTER 19

30 November 2005

Being suspended from school was a relief. Shame it was the middle of winter. If it had have been summer, I would have cycled to Cranston. It was too far in the rain. Why it was great was because I could stay in bed. Because Mum and the girls got up at different times, they just left me to myself, apart from when Jade was on the late shift, then she'd wake me with fried egg on toast, like she did Wednesday.

I'd spent all morning in bed with the curtains drawn and was smoking a spliff, watching *Pirates of the Caribbean*, when there was a knock on the front door about 1 p.m. Mum or Jade opened it. Yasmin's voice made my eyes shoot open. What was she doing here? She should have been at school. I jumped up, opened the window – Yasmin hated the smell of weed – waved my arms around, but I'd proper hot-boxed the place.

Jade shouted up to me.

I stood at the top of the stairs – time paused – gazing at Yasmin's face-like-a-slapped-ass. Something was wrong. It felt like I was moving through sand when I held my hand out. She climbed the steps with her head drooped, pushed her thumb into my palm. She was wearing her baggy PE tracksuit bottoms. Weird.

Inside my room I straightened the quilt and she lowered on to it. It felt like the sun was fading; I thought of the red ribbons in my old money box. She reached in her pocket and handed me a slim plastic finger with two lines on.

'It's positive.' I'd seen a pregnancy kit under the sink in our bathroom once; I guessed it was Crystal's and never mentioned it.

A single needle pierced into the middle of my forehead – that's how it felt. I don't know why. I really don't.

Deep pufferfish breath.

'Fuck,' I said.

'I know,' she said.

'I thought you were on the pill?'

'I took it.' She shook her head, grabbed hold of her hair with one hand.

'You're lying.' I jumped up.

She flew up and thumped my chest. Being five inches taller, I didn't budge. Anger ripped through me, I wanted to slap her.

'How dare you!' she shouted.

'You always grab your hair like that,' I pointed, 'when you're lying.'

'I'm not,' she said. 'I'm not. I mean, I got the morning-after pill. I went to the clinic with Mum the next day.'

As if she was telling me this. Lying little bitch. 'So you weren't on the pill?'

'Well—'

'I didn't even want sex,' I spat.

Big mistake. That started world war three. She was hitting me and screaming, 'As if I'd want a kid with you!' Then she pushed me and I tripped over my trainer, crashing against the wardrobe. Slammed the back of my head. I felt violent.

Jade came in.

'What the fuck you playing at, Yasmin?' Her voice boomed and Yaz looked small and pathetic. The way her eyes narrowed at Jade showed me she was exaggerating; she wasn't freaked out about the situation. She got off on it.

'It's him,' she said.

'Get out,' Jade ordered.

If Crystal had walked in it would have been different. Thankfully she was at work for once.

'Mum!' Jade yelled downstairs, leading Yasmin from the room, and then she told Mum to walk her home. After they left she looked at me. 'What was that about?'

'She's pregnant.' The words were gristle.

Of all my family I'm relieved it was Jade who found out first, she was spot on, not overreacting, and she never talked like shit was all about her. She ran her hands over her face, then put one on my shoulder and we perched on the edge of the bed.

'Wow.'

What did 'wow' mean? It was a good thing? Excitement had slunk into the far corner of the world. I knew she couldn't believe it.

'Fuck,' I said. 'I was going to end it.'

'You can't now.'

It stung. 'I know.'

The film seemed too loud in the background. Jade turned down the volume. She said, 'Did you use protection?'

I wanted to headbutt the fucking wall. There was a pint of orange squash at the foot of the bed. I downed it. 'Yeah. The condom broke.'

'And she didn't get the morning-after pill?'

'She did. She said she did – I believe her.'

A whistling sound escaped through Jade's teeth. There had never been a moment where I appreciated Jade so much for never doubting what I said, and it made me feel like elephant shit.

'This is bad luck,' she said.

Bad luck be fucked, I was cursed. Be stuck with Yasmin my whole life? I wanted kids one day, but at fifteen? With her?

'I'm gonna make a cup of tea.'

'OK,' I said. Not thirsty at all. Unless she had a litre of vodka.

Under the bed was Dad's letter. What would he say? Was he even still alive? What if the illness he had had already killed him? What if I was too late to see him? Maybe somehow the moon had turned in a way to make Yasmin pregnant before Dad died. I wanted to see him, talk to him, ask what he thought. I needed to know how ill he was. I wished he was with Mum. That things hadn't gone so wrong.

'You don't need to decide right now.' Jade appeared with two mugs. We drank silently, watching the film. The tea was strong and too sweet. Jade built another spliff and sparked up. Outside, Jord's mum shouted to Kev that their garden-shed door was jammed. That rancid bitch.

Pregnant.

Suddenly Jade gave me a tight hug. 'You always look so sad. I hate it.'

I frowned.

She phoned in late for work – lying that she'd lost her car keys – waited for Mum to get back before she changed her clothes – they stank of weed – and then left.

Mum didn't come straight up, one of her TV programmes must have been on or maybe Jade told her to wait a bit. Eventually she used her foot to push the bedroom door open, hands full, another cup of fucking tea. Almost as sweet as Jade's. We sat at the head of my bed.

'What happened, my chocolate orange?'

The air was freezing but I couldn't be bothered to close the window.

'Yasmin didn't say much,' she said.

'Mum.'

'Oh, love. Don't cry.'

'Everything's going wrong.' It wasn't proper crying; I wiped my eyes with my sleeve.

'What is? Tell me.'

The thing is I didn't want to. I felt embarrassed talking to her about sex. The idea of talking to Mum about sex made me sick because then she might start talking and I didn't want to think about her and Dad.

Dad, who was ill and wanted to see us both, but how could I put that into words? He was going to come and see us soon and he might be dying? No, I couldn't say it.

'Kai, tell me.'

'Yasmin's dad wants to meet her, she wants me to go. I can't.'

The lie was easy. Nan would know what to do, I'd ask her. I texted Jade: 'dont tell mum, plz'.

I called Yasmin the same night and told her not to tell anyone till we'd decided what to do. Before bed I pressed my forehead against the window, looking at the moon.

I asked it, 'What should we do?'

An image streaked through my mind's eye: a little girl with red curly hair. We'd go to the woods, I'd show her the grey rabbits, the birds and my den. Tell her about the silver moon planet. She'd wear our old odd socks.

Sleep hid.

After Mum and Crystal went to bed I snuck downstairs and found half a bottle of brandy in the cupboard behind the baked beans. In bed in the early hours, with a foot flat on the carpet to help with the spinning, I stared at the ceiling, gagging for mandy, weed, even more drink, to stop me thinking about when we were kids, to stop me remembering the bonfires, climbing trees, the day I'd swum with Dad in the freezing-cold river, how me and Saffie lived on the silver moon.

My bedroom walls had shrunk. It was just me and the moon, spinning a waltz round and round, like Nan did in her living room in front of *Strictly Come Dancing*.

Suddenly it all made sense: the moon was where the baby had come from. Babies were a type of magic, full of happiness and light. Tiny stars. Sparkling red-haired star. My little star was in Yasmin.

In the morning I puked my guts up.

CHAPTER 20

THEN

Kai lay under the duvet rubbing bogeys from his eyes. Blurred bedroom emerging as he heard the television rumble from the living room.

Another hot day. Yellow shone over the carpet from the window, where he heard a car speed through the village too fast. He bounded from his bed, spraying elephants to the floor, and bounced to the wardrobe. He wanted a brand-new toy rabbit, Pokémon cards and a pirate hat. He needed to make space. Inside the wardrobe he pulled out a Space Raiders crisps cardboard box, lifting the flaps to take out toy cars, which he placed on the windowsill next to the Teenage Mutant Ninja Turtles and the empty china rabbit where he usually kept pocket money. He hid Hungry Hippos under the bed then he pushed the cardboard box to the middle of the room, ready.

The smell of baking wafted from the open kitchen window into his bedroom, past the Noah's Ark border on the wall to his nose. Birthday cake. Yum yummy. A rhythmic banging sounded. Kev next door in his tool shed? Jordan had been really mad at him when he gave him back Charizard, saying he never wanted to be friends again.

The sound of laughter came from Mum and Dad. A music channel flicked on. Jumping up to go downstairs, Kai kept quiet, balancing his feet on the sides of the steps. He held on to both banister rails. He'd make his parents jump.

Kai flung open the door.

Mum was bent over, clutching the edges of the table, face screwed up – like she had with Denner – panting. Dad behind her, hands on her hips, grunting as a smoke steamed from his mouth. Pyjama bottoms were crumpled at their feet as Dad pushed against her. Hurting her? Empty cans dropped to the floor as Dad pushed, pushed, pushed.

He felt sick.

Dad pushed, pushed, pushed.

'Kai!' Mum screamed.

Dad jumped away from Mum; willy sticking out, wet. Pulling his trousers up, grabbing a Sherbet Fountain as she bent.

Mum yanked up her bottoms and squealed, 'Happy birthday, love.'

Sweat ran down Dad's forehead as he crossed the room, grinning and shoving a Sherbet Fountain at him. 'Could have let me finish, son.' He picked Kai up. 'Happy birthday, my boy.'

What were they doing? Kisses of stale beer landed on Kai's cheek. There were white spitty bits at the corners of Dad's mouth.

'I haven't finished your cake yet, Kai. The party's at lunchtime. When d'you want your present? Now or later?'

On the floor below, tiny sealy bags of talcum powder were scattered next to rolled-up scraps of paper and there was a glass thing with a hole in it and black tape stuck around it. Kai looked at Mum, then Dad. They smiled with big buzzy eyes.

'I'll wait for the girls to get up,' he said.

In his room Kai forgot the sherbet in his hand and kept seeing the image of Mum and Dad rocking against the table. The way Mum's gold hoop earring had swung. It was like the animals he saw on wildlife shows, except this wasn't normal. Underneath his bed was a gap big enough to crawl under. He lined up the elephants like a wall staring at the Hungry Hippos box, before laying his head on an elephant and whispering the words to 'I can sing a rainbow' with his eyes closed until Jade found him three hours later.

At midday, Nanny Sheila knocked on the back door, scuffing out of flip-flops and tossing a Chelsea football cap from her head to a space on the table between paper plates of Twiglets, sausage rolls, cocktail sausages and pineapple-and-cheese sticks.

'You got it all cooked, then?' she said.

Nanny had thirty hats that she kept in Leah's dad's bedroom, most of them were large-rimmed and floppy; not this one. Two presents wrapped in the *Somerset Guardian* were tucked under her arm. Kai stood up on the chair at the table with his arms wide open.

'Cheaper than wrapping paper,' Nanny Sheila said as she handed Kai a package. 'Bloody ridiculous. Happy birthday, love.'

'All right, Nan?' asked Leah.

'Yes, petal.' Nanny Sheila took the seat next to Leah. Two sets of triangular cheekbones rounded in smiles as they watched him.

They were his last presents. Mum and Dad had given him a skateboard – he was rubbish at skateboarding and thought of the bike he wanted, feeling disappointed. Dad's feet were rolling the board an inch right, left, back again. Jittery as a squirrel, he watched *The Word* recorded on video ages ago. The settee was cleared of washing and Mum had left the room smelling of polish. The blue carpet was hoovered, windowsills gleamed and balloons floated over both grey settees. Dad knocked a balloon with the skateboard, it sprung into the air. The small wheels squeaked.

'I'll ride it,' said Jade, when Kai had unwrapped the skateboard. She'd drawn him a picture of Peter Pan with 'never grow up' graffitied above Pan's green hat. Jade was being forced by Crystal to have her nails painted. Crystal had promised to braid Kai's hair for the next year. Leah had given him a Peter Pan book, the same copy Miss Butterworth read in class. 'Sarah', Leah's ex-best friend, was scrawled and crossed out inside the front cover. He hugged his sister and she said, 'I'll read it to you at bedtime.'

Scrabbling with Nan's newspaper to open the biggest present first, excitement gripped. What was it? So big and just for him. Too much tape, it was hard to get in. Kai's black fingernails found a hole, tearing, tearing, tearing. Something black, a hat? A skull and crossbones.

'A pirate hat. Yes!'

So happy, so smiley. Like the pirates in Neverland. Kai popped the hat straight on to his head and dived on the other present.

'Wait,' ordered Leah.

From the door at the other end of the living room a cake appeared. Mum walked slowly and six flames wriggled. Hair out today, frizzy, how Dad liked it. She'd painted her lips purple for the special occasion of her only son, her precious youngest, her prince. She sang.

Happy Birthday to you
Happy Birthday to you

Even Dad paused the TV, crossed the room, knelt by Kai as the whole family sang. Mum placed the cake on the silver 'Happy Birthday' tablecloth.

Happy Birthday dear Kai, my chocolate orange, my boy
Happy Birthday to you

A Bugs Bunny cake with tiny pink candles. He couldn't remember the last time Mum had baked a cake.

'Make a wish!' shouted the girls as Dad winked and said, 'Be careful what you wish for.'

Deep, deep breath, puffing out his chest. He was a big boy now. Six candles heated his brown freckled face. He wished for Mum and Dad to stop smoking.

*

As the afternoon wore on, Nanny left and everyone else turned up. Kev and Sharon brought Taylor and Jordan. They were first to arrive, Jordan still grumpy, only playing with Taylor and Crystal in the front garden, throwing the old wooden tennis bat at each other that one of Dad's weird mates, Dave, had left last summer – it usually stayed in the shed, but Crystal got it out to play AIDS because everyone said Dave had it. Then Steve, Scottie and Denner turned up; they stood at the barbecue with Kev drinking beer and talking about boxing, handing out burgers, corn on the cobs and sausages. Even Johnny the Prawn suddenly appeared from the side of the house; he had red skin and the physique of a snooker cue – that's what Dad said, anyway – and following him Saffie's mum. Kai jumped up. Saffie. He ran to her. Stood in front of her.

'Love's young dream,' Mum said.

Her mum shoved Saffie's shoulder and she was closer to him.

'I'm sorry,' he said.

'Happy birthday.' She held out a package. Inside, was a hammer with a red handle. 'It's for the den.'

'You're my best friend.'

They ran together to the apple tree next to Leah and Jade. They chose the same spot and bumped into each other as they dropped to the grass that felt spiky.

Leah nudged Jade. 'Come on.'

His sisters' matching green and yellow dresses were creased on the bums when they went inside. Kai's attention whizzed back to Saffie, who wore a Pokémon T-shirt. They were both cross-legged, with their hands on their knees, knees touching.

Bubbles popped inside, he squinted – the sun was behind her, like an angel in Nanny's stained-glass church – and she puffed her lips. Before she spoke he knew what she was going to say.

'I never want to stop being friends again.'

He knew they never would because he missed her too much and now he was reminded of Dad croaking into the pillow whenever Mum walked out if he'd hit her. The worst thing for Dad was him not knowing if she would come back and even though Kai always knew Mum would, there was no way he wanted to feel that with Saffie.

'I felt all mixy when we weren't friends,' he said. 'I know you're what Hippie Mandy said about soul – remember what she said?'

'Soulmates?'

'Yeah. It means we'll be friends for ever – I asked Leah – so till we get in the grave up Middledown church.'

'And our graves can be next to each other.'

There was a smile in Kai's chest and it popped on to his face and Saffie caught it. A breeze shifted and lifted leaves on the branches above them. Laughter exploded from the men as Denner shouted at Johnny, 'Mate, you're so skinny you look inside out.'

'You look pretty,' Kai said.

She shoved him so he fell back on to the grass and he knew that everything was OK as he sat back up.

'Staring contest?' he asked.

'I can read your mind,' she said.

'Me you, too.'

She'd be thinking about flying to the silver moon and he whispered, 'We could hide Dragon up there.'

'I'll hide you up there.'

Strange, so strange, but that's what he liked about her best. 'I'll hide you up there too.'

Crystal appeared, screaming from the side of the house, blonde hair in waves, running from Taylor, whose cheeks looked like Nanny's raspberry jam. Dad, Denner and Scottie raised their voices as she passed and Johnny the Prawn blew into the flames of the barbecue.

'It's turning white,' he said.

When Crystal neared the swing Taylor threw the shabby tennis bat and it whacked the back of her head. Her face cracked. Tears welled up, she held on to them, rubbing the back of her head – wanting to be brave – and Taylor stared, frightened, when Mum marched out of the house, dipping her head to check the pain on her daughter's face. There was a brief frown.

'You idiot,' said Sharon to Taylor. 'What d'you think you're playing at?'

Then Kev chipped in. 'You should know better than to hurt a girl.'

Taylor crushed under his parents' words, inched towards the hedge between Kai's garden and his. 'It was an accident.'

'You're all right, love,' said Mum, rubbing Crystal's shoulder. 'Suck it up, come on, I've taught you better than that.'

'I'm going to find the girls,' Crystal said, walking past Taylor like he was invisible. She passed Jordan, who took over the swing with his brother, Taylor standing on it, yelling at Jordan to push harder.

Saffie's mum came out of the house with a glass bottle and plastic cups. The kitchen chairs were placed in front of the garden shed behind Kai, and the three mums popped open the bottle. Over her macky sunglasses Saffie's mum had a big loopy fringe; her dark hair was dyed and looked a bit purple, it rested on her shoulders. She never looked happy, her top lip was pierced at the side and most of the time her lips looked pinched. Moody bitch, that's what Mum called her. Her trousers looked like pyjama bottoms and her vest was an angry mash of patterns. At the top of both arms she had tattoos of flowers and hearts. Off she went, talking, words jutty and dull like she was reading the boringest book in the world, saying Dr Lewis said she had the symptoms. Jordan's mum kept saying, 'Yeah, yeah,' and touching her frazzled gremlin hair and the mole on her arm like a beetle that might crawl up her big, pointy nose. Her vest was tight and her bra straps showed – her boobs were macky and rested on her belly. How did she balance on such skinny legs?

Leah and Jade passed Denner at the back door with bowls of chips, placing them on the kitchen table that Dad and Scottie had carried out. It was at the bottom of the garden covered in plates.

'The Turkey Twizzlers are on their way,' said Leah. His sisters went back in. They cooked instead of Mum now.

Saffie's mum moaned about the bloke she was shagging. Shagging sounded like shaggy, which meant bad hair, so she must be making his hair messy, which didn't make sense. Maybe there was a job that meant the opposite to hair-dresser. She kept lowering her voice. Kai and Saffie listened, the bloke wanted to be with her, it was obvious.

'It's much easier to talk to a mutual friend,' she said. That's how she knew his head was all over the place; he liked her, really he did, he must or why did he call every Friday night?

'Yeah, yeah,' said Jordan's mum.

Mum poured her second glass. 'Slackers.'

The other two sipped.

Mum wore a neon-green crop top and it made the new blonde bits in her hair look really bright; her thin neck looked like the curve of Dad's secret knife. Suddenly the beef burgers and sausages were thrown on the grill and it hissed as fat dripped. The men laughed like thunder, Scottie rubbed both hands over his Nike cap, Denner, on the back doorstep, tapped his foot like he needed a pee and each time he sipped from his can he looked at Mum, but she was looking at Sharon, now Kai, so Kai looked at the grass, which was getting more yellow from the sun.

Dad slapped Johnny the Prawn's shoulder. 'How you doing anyway, man? You smoking at the moment?'

Johnny the Prawn wore a top hat with a pheasant feather on, which he'd 'picked up on Green Lane', and a leather waistcoat – nothing underneath. The only bloke who wasn't wearing army-print shorts, his were blue and orange splashes. He had teeth missing, but he was handsome, Mum always said, in that junky-kind-of-way. Except Dad said he wasn't a junky, he just liked to drink. Dad said it like it was a good thing, but what sort of a person apart from bin men liked junk?

Dad offered Johnny a smoke. Small clouds spread out – once, twice and a third time, long and deep. When he handed it to Denner, who took a macky breath in, Denner said, 'It's wet, you blanket. You're not meant to blow it.'

'It's been a while,' Johnny said.

Mum looked at Denner then. Kai was glad he didn't notice. At the bottom of Steve's grey hair his neck had rolls, he wasn't fat. He kept his arms crossed. It was the first time Kai had seen him wear a T-shirt – black with a star on the pocket over his peck. He had cobweb tattoos on each elbow – they looked cooler than Saffie's mum's. Food was handed out. Everyone chewed and licked fingers, taking turns to say the funniest things. When Kai stood near anyone he smelled sweat and deodorant, Crystal kept spraying Impulse. Kai went for another sausage. Scottie was growing a beard like a big V at the front; he looked a bit like a king. He rested a hand on Kai's shoulder. 'You all right, lad?'

'Um-hmm.' He looked back at Saffie under the tree, who was pointing her number-one finger at Johnny the Prawn, who was laid on the grass behind Mum's chair; his hat had fallen off and his round blue sunglasses were skew-whiff. Mum stood up, shouting for Jade to switch the hi-fi on.

'Let's get a little wriggle on,' Mum said, twisting her hips.

Back at the apple tree, Kai said to Saffie, 'Let's go to the den.' Suddenly he wanted to be away from all the grown-ups, who acted stupid when they got drunk. They went into the shed and found nails, then to the kitchen for scissors and finally up to his bedroom and took his bottom bed sheet, shoving it into his school bag with his lock-picking pouch and the hammer. Before they snuck away he pulled on his red cape.

*

On the pavement outside Saffie's, where all the curtains were drawn, they readjusted the seats of two bikes, a red one and a pink one. Saffie let Kai use her red one so they could cycle to the woods.

'I know you wanted your own. If I could,' she said, sticking the Velcro down on her sandals, 'I'd give you my sister's, but look at the sicko colour.'

Nanny's red Fiesta was gone so she must be at Betty's. Luckily. If she saw Kai and Saffie on her street when it was his party he might be in trouble.

'Tie up your hair,' he said.

When she pulled at the hairband, this way and that, making knots of her face and the strands, he wanted to do it for her. Half of it fell out straight away. They pedalled, squeaked brakes and rang bells on tarmac-crumbled-to-potholes. Someone had sprayed lines around the holes. Probably the council, who lived in a building in town making up all the shitty rules to ruin everyone's lives. Dad still hadn't finished Mum's cupboards. Hopefully the council wouldn't find out.

'Look what I got,' Saffie said. And she held up Dragon, cycling one-handed. 'Why you smiling?'

'It's good,' he said. 'Zip it back in your bag safely.' They paused for her. A few tiny starlings darted about in the sky like tiny black triangles. So cool. Kai wondered how they knew when to turn and where they were going.

Inside the den they finished putting up the sheet they'd nicked off Kai's bed. They decided against a roof for summer because Saffie said their den was like a sweet box, which shouldn't have lids on, and he guessed that made him a chocolate orange like Mum said. What would Saffie be?

They lay side by side in blue T-shirts watching the sky, heads bumping as they pointed at animals in the explosion of cauliflower clouds. Kai picked a blade of grass and used his thumbs to make a whistle.

'I feel a bit mixy,' said Kai. The floor was slanted and their heads were lower than their feet so the world felt upside down and he had the funny feeling he was hanging by his toes. For his birthday, Saffie had painted her nails green and he thought they looked like M&Ms so that must be what she would be in a sweet box. It would look cool if his nails matched hers, except that was gay. Mum would call him batty, like when he put on Crystal's purple dress when his sister was making him play talent shows. No way would he do it again.

'We need to make our first stealing mission,' said Kai, sitting up.

'It has to be something special like Dragon.' She told him that she kept him on the dressing table next to her bed next to her purple glasses case, and also there was a green lamp and she had a special blue and green sea creature ornament. It was really cool in Saffie's room because she was allowed a goldfish; hers was orange with white fins, called Twig. Her sister had a bigger room and everything was puky pink.

Outside the den was the small dark hole where the rabbits lived, and Kai had kept an ear on it and heard nothing; he noticed a rabbit emerging. Papa Grey. Two more rabbits followed, so holding a finger to his mouth he used the other to gently poke his best friend in the ribs and point. She turned her head. The rabbits sniffed around then kept still. Papa Grey caught Kai's eye suddenly so he smiled, holding his breath. Quickly, the rabbits hopped off.

'That was so cool,' said Kai.

'They came for your birthday,' said Saffie.

He didn't tell her that he'd followed the rabbits to find out where they lived and that's why the den was by the hole.

It was weird being his birthday. Kai felt no different from yesterday and the strangest thing was thinking that he never even used to have birthdays because he never used to be here. Stranger than that was knowing his parents were here before him and a frightening thought came to him: imagine if he and Saffie hadn't been here at the same time?

'I think something went wrong before we were born,' he said. 'You should have been my twin.'

'We can be proper twins.'

'How?' He'd made Saffie go by the sheet where it would be warmer. He started drawing an outline of school into the mud and was talking about lost property because they should be able to steal something good there, when she unzipped his bag.

'Well, we're already the same inside because we swapped blood, but what about on the outside?'

Kai grinned because everyone already thought they looked the same, but hers and hims.

'I know what to do,' she said.

He wasn't sure how it started, but on the way home after leaving the bikes at Saffie's he stared at his best friend, trying to keep up with her as they whipped along the pavement, hopping, jumping, past the big posh houses with the spiky roofs and chimneys, feeling dizzy. His heart raced as his cape flapped and he couldn't tell if it was because they might get in trouble or because she looked so cool. So cool. Like he wanted to give her his cape because she was a wild girl, not afraid of anything and not like any other girl, ever, and as he thought all of this she kept looking at him. She skipped, laughed, threw her head back, puffed on her inhaler, shook her hair.

Her new hair.

'What?' she shouted. 'What? Stop making macky eyes at me!' And she whooped, so did he. Now they really were twins, more than her and Boring Twin because everyone said they were the same; they even had the same squinty eyes when they smiled and the same freckles.

Outside The Station pub stood the vicar and Bob-Cycle, who drank ale on weekends, and when Bob saw Kai he saluted. When he saw Saffie, he shouted, 'What you done, cocker?' like she was a boy. A boy! Like him! And there were chuckles in his voice. He'd seen them race up the road three hours before.

He had to get Saffie a cape. Then they'd be masters of disguise.

In the den when he'd been running a finger over the mud, describing the way to the lost-property cupboard at school, which had all the boxes and also had the Christmas trimmings and scrap left over from school plays, Saffie had opened his bag and pulled out his lock-picking kit, a hammer and his scissors. It happened so fast.

'I know what to do,' she said, snap snap snapping the scissors like crab hands. But he was studying the map of the school he'd scratched into the ground: there was a pebble where Headmaster T's office was and sticks around the open space where all the classes came out before they went into the hall for assembly; the hall had sticks round too and at the bottom there was the lost-property cupboard. That's where they had to get, to see what forgotten treasures were there.

Rubbing a stick against the entrance to the school hall, he said, 'So you stand here, be lookout and when you—'

That's when he'd heard the dull snips.

'What you doing?'

'Help me.'

She held a piece of hair out for him to hold and went to work.

'You need to do the back. I want it the same longness as yours.'

'But I can't see how long mine is because my eyes are behind my hair.'

She looked at his hair than grabbed a stick, snapping it in half. 'This long.'

It was the most exciting thing ever.

The grown-ups disagreed.

When they reached the garden, Saffie's mum's mouth opened and Jordan's mum's eyes went as big as Dad's. The men were stood by the weights they'd got out of the shed that were sprawled about the grass by the swing. Johnny the Prawn was still laid flat on his back and Mum was next to him. They were sheltered under the kitchen table; she covered her hand with her mouth. They were drunk and their words were slurred. Everyone, even Denner, stopped and stared, then Scottie laughed like he'd seen someone slip on a banana skin.

'What the fuck have you done?' Saffie's mum jumped up from her seat, bending at the waist as she moved forward, like she was trying to believe her eyes, and his sisters and Jordan and Taylor were watching from the apple tree like miniature grown-ups.

'I cut it,' said Kai, and he squeezed Saffie's hand to stop her telling the truth. This time she didn't butt in and he knew it was because of the look on all the grown-ups' faces. Saffie's mum looked like she was going to rip him a new asshole, that's what Dad said when Mum got angry at Kai for throwing her hair tongs at the wall because he wasn't allowed to wear his red cape to school.

'You little shit,' said Saffie's mum at Kai.

'Shut up,' said Saffie, twisting both arms around one of Kai's.

'Go fuck yourself,' Mum shouted at the woman, trying to stand. She bumped her head on the table and the plate of Turkey Twizzlers hiccupped from the table to the grass and cracked on the garden path. Now Dad was telling Saffie's mum to jog on and Saffie's arm was being pulled from his.

'We just wanted to look the same,' he said, watching Saffie, and she watched him as her mum dragged her round the waist across the garden.

Scottie squeezed a spot on his shoulder before he rubbed Kai's head and said, 'Young'un, you're off your head.'

Kai and the girls sat in the stinking living room. Yesterday's plates and cups with half-eaten sausages and chips cluttered the kitchen top and filled the sink. The new pipe was so stained by smoke the glass of the tiny Ouzo bottle Scottie brought last summer looked milky laid next to the overflowing glass ashtray at Jade's bare feet. The hole in the pipe pierced through the black gaffer tape wound round it looked like a bullet hole. Kai stared at it. Crack. That's what it was called. He heard Scottie do a deep voice to Dad saying, 'Mate, I'm not gonna stay here watching you smoke crack.' Kai and his sisters had been sent to bed.

Outside, the weather was changing. The sky was like whipped cream and the air felt ready to break.

'I hate wildlife programmes,' said Crystal, but she stretched her legs out and placed her feet on his lap.

'So?' said Kai. He gently poked her big toe and she picked up an old copy of *Smash Hits*.

A fight was the last thing they wanted. In the past, after Mum and Dad partied there were fights about money, who should walk to Jonesies in Hilcombe for more drink, or why Dad couldn't get his shit together, or why Mum thought she had sugar-coated tits. Crystal was in la-la-land staring at boy bands she fancied, the opposite reason of Leah reading, which made him realise why the two of them didn't get on because Crystal was like Mum. He knew Crystal was waiting, like him, like they all were, to see what mood Mum and Dad would be in when they woke up.

Leah turned pages of a book with a mountain on the front cover. Her hair looked wet at the roots, her eyes dark, she was so skinny – Nanny kept saying. Had she eaten yesterday as she'd dished out chips? Kai didn't remember seeing her eat the day before either. The pale blue hoody over the top of her pasty yellow dress had a Diadora logo on it – cheap shit, Mum said when Dad gave it to her; she'd tossed it on the back of the settee and Leah had picked it up, glancing at Dad, and he'd nodded that she could keep it. She'd worn it ever since.

The continual scraping of Jade's pencil sharpener could be heard over the low sound of the TV. Her toes, always out in summer because of the feel of mud and grass in the garden, especially at Nanny's where she was starting a vegetable patch, were scrunched up, like his. Kai splayed his toes.

Sometimes they heard a creak in the floorboard as Mum or Dad turned over in bed and it made a flutter in Kai's tummy.

Would they shout?

Kai wondered why Mum and Dad were smoking the smelly pipes more and more. Scottie hated it. It had to mean something. He was unsure what, but it felt like the sound of clattering marbles and he didn't know how to say this to his sisters. They felt it too, maybe that's why their eyes looked everywhere except at each other.

Jade held up a hand, her palms red. 'That's twenty pencils so far.' She loved the cutting sounds. As she started again the noise became a ticking clock.

'You think they're going to get up?' asked Kai.

'They're taking ages,' said Crystal.

'What time is it?' Kai looked at the hands of the clock, confused.

'Twenty to three.'

'Hopefully they'll stay up there,' said Leah.

'I'm hungry,' said Kai. Crystal agreed.

'Is Nan cooking today?' Jade asked.

'She's in Frome with Betty.'

'You wanna cook?' Crystal asked.

Jade stopped sharpening and twisted a curl around her finger, round and round, it flicked up her forehead, she pulled it down and twisted. 'I don't mind cooking.'

'What about the washing-up?'

All four of the children looked. With the kitchen table still out on the back lawn the room felt unnatural and they were missing seats. Who would sit where when *they* woke up?

Leah sighed.

'We can all help,' said Kai. 'How can we bring the table in?'

'We can get the chairs,' said Jade, standing. Kai and Leah followed her outside and between them they pulled the chairs in. There were greasy fingerprints and mayonnaise stains on the seats and arms, so Leah rinsed a cloth to clean and Jade pulled a dirty towel from the washing machine and followed her, drying.

The ceiling creaked and their eyes darted up. The bulb swung a little and Leah and Jade rushed to the settee and sat upright. If they argued it would be OK, things always ended up OK.

It just felt scary when it happened.

On the TV, two grey hares stood on hind legs, fighting like skinny boxers. This room was like their warren under Mum and Dad. Saffie should be in their warren too now that she was his twin. Yesterday had been crazy, how angry her mum got – would her mum hit her? How hard? He'd heard stories on TV about terrible things that happened to children and he desperately wanted to go to her house to check she was safe, that her mum hadn't hurt her.

Nobody spoke when Mum came down. Leah moved to the floor in front of Kai and Mum sprawled in the spot she'd left. She yawned loudly and wobbly, opening and closing her mouth, then she closed her eyes.

'D'you enjoy your birthday?'

Leah snorted. 'Doubt he had as much fun as you.'

'What's up with you?'

Leah held her book with one hand behind her bent knees, the other hand was curled into a fist and she was squeezing her nails into her palms so that her nails looked white where the blood was pressed away at the tips.

'Kai?' asked Jade, who, hearing Dad start downstairs, stood and crossed to sit next to Leah.

Had he enjoyed his birthday? Parts of it, before everyone got too drunk and smoked and before Saffie was dragged off. His favourite bit was when Saffie turned up and gave him his present because that really had been a surprise and when he and Saffie had snuck off to the den, when she'd snipped her hair, but this stuff had nothing to do with Mum and he thought carefully about his answer. His worst bit was seeing Mum and Dad bent over the table when Dad's willy was out, in, out, and when they got too drunk.

'Yeah,' he said.

Dad entered the room and crashed next to Mum, resting a head in her lap, and she touched his hair.

'Good birthday, my boy?'

Leah snorted.

'Yeah.'

'Best part?'

He hadn't even wanted the skateboard, which lay abandoned on the front-garden path.

'My pirate hat,' he said. He loved Nanny so much and wished he and the girls were having roast at hers today.

'What we gonna do about all this shit?' Leah flicked a hand towards the kitchen.

'You offering to tidy?' asked Dad.

Kai was sure he felt the heat rise from Leah's neck, his hand was right by her, and he knew the reason she didn't answer was because she was angry.

'Let us wake up first,' said Mum.

'It's three p.m.'

'Oi, touchy. It was his birthday.'

'Yeah, his, not yours.'

'Everyone has fun when it's a birthday, that's the point.'

Crystal frowned at her magazine.

'As much fun as you?'

Mum rolled her eyes and Dad asked for the remote. He flicked over to *Antiques Roadshow* and Jade groaned.

'Why are you smoking and drinking so much?' Leah asked.

'Are you serious?' asked Mum. 'It was one day.'

'Was it?'

Kai was on Leah's side.

Dad always stayed out of arguments between Mum and the girls. He used a foot to push the smelly pipe round the side of the settee so it was out of sight then looked at Kai, who looked back at the TV. No way was he going to smile. Kai hated the smoking and drinking too.

'So? What about the mess? I can't relax.'

'So get off your ass and help do it,' said Mum.

Suddenly Leah jumped up and raised her voice. 'Me? Me and Jade did almost everything yesterday when all you did was drink.' She threw her book across the room. It bounced off the wall towards Dad, who crossed his arms over his face. She shouted, 'Why say you're going to quit all the time? You're a liar.'

Mum's face looked guilty, a cross between wanting to tell Leah off and knowing she was right.

'Why?' shouted Leah.

Jade stood up. 'I'll do it.'

'It isn't that easy,' said Crystal.

'Trust you to stick up for her,' shouted Leah.

'Relax,' said Dad.

'No!' she shouted, grabbing Jade's arm. 'Stop it, Jade, they're the grown-ups. They should do it. They've been in bed all day.'

'Christ.' Mum stood, rubbing her head as she moved to the sink, flicking on the old radio with the coat hanger sticking out. Barry White's deep voice filled the room as plates clattered in her hands. 'Happy now?'

Leah picked up her book and slammed out of the room and then the house.

'Mardy pants,' said Dad.

Kai ran to the window and watched Leah run up the road under the dark clouds. She'd be going to Nanny's, would have to wait in the rain till she came back from Frome. Dad grabbed Mum round the waist, singing into her ear as they moved with closed eyes in the middle of the living room. Her fingernails scratched through his red hair. They weren't smiling.

Jade started scraping food from plates into a black bin liner that was placed on top of the new black kitchen worktops Dad still hadn't screwed in, so Kai joined her and scraped plates too before she filled the sink with bubbly water and he knelt on a kitchen chair drying with a tea towel, watching as raindrops started to hit the kitchen table that was still outside. The Turkey Twizzlers still on the path next to the broken plate.

CHAPTER 21

1 December 2005

Hangover be fucked, I was dying. I wondered if Mum's brandy was out of date, but doubted it. I popped next door to see Jord when he got in from school and he managed to nab Taylor's hip flask. He filled it with JD when his mum was in the shower, we both swigged from the bottle and by 7 p.m. I started to feel normal. Luckily. It was the night I'd promised old Wheeler I'd play skittles at The Station.

A bloke came in. He wore a navy-blue Ralph Lauren top and tight jeans; he handed the fake-lashed bar girl – a girl called Laura who was in sixth form at school – a bunch of lilies.

I hated lilies.

I carried on playing skittles with old Wheeler and his team. It was boring and between throws, I snuck to the toilet to swig the JD. Hip flasks were small; it must have had five shots in, tops. Fuck all. I'd been fine. Until that bloke brought in the lilies.

'What d'you think of lilies?' I nudged old Wheeler, pointing towards the bar. Badger was following me around like a new-born duckling. The fire was crackling next to me, my leg was on fire. There was a Santa puppet hanging in front of the fireplace and a red stocking – Christmas had pre-jacked all over the place.

Old Wheeler looked at me like I was mad. 'Come on, lad, it's your shot.'

We were winning and, being good at sports, I wasn't letting the team down. It was obvious old Wheeler was chuffed he'd asked me to play even though I wanted to shoot my brain out; it was doing my swede in doing the chit-chat about the weather, why pickled eggs were good in salt and vinegar crisps and what the fuck Shove Ha'penny was with all the old codgers. How could I think about all this when Yasmin was pregnant? I went to the bar.

It was my first time in The Station and seeing what an old man's pub it was, it would be the last. It was built nice, though, pine-clad walls and an oak-slabbed floor. The smell of ale like a raised middle finger because all I could buy was Coke or lemonade. I texted Jord, asking if Taylor could get me a bomb of mandy, then thought of Mum and Dad, and regretted texting him so texted him again telling him not to bother, then I texted him again saying, 'Fuck it, see if he can.'

The bar girl was fiddling with the lilies. I imagined huge greenhouses filled with identical lilies. Long white petals. I knew a bit about flowers because we'd done it in science; the stamen had anthers and that was the coppery-orange bit in the middle that made pollen. I pinched one. It left brown powder on my fingers. Laura, the bar girl, was talking to one of them 'cultured'-looking couples, the sort who look natural and wear creased clothes. Like they were artists. I shoved the vase and it smashed behind the bar.

'Ey up,' shouted Laura, until she realised it was the flowers and not a pint.

'What does it take to get served round here?' I asked.

'Did you do that on purpose?' she asked.

The bloke in the navy-blue Ralph Lauren T-shirt appeared next to me. His skin looked as potholed as Brewer's Lane.

'Say sorry to the lady,' he said. There were shitty tattoos drawn over his knuckles.

'What for?' I asked. I grabbed a half-full pint glass that I guessed was his and gulped.

'For being clumsy.'

I wasn't in the mood for a jumped-up little prick. He had one of those stiff beer guts and was shorter than me by three inches.

'You're having a laugh,' I said.

'Kai,' called old Wheeler from the other side of the room. 'It's your turn.'

'You need to get out my face,' I said to Beer Gut.

'Watch your mouth, young'un,' he said.

'How old are you anyway?' I made a point of looking at him and then eyeing Laura up and down, letting him see me stop a moment at her tits. 'Oh, I get it, you're her dad.' I laughed.

'If you don't shut up, I'll knock your teeth out,' he said.

'You're all fart and no shit,' I said.

I was enjoying myself, I took another gulp and he grabbed the pint from my hand and Stella spilt over the bar into the cultured couple's packet of salted peanuts, which were opened so they could share. It pissed me off.

'Laura,' I said, 'let me take you on a date. I'll show you a good time. I think your dad here likes me.'

'Fuck off,' she said at the same time as he grabbed my shoulders. He pushed me towards the door; I pulled out of my hoody, leaving it in his hands. Dad taught me to stay calm in a fight so I watched him, he thrust his left fist and I dodged, jabbing his ribs, one each side before he cracked me in the jaw. He was a big cunt, mind. I felt the half-barrel flower pot thud my head when I went down and old Wheeler was there trying to pull Beer Gut off me with Badger biting at Beer Gut's feet – I loved that fucking dog. Old Wheeler's dickie bow twisted up and his monocle fell out. I started laughing.

'Come on, then,' shouted Beer Gut.

But I couldn't stop laughing and I shouted, 'I'm gonna fuck your slut daughter.'

Old codgers were holding Beer Gut back by then – gutted, I wanted him to smash my head apart like it was a watermelon – they yelled at me to shut up.

I looked at old Wheeler and said, 'I'll buy you a new monocle.'

CHAPTER 22

THEN

Morning playtime was the best time to steal from lost property because all the kids were everywhere and there was no way teachers knew where each child was. Everyone played tag with the sticky bush leaves in the playground, raced on the lanes or hid in the secret garden because the sun was back, except for Kai and Saffie, who were sat on a bench outside the middle door.

'Come on.' Kai stood and pulled open the door.

'If someone finds us, we say we lost your Pokémon cards.'

Their shoes shuffled across the tiled floor of the corridor where coats hung either side next to name labels and underneath were wooden benches where everyone sat in the mornings to take their hats and gloves off in winter. The benches homed lunch boxes.

'What's Adam having for lunch?' asked Saffie. Kai stopped at the *Lion King* lunch box and opened it.

'Cheese and he's got a Penguin.'

Saffie opened Harry's next to Adam's. 'Cheese too, and Space Raiders.'

'Keep them for Jade,' Kai said, and he put them in his school bag when they passed it.

At the end of the corridor, right took them to Year Five and Six classrooms and the small room where people like Ella played violin. Kai had heard conga drums on TV and that's what he wanted to learn, they sounded well cool, like a forest heartbeat. They turned left to the huge room where the other classrooms' doors opened outside the assembly hall and Headmaster T's office. He was outside in the playground talking to Hippie Mandy and she kept pushing her hair behind her ear and looking at her sandals.

The sunshine-filled hall where they had gym class was empty apart from a piano and a gymnastics horse. Kai loved backflips on the trampoline and last week he'd learned how to walk on his hands; he needed to show Nanny. The hall was out of bounds.

'Shh,' said Saffie.

Through the window, Tom B the bumhole was racing Harry on the monkey bars. Kai felt prickly.

Their shoes squawked on the shiny yellow floorboards. The lost-property cupboard had grey doors and was at the other end of the hall; it was unlocked. Kai felt his heart pump harder. Saffie climbed over a Christmas tree making it jingle, like a proper burglar, like she was made for this, her face relaxed, concentrating. There were decorations from Christmas, Easter chicks and bunnies, a string of lights left from Diwali because Ali in Year Six was a Hindu and they had a school assembly about it and Mr McRitchie put fairy lights round his classroom, and there was a crib from the Nativity play. Kai stood on a cardboard donkey. He could smell its grey paint and PVA glue.

'Yee-ha.'

'Look.' Saffie pointed at a box on the middle shelf. It was the lost-property box. It was too high to see in. He tried to pull it. Too heavy.

'Get that,' said Saffie, pointing to a step ladder.

They shared the top step, dipping their hands into the box, turning over pogs, dinosaurs, pens; marbles rolled round the bottom.

'Pokémon!' Kai grabbed the Metapod card, a green lump with a face. It only had fifty HP points. He unzipped his pocket and pushed it in anyway.

Saffie picked up a Barbie. 'Ugly.' She threw it over her shoulder and it slammed on the floor under a mini trampoline.

'Here!' Saffie's voice threw excitement as she dug her hand to the bottom and pulled out sparkly gold. 'They sell it in the shop down Cheddar; I saw it when Mum took us to see the caves. It's real gold.'

It was fool's good; Nanny had some in her fairy cabinet. Saffie looked so happy, he said, 'It's pretty like you.'

'This is what we'll nick, yeah?'

'Come on. We gotta go before the teachers see.'

They left the cupboard and started across the hall.

'I don't have pockets.'

'You need some like this,' he tapped his trousers, 'with zips. And you need a cape like my red one.'

'Will you get me one? I don't know where they're from.'

'Dad will.'

'Cool.' She scratched her fluffy hair. It was exactly the same length as Kai's – long enough for plaits, but short for a girl – and stuck out all round her face like sunshine.

'I like your hair.'

It was the first time they'd been alone since Kai's birthday.

'Did your mum whack you?'

'Real hard,' she said. He felt a twist of anger. 'She left a handprint on the back of my legs, here.'

'Your mum's a bumhole.'

'Yeah, she is, and yours is the pooh.'

Kai laughed. 'Pooh liar. We could tell the police; Dad calls them pigs.'

'No and anyway, even though,' she made a small breath, 'even though it's my hair, I am her fluff—'

'No, you're my fluff.'

'No, you're mine, anyway, and I gotta do what she says till I'm eighteen so when I'm eighteen I'm gonna get a tattoo.'

'What of?' He thought of Steve's cobwebbed elbows and decided if Saffie was having one so was he.

'A dinosaur coming out of a volcano.'

'I'm gonna have Mike Tyson's face on a dragon body.' He held his hand out for the gold.

'But it's mine, Kai.'

'I know, beef head, give me it, before someone—'

They heard footsteps and looked up. Miss Butterworth. Her boobs looked macky and her eyes like a bald eagle. He slipped the gold in his pocket, imagining her with a bald head, and snorted.

'What was that?'

'Nothing.' No way give her it.

'Why is the cupboard door open?'

'We got lost,' Kai said.

'You got lost in lost property?'

Saffie inched closer to him.

'What's in your pocket?' She held a palm out.

Teachers were so nosy. 'Metapod.'

'The other one.'

'The reason we're here is because of something that happened yesterday.'

There was a pause to make everyone think back. Kai knew, they all knew why they were there, him, Saffie, their mums and Headmaster T, who looked like he'd just come out of Nanny's tumble drier crumpled. He was wearing his jacket for once, the collar looked bubbly. The way he looked at Mum and Saffie's mum was too friendly, like he wanted to be their boyfriend, almost touching their backs when they walked in the office. Who cared what he said? He thought he was the big-I-am.

'Kai, you listening?' asked Mum.

He gazed round the room, the spot Dragon had been, the plant with macky leaves in the corner, the paintings on the wall of the surfboard and guitar. He wondered what beach it was meant to be. Saffie was staring at the pictures too then she looked at him, wrinkled her nose, and that made it easier to sit in the room.

Mum was a liar – there was the ice-cream-van lie, the one about loving Leah's dad, she let Denner put his hand up her skirt, all she did was drink and drink and say that she was going to stop and she didn't. She was a grass, telling Nanny about Dragon, too. The more he thought about her, the more he wished Dad was there instead.

Sir suddenly looked like he'd just seen Saffie for the first time. 'You had a haircut?'

'Yeah,' answered her mum. 'Yeah, Saffie's had a haircut.'

'I cut it,' Kai said.

Sir looked surprised.

'On his birthday,' said Mum, 'they snuck off.'

'They wanted to look the same, apparently.' Saffie's mum's cheeks looked like pig fat. She was a pig. Pig-mum. She drank too much too, Saffie told him.

Headmaster T cleared his throat. 'As if they hadn't looked enough like twins already.'

'Exactly,' said pig-mum. 'It's ridiculous. Why d'you wanna look like a boy, anyway?'

'She doesn't,' said Kai. 'Maybe I look like a girl.' He hated to say it because that was gay, but he hated pig-mum saying it and enough strangers had said it to Mum anyway, that she had a pretty little girl when he wore his hair out.

Saffie's hand was making a little signal, her thumb stuck up like a little friend, and he did the same. Who cared if he was in trouble? Mum and Dad only cared about smoking. Bet Mum was only at school so she didn't look bad to the teachers.

They talked and Kai ignored, until Mum said, 'There's a lot going on at home at the moment.'

'Oh?'

Mum put on a fake sad face. It was the same one she put on when she tried to get Dad to buy drink on a Wednesday.

'There's nothing wrong at home,' Kai said. He didn't want the family to get in trouble. There were stories of kids getting taken away by horrible grown-ups and they had to live with other families.

'Course there has been, Kai,' she said. 'When your dad stayed at Steve's, remember?' She looked at the Head. 'Only for two weeks.'

In a rage, Kai stared at the grey cabinets. Headmaster T was scribbling notes and he wanted to pull the sheet of paper from his hand and jab jab him in the ribs.

'So, Kai and Saffie, the reason we're here is because you've done something really bad. You stole from lost property—'

'It was me.'

'No, it was me.'

'I'm sure it was both of you. Do you think it's OK to steal?'

They kept quiet. Kai watched Saffie's thumb again, which slowly turned into a little friend thumbs-up, and he copied.

'Do you think it's OK?'

'No,' said Saffie, in the same make-believe voice she used when she spoke to the furred hunters on the silver moon. Kai said the same.

The meeting went on and the mums hummed and agreed with Mr T about things called behaviour management and coping techniques. Outside, the sun broke through the clouds like the sky was splitting open and God was having a party. Suddenly there was a creak in the door and Mr T waved a hand for Hippie Mandy to come in; she grinned at the mums. A soapy smell filled the office. Her hair swished like a long black river over her shoulder when she crossed her legs.

Another grown-up to tell them off? What did she have to do with it? She was usually cool. Adults always made stuff up, he'd had enough, they lied, they smoked, they drank and made his sisters cry. Why should he listen to any of them apart from Nanny? He had a weird feeling that Hippie Mandy was going to go against their friendship because she always acted like she liked them, then in a moment, her face turned like the wind, fresh and kind.

'So,' said Sir, 'Miss Dawson's had an idea. She says she's already doing mindfulness with you . . .'

'Big pufferfish breaths and counting,' explained Hippie Mandy. She blew out her cheeks and her peanut face looked funny.

'Do you enjoy it, Kai?'

'Yes.'

'Saffie, have you tried it?'

She nodded.

'And?'

'It was OK.'

'What did you like about it?'

'It felt like clouds in my brain.'

Crazy, that's how it felt to him, too.

'So what I thought,' said Hippie Mandy, 'is that us three could have two hours a week where we do our special breathing and counting, which helps us relax and be happy. Perhaps in these sessions we can talk about things that might be bothering us. If you want?'

'So,' said Headmaster T, 'I'm going to be getting a report each week from Miss Butterworth so I always know how you two are getting on, and Miss Manners and Ms Fellers, if you could keep me updated on anything happening at home that might be bothering Kai and Saffie that would be great.'

More nodding heads.

'That would be great, yes, and Kai and Saffie, during this time, it's expected that you will stay in the parts of the school where teachers are and where you're allowed, OK? The hall is out of bounds.'

'What about a punishment?' asked Mum.

Kai made a big breath.

'Yes, yes.' Sir rubbed his stubble. 'Detention on Thursday, which means you stay an extra hour at school at the end of the day to write lines.'

Kai hated writing and clenched his toes together; he couldn't even get his letters the right way round. He wanted to scream.

'Thanks,' said Mum.

For the first time in his life Kai hated Mum.

After the school meeting, Kai was allowed out because he was so good in front of Headmaster T. He went with Jordan, Jade, Crystal and Taylor on a walk with Kaos. Cow-manured fields suffocated their noses as they skipped, hopped and ran to the gap in the wall at Middledown Woods, where the stink thinned. Sun pickled the leaves and shadows waved from the floor. Kaos dashed about, dipping, jumping, sniffing, pissing. Rushing over stones, twigs and tree roots to check the path ahead. He was the fastest Bull Lurcher about.

Kaos was off lead.

Kaos was off.

'Must have seen a squirrel,' said Taylor. 'Or a rabbit.'

Jade looked at Kai.

'What?' he shouted.

Kai stopped breathing. It couldn't be a rabbit, it wasn't dusky enough yet. He started running. Nanny Sheila said to pray to God when you were scared, but he didn't know how. Jumping over tree roots to sounds of scuffling. Kaos was bent in front of a broken-limbed rabbit. Big paws ravishing.

'No!' Kai yelled. He froze. Waves crashed in his ears. Was it Papa Grey? Was it?

When Kaos spotted Kai he teethed the grey rabbit around its neck. Shook his head. The rabbit flopped like a rag doll. Eyes reflected like twinkling marbles.

Taylor squealed and jumped up and down. 'Go on, boy. Kill. Kill.'

Jade drew towards Kai and Jordan and placed a hand on her brother's shoulder. Crystal followed Taylor, watching the death closer. Kai shook all over. A sharp taste filled his mouth. Papa Grey.

'That's horrible,' said Jordan.

Jade pulled Kai's arm and whispered, 'We're going home.'

He'd already learned to cry silently.

CHAPTER 23

15 December 2005

I drink and smoke every day now. It helps dull the thinking. Obviously I'm ashamed of it. It makes me the same as them.

Deep breath in.

I crawl out of the den. The muddy floor is hard and icy. Sticks and twigs dig into my hands and knees. The moon watches me. The entrance to the grey rabbits' warren is directly in front. I have half a spliff left. I spark up. Laid on my front, cheek to the ground, blowing smoke towards the rabbit hole.

This limp thing I've become has slithered around inside of me for years. Recently it's taken over, drowned me from the inside out. I take another toke and stare at the rabbit hole, thinking of Neverland. Wanting to be there.

Deep breath in.

Leah gave me a book on my sixth birthday, *Peter Pan*, because I'd watched it over and over on video to the point

Dad mouthed off if he walked in and it was on. Mum didn't mind. She liked us quiet. Everyone wants to fly at some point in their life because of that film. Saffie was sure she could. She *believed* it. I should have told her that day at the tower that it was impossible.

When we talked about *Peter Pan* in English, it freaked me out because Mrs Toghill said Neverland was a metaphor. I forgot what that means, but she said it was heaven and that the Lost Boys were already dead. Middledown Woods is Papa Grey's Neverland and I'm in the middle of it, staring at the gate. Once, I tried to paint him in art – he ended up looking like a grey sausage roll. I tore it up.

I roll on to my back, fold an arm under my head and close my eyes, shutting out the black sky, feeling winter press my face and fingers, wishing it would freeze me. I want to sleep and not wake.

2 December 2005

'Why don't you stay with Nan for a bit?' suggested Jade.

We were watching *Top of the Pops*. Craig David was singing 'Don't Love You No More', Crystal humming along. I'd just taken two bombs of mandy to feel happy.

'That's a really good idea,' said Mum, wagging a finger at Jade, nodding her head and staring at a pair of slippers on the floor next to the ashtray.

Jade reminded me of an oak tree. The mornings I did the paper round I would cycle up the road and stop by the gate to the field for a roll-up to wake me up; across the fields there was a dead oak tree without any leaves, even in August. It was creepy. Like something from *Dracula*, with long knobbly witch's fingers for branches. Leah was into Gothic books. She said that tree was the only beautiful thing in Middledown apart from Midnight Mass at St John's Church on Christmas Eve. Anyway, I understood what Leah meant: it was beautiful, and the reason it was was because it was solid. It never changed. That was why it reminded me of Jade.

When Jade suggested, as she handed me a pint glass of orange squash and a cheese sandwich, that I go to Nan's because I'd got into trouble up the pub, I thought how much I trusted her, even though I was sure I didn't want the sandwich because I didn't want to ruin my buzz.

'What's the point in him going there?' asked Crystal, who was sat on the settee next to Mum, opposite us. She had a towel wrapped round her head, deep-conditioning her hair with coconut and mango something. It needed it, apparently: she had split ends where she was always straightening it – it was straight enough – and dying it black to match Jade's, whose hair was long, finally, after years of refusing to go to a local hairdresser because they didn't know how to cut Afro hair. Jade had her crinkly hair tightly twisted into a French plait. It was longer than Crystal's.

'The point in him going to Nan's,' said Mum, 'is that when Kai's with Nan, he behaves better.'

Both Mum and Jade were wearing pyjamas and drinking tea, as always. The sandwich was good, actually, the margarine spread thick and the Cheddar cut as wide as a door stopper; I tasted salad cream and black pepper. I realised I'd not eaten since the day before.

'What have I done now?'

'What happened at The Station?' asked Crystal.

'Sounds like you already know,' I answered.

'What happened?' asked Mum.

'Ask Mouthy,' I said.

'Becky said Laura said you started on her bloke.'

'Get the brandy,' Mum said to Jade. 'Then what happened?'

'What happened next, Crystal?'

'You tell me,' Mum said.

'It's not in here,' said Jade, raising an eyebrow at me and holding out a bottle of Pernod that was a million years old instead.

'Who drank that, Kai?' Mum said.

'Fuck sake, all right. Sorry.'

'You're definitely going to your nan's. You shouldn't be drinking like that. That's terrible! So, what happened at The Station?'

I told them. They laughed, even Crystal, when I told them about Badger trying to save me. Truthfully, I knew I was a prick and had embarrassed old Wheeler, and I admitted it was stupid when Mum called me out on it being out of order.

'I'll buy old Wheeler a new monocle,' I said. 'I felt bad when I saw it mashed up.'

'So you were fighting over a girl?' Mum said. 'What about Yasmin?'

Fucking crackhead-retard. I rested my head on the back of the settee and looked at the round white lampshade. I wished the mandy would kick in.

'It wasn't the girl,' said Jade. 'It was the lilies.'

The lilies.

There had been a time I used to think the lampshade was a planet and there would be polar bears roaming around it. Everyone stayed quiet listening to Reggie Yates and Fearne Cotton introduce the next song.

'Jade's right,' said Mum. 'Going to Nan's will sort you out. You haven't been your normal self recently.'

'I'm fine,' I said.

'He'll be OK,' said Jade. 'We just need to find him something to love.'

I knew she was talking about Yasmin being pregnant. I felt ashamed when my eyes filled up, so told them I was going to bed. Couldn't be around them when I was coming up anyway.

Before I left the room, Mum said, 'I'll call Nan. You can go up tomorrow and stay for a few days.'

A bit later, Mum knocked and walked into my room.

'What's going on, Kai? I know something's up. I'm your mum.'

'I'm trying to sleep.'

'It's ten, you think I believe that?'

The light was off so I couldn't see why not.

'You're an insomniac.' The light from the hallway traced her outline; she was holding the glass of Pernod. 'What did your dad say in the letter?'

'He's ill. He wants to see us.'

My tongue felt looser and I wished I could see her face. She pushed the door so it was left slightly ajar and went to sit on the bed so I dragged myself away. The little light there was landed on the surface of my rabbit piggy bank on the windowsill, the Teenage Mutant Ninja Turtles next to it, the cannabis leaf poster on the wall, the pirate hat Nan had given me years ago. The white of the skull and crossbones stood out. Mum's hair. The dim light hit the surface of the curved bridge of her nose, her forehead, cheek.

Seconds slowed. We listened to the mumble from downstairs and heard Jade suggest spicy egg fried rice.

'You can hear a lot in here, ey?' Mum said, sipping from the glass. The liquorice-smell slid around my room like a viper.

'I keep my headphones in.'

The room was blacks and greys. The liquorice viper swelled out and zoomed in and out of my nose as I breathed. All the darkness in the world was slipping down my throat; there was no room for it in my head because my mind was already sludge.

'What's wrong with Jesse?' she asked.

I gulped; the liquorice viper filled my throat, found my chest.

'I don't know. I think it's bad.'

'They say it's easier to get drugs there than anywhere else.'

Watching Mum and Dad when we were kids meant I was used to hearing horrible shit. But knowing he'd still be fucking up his body clenched my jaw. Why couldn't he just sort his shit out?

'It might not be that,' I said.

'No one knows your dad better than me.'

'You don't know him any more.'

'He'll always let us down.'

I rounded my fists. 'Mum, I'm trying to sleep. Go away now, please.'

She didn't move. The viper was still in my chest. I moved my tongue over a back tooth and tasted black pepper and then the smell of Jade's onions and spices jumped in and cut up the viper and I thought how the smell of spice was home.

'You shouldn't talk to me like that,' she said.

'Why did you stop loving Dad?'

A small groan came out of her.

Fuck. A metallic light glowed in the corner of the room beneath the piggy bank. I blinked hard. Never? Swear I'd just seen Silver the rabbit, only smaller. I blinked again. Nothing. What the fuck?

'I don't know if I stopped,' she whispered, and I saw the murky light reflected in a tear. The tear was Silver, tiny, hopping down her cheek to her jawline and then Silver was gone.

'You were fucking Denner.'

'We never slept together.'

'I saw how you acted with him.'

Her liquorice breaths were pulsating around the room and were too close to my face.

'Everything was hard back then, Kai. I . . . sometimes it was just easier to go along with . . . You remember what a cunt your dad was.'

'You shouldn't have let Denner touch you.'

'We both fucked up. You understand that. You're not exactly perfect.'

Yeah yeah yeah. My eyes had started shuddering and I wanted her to fuck off, so I said again that I needed to sleep, but I was planning to sneak out to the den, so I'd have to put more layers on even though I was hot as fuck. Mum being in the room wasn't helping.

'Mum, I'm tired, please.'

'OK,' she said, then she was leaning towards me for a one-armed hug and I could smell the Pernod but also the Dark and Lovely cream in her hair. 'I'm sorry,' she said, and I knew that the smell of home wasn't spice, it was the sweet-cream and headiness of her unwashed hair.

CHAPTER 24

THEN

He runs through Middledown Woods, but the trees are different, growing in lines with black shrivelled leaves. No rustling wind or singing birds. A scuffle ahead, a bark. Kai runs with his fastest running legs, fast fast faster towards white light, a clearing ahead. Looking down at his feet.

'Faster faster.' A wise voice whispers so close it feels like it's in his head. Whose voice is it?

A bark ahead, a growl.

'Run faster,' the wise voice whispers.

Run faster, faster, with his fastest running legs. Where's Dad? Kai needs him. Dad runs faster than him. Now Dad's missing.

Black leaves silent, still, as he whizzes as fast as he can, yet the white-lit clearing ahead is far away. A black blob on the side of the path gets closer. A settee; someone laid on it, thumping his arms. Dad, but different.

Kai cries.

'Run faster.' The wise voice groans inside his head.

Fast fast faster. The growling in the clearing is closer. There are fewer black trees, no shrivelled leaves, only twisted black branches like arms and elbows, they ooze black gloop. He's almost there. He listens for the wise voice telling him to run faster. The voice has disappeared. Last black trees – he runs past. White light blinds him for a second, then he's in the clearing.

There's a white-and-black furred dog in the middle whose tail is stiff. The dog faces the other way. Silently, Kai creeps up to it. A snap beneath his foot, a black stick. The dog whips around.

Kai bolted upright in bed, wailing, tears streaming. Kaos was barking outside. The bedroom was too dark. Kaos barked again. The more Kai listened the more strange the noise sounded. Like coughing. The front gate clanged. Dad and Denner had been gone for two days. Now they were back. Kai sat up, rubbing his eyes. Footsteps crunched round the side of the house and then they were in. On the other side of the wall Mum's light switch clicked.

He wanted to run to the girls' room and shake Jade awake; he stopped himself. Something felt different. Why had it taken two nights? Why weren't they laughing? Why hadn't Mum gone down yet? Their voices were low and the kettle started boiling. Mum's door handle sprang and then she was in the living room too so Kai crept out of bed, slowly opened the door and tiptoed, extra quiet, across the landing into the girls' room. The curtains were wide open and the window was cracked.

He felt uneasy.

'Jade,' he whispered.

'I'm awake.'

He jumped. Her voice was lower than his waist and in the corner of the room by the wardrobe, where her shadowed outline looked like it was sitting.

'What you doing?'

'Waiting for you.'

They shut the door behind them and sat at the top of the stairs, feet on the next step down.

'Why were you on the floor?'

'I like sleeping on the floor. It stops the dizzy.'

'Dizzy?'

'Like, when everything feels wrong.'

The last picture she'd drawn was of a face looking out of cracked glass. Jade felt dizzy because of Mum and Dad. It was obvious. Her knee felt soft and warm under his hand. They couldn't hear any voices.

'Shall we go down?'

Jade didn't answer. Must be for the same reason he was unsure; what had they been doing? They crept to the bottom of the stairs and Jade told Kai to hush when he got bored and talked loud enough for the grown-ups to hear.

'They're not even coming out,' said Kai, wanting Dad to open the door. 'Let's just go in.'

Jade hesitated. So did Kai, before remembering he was a big strong boy. Jade must have thought about being older than him because they both jumped on the handle.

'What you doing up?' Dad, in his neon-yellow security coat, yawned from the settee next to Mum. The lights were off, the TV glared black, dark blue and white, outlining them and Denner, opposite. On the floor was a pile of money, a big pile. The room was too quiet.

'Turn the light on,' said Dad. The treasure chest was wide open. There was the green stuff and the hash Mum made for smokes and milky-brown powder like what he stole from Steve's that was hidden in a sock under the bed. All small. Nanny said the best things in life came in little packages. She was wrong. Dad had a rectangle of tin foil and sprinkled some of the light brown powder on it; he asked Denner to light it underneath and then he used a metal tube to suck in the smoke.

'I'm knackered,' said Mum. 'I'm not getting any sleep.'

'Have some of that,' Dad slurred. His fingers went limp and the pipe rolled from his hand to the carpet.

'I'm not touching that,' Mum growled. 'Why—'

'Give me a break, woman.' He looked like jellyfish man.

'It was full on,' said Denner. 'The alarms went off.'

Strange for Dad to return with money instead of Santa's sack to dive into. Every other time they'd visit Scottie or Steve and the money would follow a day or two after, but it was never this amount.

'Are we rich now?' Kai asked. Dad slumped on the settee, mouth ajar and eyes like white cuts. Kai reached over, shook his knee. Wet sand caked his trainers.

'He's all right, love,' said Mum, pulling a plate from the microwave. 'He's just had a smoke.'

He looked dead and Kai rested his head on Dad's knees and threaded a hand through his legs to rest on a gritty trainer. Denner took white powder from his pocket and Mum tipped it on to the plate and started chopping it up with a blade from Dad's penknife. Kai didn't know what to say. The world felt like he was lying with his head hanging off the side of the bed.

Jade stood up, holding out a hand. 'Come on.'

'No,' said Kai. No way was he leaving Mum in the room with Denner when Dad looked knocked out. 'I want to count the money.'

His sister chose a chair at the table where her pencil case was; he heard the scraping of sharpening a moment later and then the rustle of sweets and they shared a giant bag of Smarties and a big bottle of cola while Denner's low voice grumbled how him and Dad, Scottie and Steve had lifted a safe into a lorry.

In the morning Kai woke up wrapped in Dad's arms. Beast breath. Kai pushed Dad's elbow and turned to face the room. He felt safe. Maybe today they'd go to the den or the tower. He'd love to show Dad the valley from the window where he and Saffie sat watching the rabbits and he was desperate to get back and see them after Papa Grey had been killed. He'd keep it a secret from Saffie about showing Dad because she wanted it to be just theirs. The TV flickered. A TV presenter was talking about a man called Nelson Mandela visiting the UK. Mum and Jade must be in bed. Brightness shone round the edges of the curtains. A whole new day. Kai felt suddenly like something bad might happen and he didn't want yesterday to end. He closed his eyes and listened to the TV, the ticking clock, felt the rise and fall of Dad's chest. Out the window, Kaos barked and the bin men's lorry bleeped. Horrible dog. The empty Smarties packet rustled underneath him; he chucked it on the floor. Hopefully, someone had remembered to take the bins out, they were overflowing from missing the last collection.

He was definitely going to the den to see if the rabbits were OK without Papa Grey. He'd take lettuce and carrots from Nanny's. They'd be sleeping now. There was nothing worse than the idea of Dad not being there. Kai squeezed his eyes tighter and pulled Dad's heavy arm further round him like a shield. What Kaos needed was some of Dad's special smokes to calm him down. To stop him barking.

He opened one eye. Across the room next to the cup filled with ash and butts, the treasure chest was open. The twenty-pound notes that had decorated the floor last night were gone. Denner was hiding some and Mum had taken a few upstairs. What had Dad done? Last night after Denner said bye and Dad had fallen asleep on the settee, Mum said to him and Jade between two sniffs through a straw off the plate, 'What's the worst thing in the world?' and they answered, 'A grass,' and Mum said, 'That's right. So, if a policeman ever comes and asks if Dad stole anything, what would you say?' Jade made a big breath and Kai stared at the Queen's fat cheeks on a money note remembering Dad telling him the same thing when he met Tony-teeth and Elf. Kai said, 'No, he didn't.' Mum said, 'That's right.' Then she stared at Jade. 'You always deny everything, right? Even if they tell you one of us has admitted it, OK?' They'd nodded.

Kaos growled, meaning the bin men were at his garden gate.

'Dad?' Kai whispered.

Nothing.

Carefully, he lifted Dad's arm and crept to the treasure chest. He picked up and dropped down the different bags of smelly green leaves that Dad put in his Js – J meant joint. There was a bag with brown powder in like what he'd hidden under the bed. Kai picked it up, held it towards the light of the TV. It was what made Dad look like he'd been knocked out by Mike Tyson. Dad snored. Kai took a grey rasher of bacon from the fridge and sprinkled half of the powder on top, rolling the meat up, careful not to put it near his face because he didn't want to look like jellyfish man, before going up the garden and checking the curtains in Jordan's house were pulled. He threw the bacon over the fence.

Kaos stopped barking. Dogs' mouths sounded slobbery when they ate.

'It's to make you feel calm like a pufferfish,' whispered Kai. 'So you don't kill any more rabbits.'

The bin lorry's bleeps were quieter, must be off up Middledown main road towards Saffie's. From the back garden Kai saw the china rabbit money box on his bedroom windowsill. Four pounds' worth of change that Denner gave him last night were in it, and even though he hated robot head he wanted strawberry laces. He wanted to count it again. He liked making money towers.

Upstairs, Kai pulled the black rubber circle from the bottom of the money box; he poured out the fifty-, twenty- and ten-pence pieces. Maybe Dad would give him some notes when he woke up. It was safer to hide them for now. He pushed the net curtain aside to let the light in. The birds were extra sharp sounding. As he piled coins, a movement caught the corner of his eye. Jordan walked up his garden path to Kaos, who was lying in front of his kennel.

'Kaos,' Jordan said, then his voice rose, 'Kaos!' He rubbed the dog's shoulder and then screamed at his house, 'Mum!'

His voice was mad, high-pitched like a girl's. Kai knocked coins off the windowsill as he leaned close. When Jordan shook Kaos with both hands nothing happened, like with Dad. Jordan's mum and dad ran out.

'What's wrong?'

'It's Kaos. Look, Kaos—'

Coldness swept through Kai. From where he stood he saw Kaos's floppy legs and Kev's wide back and builder's bum. Jordan hopped from foot to foot and Shar clutched her neck. Her T-shirt had letters on: **d i p p y c o w**.

'Fucking hell,' croaked Jordan's mum.

'Take him inside,' yelled Kev, and Shar dragged Jordan over the grass, kicking. Kev's shoulders heaved up and down like the kiss of life on *Baywatch*, but without breathing in Kaos's mouth, then he stiffened and sat next to the dog, his face still; he rubbed his eyes then looked at the house where Kai heard the door whacked open. Taylor.

'Go back in,' Kev shouted. Instead, Taylor ran the length of the garden and threw himself on Kaos, balling.

Taylor's words caught in breaths. 'But, he's, my, best friend.'

The bedroom felt mixy. Dad. On the settee he had been breathing, he had. What if? What if something happened like with Leah's dad? Kai stepped away from the window and felt a fist hit up from the bottom of his tummy. He threw up over his coins before his knees buckled and he fell. The sick was green from last night's Smarties.

*

'Why didn't you get up when I told you?' asked Leah. She'd cleared the sick. Mum stood in the doorway to his room an hour later, asking what the stink was. 'You should have been awake. Or Jesse.'

Their voices faded when Kai put a hand over his ear. His bed felt damp from sweat. He'd killed Kaos and that stuff could kill Dad. He cried. 'I want Dad.'

'He's downstairs,' said Leah.

The elephant and the horse on the Noah's Ark border on the walls looked too happy. The walls were light blue like starling eggs. His sister on the edge of the bed held the Peter Pan book and each time she turned a page she checked on him. He hadn't stopped sobbing.

Mum crouched in front of Kai. 'You're really poorly, huh?'

'I want Dad.'

'Go and get him, Leah,' Mum said, and then he felt bad that Leah was ordered away when she took good care of him. He loved Leah so much. More than Mum. Tears heated his eyes afresh.

Ten minutes later, Dad lay on the bed next to him. 'You all right?'

'Kaos,' he said. 'Kaos is dead.'

'What?' Mum stood up and looked out of the window. 'He's not even out there, Kai—'

'Please.' Kai grabbed Dad's hand tighter over him. 'Please stop.'

'Stop what?' His voice was whiskery like it always was, soft as rabbit fur, and Kai remembered Papa Grey's shining eyes catching the sunlight when Kaos killed him. Maybe it was good he'd killed Kaos? No. The hurt in his tummy squeezed and he wanted to tell Dad to stop smoking because it was so terrible, far worse than Denner's elbow wriggling.

He couldn't breathe and was hiccupping and Mum was telling Leah to grab the can of Special Brew in the fridge and a moment later they held a pink plastic cup to his mouth, saying, 'Drink, love, drink, it will help calm you down,' and even though Leah crossed her arms over her chest her face was worried and that's when Jade and Crystal pushed the door open asking, 'Is he OK?' and Dad told everyone to get out, but Mum watched a moment from the door and that's when Kai said, 'Dad, please don't smoke again,' and Mum put both hands to her scraped-back hair and he spotted a grease stain on Leah's Diadora hoody that she had on. Dad's arm tightened around his body and the other rested on his forehead.

'He's right,' said Mum, before she closed the door.

Dad's lip pressed Kai's ear. 'I'm sorry,' he said. 'I'm sorry. I'll stop now.'

It was almost summer holidays and the weekend before was the Blueberry Fair at school. Cake stalls heaved with Victoria and chocolate sponges, crafts made from paper, wool and wood were being sold as cards, cardigans and cats. There was face-painting, karate presentations, Morris dancing, willow weaving, bush craft, and games like Twister. A raffle was being called by Headmaster T next to Flopsy's hutch. His voice was distant. Kai and Saffie had come with her mum and sister, who were checking their raffle tickets by the sandpit.

Kai lay by the pond in the secret garden among strips of bamboo listening to Saffie, who was doing her frog crouch as she talked about the silver moon and the Grey Tower and how Headmaster T was a scum of the earth, and a scum rhymed with crumb so now she was gonna call him Scum-Crumb. It would be their code word.

'Why aren't you laughing?' she asked for the millionth time.

No one knew about Kaos. Not even her. He wanted to be good and admit the truth, he just couldn't. There was no way she would like him after, nobody would. He was a killer. The afternoon Kaos died, Kev and Taylor had buried him in the garden and they made him a wooden plaque that the boys had painted and varnished and propped into the earth by his hump, which was next to his brown kennel. The same day after making his promise Dad had smoked again, the same terrible stuff, and Mum called Denner and made him take Dad away. When Kai next checked his china rabbit money box, his coins that Leah had cleaned of green sick had disappeared. He knew it was Dad. It hurt more inside. That felt the worst.

'It's too much,' Mum had whispered to Dad at the front door, thinking Kai hadn't crawled along the settee so that his ear was near the hallway. There were red smudges round the door handle and when he touched them they were sticky and tasted like jam. Probably from his toast.

Kai woke from nightmares every night – of Kaos, Papa Grey and Dad and the sound of barking. Leah would always be there, folding herself around him so he slept again. The piles of cash had come from a safe. Middlevalley's building society in town. They'd dumped it on the beach and it hit the local news: 'Missing safe turns up in Weston-super-Mare'.

'See that?' Mum said. 'Your dad would be brilliant if he could sort his shit out.'

Why there had been sand on Dad's trainers.

Then Saffie was shaking him. 'Why aren't you listening to me? You're so annoying.'

'Sorry,' he said.

That morning Crystal, concentrating and biting her lips in Nanny's front room, had braided Saffie's hair into two plaits and she looked as cool as Nanny's big green hat. There were tiny red ribbons threaded in two of the plaits, the ribbons were longer than her hair and hung lower than her shoulders.

'What shall we steal next?'

One of the stalls round the front of the school was Hippie Mandy's. Crystals and precious stones covered a black velvet throw; some jewels were shaped into teardrop earrings. For a couple of weeks they'd done big pufferfish breaths and talking and listening to the wind. Hippie Mandy was kind, even though shc asked him how things were. Dad was gone and Kai's mouth was tightly zipped.

'Kai!' said Saffie. 'Answer—'

'One of Hippie Mandy's stones,' he said, noticing how the sun touched the leaves on the helicopter tree. Bright on some sides, till they rippled and darkened. 'One of the bright orange ones.'

'That's called amber,' said Saffie.

'How do you know?'

'The label said.'

'They're tiger eyes.'

'So, how we gonna do it?' She lowered her forehead so her eyes looked shadowed and glaring.

Kai sat up. The plan came to him quickly as he placed various pebbles to represent him, Saffie and Hippie Mandy. How they would wait for a customer to distract her and one would lean across the table pointing at the big purple-and-white crystals at the back while the other slid a hand over the cloth to grab an amber.

'Will I take, or you?'

'It should be me. I'm the boy.'

'I don't care about you're the boy.'

'You take it then.' He flopped back down; a robin landed on a branch. He could smell hot dogs and popcorn.

'No, you can.' She tugged at his *X-Men* T-shirt. It was too tight. He loved it and was scared Dad would never surprise him with another and though he wore his red cape he didn't feel like he could fly any more. Saffie added, 'You're the best at taking because you never get caught.'

Untrue: Mum had found out about Dragon and Charizard. He couldn't be bothered to tell Saffie.

They decided to play rock, paper, scissors, which they always drew, second-guessing each other. Saffie laughed, then Kai won with paper. He'd be the taker.

'Fine, I'll take it; it will be a present for you.'

Saffie watched him a moment, she lifted one green Velcro shoe then the other like she needed to pee. 'Come on.'

She hopped over the stepping stones through the garden and Kai followed – dragging his feet, his hands deep in his pockets, his shorts had mud stains on and smelled like smoke from the barbecue on his birthday. The morning of the Blueberry Fair, Leah and Jade had read the packet of the washing powder before fumbling with buttons on the machine because they wanted clean uniform next week and they couldn't ask Mum because she was always in bed, missing Dad and wanting and not wanting him home.

What if Dad died like Kaos?

They passed over the playground and hopscotch, where families were talking to teachers about the science displays spread round on school tables. Saffie waved at her mum and sister. Year Six had made erupting volcanoes and they were spilling over tables. Flopsy was being cuddled by a girl in Jade's class, who everyone called Bacon because of her shiny lips. They passed the 'Grow our Future' herbs, where Jade shouted, 'Hey', and carried on to the lanes, where a couple were chatting to Hippie Mandy.

Easy. Saffie reached out, saying how beautiful the big purple stone was, and Kai picked up a small amber like it was a pebble on Weymouth beach and they walked along one of the lanes with him squeezing it tightly in his pocket and Saffie said, 'Let's go, just in case.'

Vells was a small village on a hill and Vells Primary was at the bottom near the bridge. They passed the farmhouse and the huge open-sided barns, tractors in the yard, the old church with the wooden porch leading into the graveyard, the closed Post Office. At the top of the hill their breaths were jagged. Saffie took big pufferfish breaths on her inhaler. They met the crossroads that led into endless fields and took a left towards the cycle path before heading to the den in the woods.

Saffie wore a purple dress, which looked really nice. She hated it; she whacked tree trunks with a stick. In a flash, Kai felt the amber in his pocket burn because he shouldn't have taken it. He liked Hippie Mandy.

'Here.' He chucked it at Saffie; it bounced off her hand to the floor. She swooped to pick it up.

Inside the den Kai lay down next to the huge needle tree and Saffie sat at his feet, rubbing two sticks together trying to make fire. She smelled of toffee popcorn from what her mum bought earlier and he guessed he did too even though he only ate two pieces. Through a gap in the branches around them Kai spotted the dark rabbit hole. Some of the greys searched for food in the day, others might be sleeping in the warren. If the rabbits knew Kaos was dead they might feel better. Kai made a big pufferfish breath.

The amber reflected the sun when Saffie held it up to the sunny part of the den. 'It's got yellow bits in.'

For ages Kai thought Dad was the coolest. He got his hands on anything, dressed the best, had muscles and taught Kai everything, but all the things were getting mixy and mixier recently and he knew it was to do with smoking. Horrible. He turned on his side and wrapped his arms around his legs. Lots of grown-ups smoked, but the smelly pipes were different.

'Have you ever been back to the tower?' Saffie's voice was quick, and he knew her eyes were creased almost shut. 'I want to. It was the best seeing the whole valley and watching Raven fly over it.'

'I wouldn't go there without you. That's our special place.'

'I dreamed my dad was there,' she said. 'We were holding hands, watching the valley.'

Saffie said the tininess of Vells Primary School was like Lego from the top of the Grey Tower and asked if he had his lock-picking set, he mumbled no and said he'd bury the lock-picking set in the den next time he came – he didn't want it at home any more.

'Why?' she asked.

But he couldn't explain.

The picture of Kaos punched Kai on the inside of his eyes over and over. In the mornings he woke up with headaches and wished he could drink Mum's can like when he couldn't stop crying and it made him sleep. That was bad, too. It made Mum cry and made her hang out her ass. Apart from Nanny, grown-ups acted bad. He didn't want to be like Dad. His tummy bubbled.

'What's wrong?' asked Saffie, crawling over and resting a hand on his arm.

'I don't want to be a thief any more, Saffie. That amber is Hippie Mandy's and she's kind.'

She shook him. 'But, but—'

'No!' He sat up. 'I'm not doing it any more.' He shouted, 'Nanny says it's wrong and it is.'

There was wet on his face.

Saffie pulled his hand and led him out of the den. They walked to the deepest part of the woods where a wooden bridge crossed spluttery Middle River. The path turned into three, leading to Middledown, Vells and Hilcombe, and they climbed the wooden fence on one side of the bridge.

'Put your arm here.' She pointed at her back and so he lowered down a step and held her. 'Hold tighter.' He squeezed. The toffee popcorn smelled sweeter and his ears got hot. Quickly she leaned back and threw the amber with all her muscles, skimming it along the river until it plopped out of sight into the black-green water. 'There,' she said. 'We'll never do it again.'

'Saffie,' he said, 'will you marry me when we grow up?'

'Obbiously.' She smiled.

Then she kissed him on the cheek and inside his chest felt like one of the volcanoes he saw at the fair when they burst. Kai decided that one day when it wouldn't make her cry he would tell Saffie about what happened to Kaos.

CHAPTER 25

15 December 2005

The rope is thick. It shouldn't break. The temperature feels like it just dropped. I'm wearing two scarves; one is Jade's, I'll leave it here. As much as I love my den, it's stupid to stay here at night, although I have done a few times in summer. After tonight, it won't matter anyway. I imagine Jade coming here after I've gone. She will be sad and quiet. My thoughts would have stilled.

Where was I?

Sandy Cove.

When Jade and Mum said I should go to Nan's it was the same week that Nan was going away with Betty. That week I slept a bit better and finally saw part of the nightmare that made me go to Cranston on the bus a month before. I've had trouble sleeping for ever. When I was little Leah told me to count if I'd not fallen asleep to her reading.

The aim was to be asleep before I reached one hundred. I asked her what came after.

'Darkness,' she whispered.

She slept with me heads-and-tails and pressed her foot against my arm so it was the last warmth I'd feel. As we got older, we stopped sharing, and the nightmares had eased off till that night before I went to Cranston.

3 December 2005

Nan knew of a small caravan park that opened during winter; she liked the smell of caravans and how everything was miniature. She was five foot ten and must have imagined herself as a queen in some fairy tale where everyone else was the size of ants. Nan had this funny streak in her.

When we reached Sandy Cove, she and Betty jumped out of the red Fiesta – it had patches of orange from being so old – went to reception to ask for an upgrade, so I could have my own room, and were told they were sold out, which made Betty tell them I had some hidden disability called autism so we could get a disabled caravan and then Nan got in a piss with Betty because she 'couldn't abide people lying' and so the first hour in the caravan it was only me and Betty because Nan had gone to buy a bottle of wine. That meant she'd gone to calm down. Betty cracked me up; sometimes she wound Nan up on purpose.

'What do you think of the view?' Betty asked, pulling the net curtain aside. There was so much hairspray in her hair and dark purple eyeshadow round her eyes, she looked like she was from that band KISS.

We were on a hill, at the front of the park – due to my 'disability'. Knowing Yasmin was pregnant, Dad writing that he was ill, seeing the grey sky, sea and drizzle were so depressing I felt like all the sadness in the world had slipped into my heart and was trying to strangle it.

Betty tucked the curtain back, folded her arms and stood in front of the window. 'I'm not sure.' She pointed at another caravan across the path from us. 'Perhaps their view is better.'

'Maybe,' I said.

I sat down with Jade's old school bag filled with clothes at my feet – at least I had a week off – wondering what the fuck I was going to do for five days. What were they going to do? Drag me to? What the fuck had I done? I should have gone to Nan's the week after. A part of me wanted to come, though, wanted to be near Nan. But for what?

Betty moved to a bag on the table and started taking out food.

'Here.' She handed me packets of bacon and sausages. 'Put those in the fridge.'

I did as I was told and kept on putting away cornflakes, eggs, spaghetti, feeling too shy to find a bedroom. From the first time I met her, she'd been kind of, well, intimidating. The sting of her perfume had started a headache. There's no way my little girl would wear perfume.

The door opened: Nan with a bottle of Merlot – she took out glasses – and orange juice for me. It made me want to stick my head under the tyres of the caravan. Hopefully I'd get served drink somewhere down here.

'Thanks,' I said when Nan pushed the glass of juice towards me. I felt the landslide again, realising that there was no way I'd be able to drink with Nan around and I only had enough weed for two spliffs the entire week.

'I've got a headache,' I said.

Nan found a packet of paracetamol but I ignored them and asked which bedroom I could have of the three doors. After checking, she pointed to the nearest. A twin room. The beds so short I'd be scrunched up like Johnny the Prawn that Halloween he slept on his front lawn in the white and purple vicar's outfit.

I went to bed and slept. For a day. One dream was back in the tower – Saffie was there with her dad. My hand throbbed as I watched.

What woke me was chatting – the bedroom window was open so I would hear the birds – it was light outside, it was Nan and Betty. Probably smoking, thinking I wouldn't notice.

'Everyone's worried about him,' Nan said, and I knew she meant me. I felt guilty. I held my breath.

'What do you think brought it on?' asked Betty.

'Could be any of it,' Nan said. 'The rabbit, issues with his dad, Jade said something's happened with Yasmin. Maybe . . . I think, maybe . . .'

Her voice went quieter as she moved.

'Oh, don't,' said Betty. 'That made me go cold.'

She'd probably said that I was depressed, I'd overheard her say it to Mum once. It shocked me when I checked my phone that it was 2 p.m. – I'd slept about twenty-three hours and Nan had let me. Their footsteps up the ladder to the caravan made it shudder a little.

My bedroom door clicked as Nan pulled it open.

'Finally,' she said.

Nan was trying to guess what I was thinking, her eyes were direct – unmoving. She was wearing a black dress that reached her knees; it looked thick and warm, a blue scarf round her neck. I was still tired.

'I could sleep a million years.' My voice was croaky.

'We're doing breakfast,' she said. 'Get up.'

'You mean lunch?'

'Both. Then we're going to the beach.'

Getting out of bed? I didn't want to. She left the door open and started clattering pots and pans. Through the crack in the window I heard rain start. A walk on the beach? She was having a laugh.

I spent the whole week under the duvet. A couple of hours on the sofa because Nan wouldn't let me eat in bed. I thought of Yasmin – because she kept texting me wanting to know what I was feeling, what I was up to, when I would be back – and of Dad. Mainly, I kept thinking about having a baby. I knew it would be a girl; would she have an Afro like me or would it be like Yasmin? I'd teach her about wood because by the time she was a teenager I'd know how to build tree houses.

At night, I missed the stars; the clouds were a mask for the night. I had a toke out the window before sleep. There were nightmares. Most times I jumped awake and couldn't remember them.

On the Wednesday, when I suddenly thought I'd be missing I.T. and sitting next to that new girl, Ammi, who made me think of starlings, I felt a bit weird. Like dizzy. And sick. In the small living room, the gas fire was blazing. I found Nan on the sofa, reading a book about the Royal Academy of Dance; Betty was at the table doing a crossword. I lay down with my head near Nan's lap and she placed a hand on my hair, which I knew she loved because it was long – she said it was coarser since I'd got older – and it was like some man in the Bible called Samson, who got his strength from his hair. When she touched my forehead her fingers were cold from bad circulation.

After a while, she asked, 'What's on your mind?'

Suddenly I knew; I wished I was dead. I breathed in long and hard a few times so I wouldn't cry like a girl. The thought had come to me a few times. Like that time in the abandoned house when I stood at the window and when I started on that bloke at The Station. I usually shut the feeling away. I couldn't tell her that, and I so badly wanted to tell her that Yasmin was pregnant, how terrible I felt. How I'd fucked up. That I was like Mum and Dad when they'd been bad when I was little. I felt so angry at Yasmin. Not wanting to have sex in the first place, it kept going round and round in my head. I felt sick remembering that nasty little pink outfit she'd worn.

'Hey,' said Nan. She ran a finger over my cheek.

The pattern on the brown and beige sofa looked like rooftops. In some places it looked worn. Apparently, Nan had been holidaying there for years; it surprised me because I thought she would have brought me and the girls. She took us to Weymouth a couple of times. Probably more to do there.

'Kai,' she said. I felt like my rabbit must have when she was dying, like there was only bad in me – Dad, drugs, darkness, death. It was hard to know why I felt this way; Jord and Richie always seemed chilled out and happy and like nothing really mattered. I thought the last thing, too, but it was for some other reason. It didn't make sense.

Betty reached for her handbag and pulled out a blue and gold embroidered purse. 'We're out of bread.'

The room fell silent when she left. A clock ticked somewhere and a pattering of bird feet scuttled over the roof. The bird sounded mad. Like an escaped prisoner.

'I'm a bad person,' I said.

'Don't be ridiculous,' she said.

Annoyed, I moved away.

'You want tea?' she asked. She'd spotted my eyes land on the kettle. I shrugged and while she brewed, I counted the curtain hooks on the cheap plastic rail that ran around the three sides of the room.

If she knew I chewed mandy for fun, how much school I missed, that Yasmin was pregnant it was obvious I was a bad person. If Nan knew how I wished I wasn't here – Church told her suicide was a sin – she'd think differently.

The teapot, cups and saucers chinked as she lay them out next to a plate of Digestives and Jammie Dodgers. I moved to watch her slosh drops of milk in. We waited for the steaming tea and she opened a window; the sound of the sea crashing against the cliffs below was loud. Crazy. I pulled off my Nike hoody with my head turned towards the window and my hand resting on the book she'd been reading. I thought of Saffie. The scar on my palm was pale and shiny.

Yasmin was pregnant with my baby.

'I don't want to be a bad person,' I said.

'What makes you talk of "badness" like it's a quality you innately are?' She poured the tea and I watched the brown liquid swirl and mix into the white. It made me think of when Mum and Dad taught me that I was mixed race.

Dad told me once that he'd stolen off his mum when he was seven like it was a job to be proud of.

I answered, 'Some people aren't born good.'

Like those kids who purposefully killed James Bulger. Crystal got so creeped out when she overheard Aunt Shad talking about it to Mum when we were little that she had to sleep in bed with Jade for three weeks.

A child that could kill meant some people were born bad. I scooped four sugars into my cup. 'What about killers?'

'People aren't born bad, Kai.' She ran delicate fingers over her dress, just like Leah did. There weren't two more similar women in the world in how they moved and acted like ladies and were ready to rip a head off if they were crossed. 'And more importantly than that, people can change.'

'I thought a leopard couldn't change its spots?' I said. I fucking hated my memory.

'You aren't a leopard.' She reached for a Digestive. 'You're more of a rabbit.'

That night, I woke myself up from a groaning that was trapped in my throat. I could see a figure, a man, on a sofa. I thought he was dead. It was 3:38 a.m. when I called Leah.

'Hello?'

'Leah,' I said. Her voice sounded sleepy and alert at the same time.

'Kai. Are you OK?'

'Yeah.'

'Where are you?'

I heard shuffling; probably she was sitting up and turning on a light next to that old-codger-crisp-packet boyfriend she had, 'Dean'. Be better if she left it off.

'With Nan in Dorset.'

'Oh, nice. What's up?'

'I just wondered how you are.'

'At three in the morning?'

'Did I wake you?'

She did her machine-gun cackle and I heard someone grunt in the background. I knew she wouldn't mind.

'What have you been doing down there?'

'Nothing,' I answered. 'Nan and Betty have been out a few times, but I'm not really feeling it. Going out, I mean.'

'Well, you should,' she said. 'Go out and find some fossils.'

'You taking the piss?'

'No.'

I yawned.

'Is there a club at the campsite?' she asked.

'Yeah.'

'Well, get down there,' she said. 'Nan will buy you a couple and she'd love you to do the twist with her. Get your blue suede shoes on, it will do you good.'

That was a good way of getting alcohol. Maybe tomorrow I'd sleep properly if I blagged enough drinks. 'OK.'

Our last night, Nan refused to buy me more than two pints, but I managed to slip a bottle of Bacardi from a storeroom out the back into Jade's school bag and kept topping up my glass of Coke. It tasted shit. To Nan's delight, I danced with her under purple and green disco lights. Even Betty got up and twisted about. They looked so good in their flouncy dresses – that's what they called them, 'flouncy'. The skirts spread out like flower petals.

I'll never forget the grin on Nan's face when I twirled her under my arm: she looked five years old, like she'd just stumbled across a real fairy down the bottom of the garden.

'I love you, Nan,' I shouted.

She didn't hear. She was too pissed and singing along to Tom Jones.

CHAPTER 26

THEN

'Thank God he didn't do it here.'

That's what Mum said. Over and over.

Behind the crack of the living-room door Kai watched from the bottom of the stairs, rubbing the end of the banister, forgetting the last time he got a splinter.

'Fucking smackhead,' said Mum. 'I knew he was injecting. Knew it. The lie ... the lying bastard.'

Outside the sky was grey, but September felt warm.

Mum clutched Leah's and Jade's arms, begging from the chair. She looked ill, shadowed eyes, brown skin powdery pale and cheeks pointy. She'd just had a phone call from the hospital saying Dad was there. He'd OD'd. Lucky Dad wasn't at the house otherwise the officers would be there now. Without warning. Crack wasn't as bad. Just Coke cans. Not as bad as smoking smack, but Mum *knew* Dad had been injecting.

'We need to get rid of everything, everything. Everything, girls,' she stuttered. Kai held his breath, wondering what OD'd and injecting meant. Bad, if Dad was in hospital. It had to do with that brown powder he smoked. It had to be. A stone grew in his throat. The girls knelt at the cupboard under the sink next to the churning washing machine. Leah told Jade to hold out a Tesco carrier bag.

'Don't move,' she whispered as she threw in cans, tin foil, nails and blades. 'Watch your hands.'

'Wait,' said Mum. 'Wait. Bring that here.'

Leah stood in a grey hoody with her frizzy fringe as miserable as her face. Mum grabbed the Coke can and a nail. Eyes focused. Task most important.

'Calm.' Mum spoke with trembling hands. 'Calm, calm.'

She took paper from her pocket – a wrap, Mum and Dad called it – the little red pot of Dr Cook's Bicarbonate of Soda at her feet, and asked Jade for a tablespoon with a tiny bit of water on. Kai swore he'd never give that stuff to Mum. On the spoon Mum added the two white powders. In a shaky voice she told Jade to hold the spoon. 'Steady, steady. Like Jesse does when he holds it for me.'

Mum held a lighter underneath as she used the nail to stir the tiny cauldron. Leah stood by the table covered in yesterday's school books, Guess Who? and dirty plates. She stared at the floor with clenched fists. If Kai was in there he'd give her a cuddle.

It stuck to the needle like a tiny white toffee apple. Mum waved it in the air before scraping it off.

'Crystals for a clear head,' she whispered.

Mum pinched ash from the ashtray at her feet and dab, dab, dabbed it over the ten tiny holes at the end of the Coke can, then 'careful, careful, hold-breath, careful', placed the crystals on the ash. Wrapped her cracked lips around the broken ring-pull, lit a lighter, burned the crystals and sucked in. Eyes closed, hanging on to it, chest puffed out. Denner had left a newspaper on the settee and it rustled against her hand.

They watched her use all of it.

Then she had energy.

She stood, shoulders hunched, and smiled at the girls. 'We need to clear up everything. You don't want the social workers to take you away, do you? You wouldn't want that, would you? You love being here. We're the dream team. Let's get this house clean.'

Kai felt weak. She always changed so quickly. Leah's clenched fists and Jade's silence made him open the door.

'There you are, my prince. Come here.' Mum grabbed him, planted a kiss on his turned-away cheek. Leah's eyebrows wrinkled in the middle as though she might cry, her dark brown eyes like a trapped animal.

It wasn't until the house was spotless, Mum had her first bath in weeks and put on clean clothes that made her look fatter. She asked, 'Where's Crystal?'

'With Taylor.' Jade kissed her teeth before adding, 'As always.'

Then came the officers in black jackets, black trousers and with stiff backs in white shirts. The man had a double chin below a bum-nose and the woman had shorter fingernails than Dad.

'Will he be OK, Officer? I can't believe what's happened. He wasn't at the house ... No, of course not. We've got four kids. He wouldn't do that here. Do I? Never have, never would. I promise you that. We don't use smack, Officer, we don't do that. Check the house, look around. We don't do that.'

'Perhaps your children could go upstairs?'

'Yes yes, of course. Kids, go upstairs. Leah, read *Peter Pan* to the others. My girl's a proper bookworm, Officer, she is.'

The girls' feet rumbled upstairs. Leah ran to the bathroom, slipped the lock and turned the tap. Jade put the radio on. Kai stood at the bottom of the stairs spying on Mum, whose eyes focused on the officers in the same way he'd opened his eyes at Headmaster T when he was asked about fighting Tom B.

'You don't use heroin?'

'I don't. It's poison.'

'Do you use any other substances?'

Mum shook her head.

Dickheads. The first thing Mum said when the officers left. At least they hadn't searched the house.

Kai stood at the top of the garden near the slow-worm snake cake watching Mum, who dropped to her knees at the bush that had macky blue flowers in spring. Dad had once said slow-worms 'existed to eat shit like slugs and snails at the bottom of the food chain'. They were different to snakes because they had eyelids and ear holes – that's what the man said on the wildlife programme.

Moments after the police officers left Mum shot up the back garden to where his sisters had hidden the bag. As Kai watched Mum wriggle with effort to get her poison, he felt the urge to kick her and send her into the mud. Imagined her eye pierced by a twig. She pulled out the Tesco bag Leah and Jade had packed, so carefully, with fingertips.

That night, Kai woke up. The pipes churned, a tap was running in the bathroom. Leah. She usually spent hours in there. The tap turned off. Silence.

He lay there with the sound of his heart filling his ears, too quiet without Kaos barking; he listened. Moonlight highlighted his room, and green glowed from his night-light. What would the rabbits be doing? He'd love to go to the woods, find them, play with them. See how they scurried at night, even though the dark was scary. If Dad got better they could spy on them together. Kai had been eating more carrots. Miss Quiller said they had beet-a-carrot in which was good for eyes, and he hoped to see in the dark. It would stop him being scared.

Silence still from the bathroom. What was she doing? It was too late for a bath. A tiny wave rippled inside him. He climbed out of bed, quietly opened the door, crept along the landing and saw the bathroom door ajar. Strange, Leah always locked it. Eye to the crack he saw the light was off. His eyes readjusted.

Leah, in a long white nightie, was bent over the sink, hands tightly gripping it, elbows sharp, her face pushed into water. Kai's heart leapt. She was holding her breath.

'Leah!' He jumped forward, pulled her arm. She raised her head, wheezed. Water slopped to the floor as she dropped to her knees. The streaks of her wet fringe were so dark they looked like blood.

'You might drown.'

She rubbed her eyes and stole fast breaths. Kai pulled the light cord on, he grabbed a towel and she kept quiet as he dried her face. When Leah opened her eyes, he saw her sadness and wished he could find the end of it, pull it and wrap it into a ball for him to look after. If he was bigger, older, he'd know what to do. How to take care of her.

'Stay in my room,' Kai said, taking hold of his big sister's hand. He led her to his room, threw the elephants to the bottom of the bed and made her lie by the wall so he would know if she climbed out.

'Sorry,' she whispered.

He placed his hand in his sister's. Kai stayed awake until Leah shut her eyes and her breathing deepened.

His face had started to ache from frowning at Denner, who was sat at the kitchen table by Mum as she made her tiny white toffee apples and sucked on a pipe, jumping up to pace the room as she talked about Dad and why he was such a wasteman, then the next second she'd be thumping the table wanting him back, rubbing her forehead, and those were the moments Kai felt his tummy curl like a spring. Jade and Crystal listened to headphones, Jade sharpening already sharp pencils, Crystal humming. They were hungry, tired, Jade hadn't drawn for weeks. Leah had slept at Nanny's the past two nights.

'I'm shitting myself, really, though, mate, shitting it. What if he'd—' She looked at Kai, who stared at the back of Denner's black-haired robot head, wishing him in hospital instead of Dad.

Mum whispered to Denner, who grunted, before adding in a normal voice, 'I can't be without him, you know what? Him and I, we're like Bonnie and Clyde, aren't we, though? Aren't we? We're meant to be? Yeah, things go wrong, but he's the fucking one, you know?'

Denner took a massive puff of his fag and blew a cloud around Mum's face. 'You got enough money, Sherry?'

Confusion caught Mum for a second. Her finger froze, before it rested again on the table. She nodded her head. 'Yeah, course. We've still got two hundred. I had to hide it from him, you know?'

'Make it last mind, sweetness. You dunno how long this could go on for. And the kids look like they could do with a new set of clothes.'

Mum groaned. 'I don't want to be a shit mum; the kids are my life. It needs to stop.' She shoved the cola-can pipe across the table as she sat. 'We need to stop this shit. It's no good for the kids.' She lowered her voice, saying something about the social.

Silly Putty wasn't hard enough. Kai had a green blob in his hand that Hippie Mandy gave him to use when he felt the bubbles in his tummy or if he felt angry. He pulled it apart until it went white and snapped. Snap snap snap. Denner's neck should snap.

'I don't even care about all this.' Mum pointed at the black kitchen cupboards still in a pile, which the girls used as a step in front of the sink. 'You know we've been reported for that? Changing the kitchen. Reckon it was her,' she pointed as though out of the house and up the village, 'that fat pisshead. You know what she's like. Jealous. Jealous, fat pig. I'll fucking knock her out, Den, you know I will.'

At this she stood up and yanked off the hoody, tossing it at the pile of washing in front of the machine. Underneath she wore a bikini top, and her hip bones stuck out.

'I'll do the cupboards.' Denner pushed back his seat and knelt on the floor, holding the fag in his mouth as he lined up the fronts.

'You reckon? He was meant to bring the right sized screws back. Nothing happened after that. All talk, as usual.'

'They're in my car.' Denner crushed the fag in the chipped red teacup and rubbed the front of his T-shirt when he stood up.

'Sounds about right, couldn't even remember to bring them in. Fucking hell, Den, I'm so scared. I just, I don't know what I'd do.' She squeezed her eyes shut.

'I'll get the nails.'

Kai scraped his top teeth over his bottom lip a few times. Whenever she smoked she jumped around and changed her mind about things; she'd want to dance, eat, not eat, hoover. The living-room carpet was the only clean surface in the house. Mum jumped up and pulled the hoody back on. Kai was so worried about Dad he couldn't sleep; well, not until everyone else had gone to bed, and sometimes he sat up wrapped in his duvet in the corner of the room, counting the green stars on the bedroom ceiling or watching the breeze from the window blow the curtain in the shadows. There were twenty-three stars. When he finally fell to sleep he'd be shaken awake by Leah or a nightmare strangling him to shout for her. When would Dad be better? Not being allowed to the hospital was the worst. Probably because Dad was so ill, he'd overheard Mum say to Nanny on the phone that Dad was too ill and there was no way she'd risk Nanny catching it, then she'd forced him and the girls to promise not to tell Nanny that Dad was in hospital. Their little secret, she'd said. Another lie.

The dream team – that's what she kept calling them. Kai's only dream was for Dad to be OK and come home, that the smoking would stop, that he'd show him the den and the grey rabbits.

Two hours later, after fag and tea breaks, Denner finished fitting the black kitchen cupboard doors with the sparkly handles and Mum sat with her face in her hands and her elbows on the table, asking, 'Why, though, why's he doing it?'

Denner made a big breath, sat next to her and ran a finger down her arm. She straightened up and hugged her arms in, and he said, 'Behind every man's a scared little boy.'

Dad wasn't a scared little boy, and if Denner touched Mum one more time Kai would do something real bad to hurt him. Make him a scared little boy.

'Sort me out another twenty's worth, Den,' Mum said, tossing him a note from her back pocket.

After school two days later, when Kai, Jade and Crystal reached the garden fence, he just knew – something about the way the net curtain in Mum and Dad's room was shoved to the side – that Dad was home.

'He's back,' he whispered, stopping with his hand on the gate, wanting to run to him, before remembering how Dad had walked past him as though he wasn't there the last time.

Jade placed a hand on his shoulder. 'Come on.'

The gate creaked. Round the back of the house, the drain gushed water, Leah washing up. Through the window her face was lowered and he couldn't guess her mood. Over the fence next door he heard Kev ask Jordan and Taylor how school was. 'Boring,' they answered. The air too silent without Kaos.

'Why do you keep stopping?' Crystal pushed past him into the house.

Kai followed Jade. He chucked his school bag into the indoor shed opposite the living-room door on top of a bucket and it knocked a sweeping brush that toppled over.

The girls said hello to Dad and disappeared upstairs, Leah dried her hands on a tea towel and touched Kai's shoulder before she followed the others, leaving him, Mum and Dad in the room. Dad jumped up from the settee, his sleeping bag dropped to the floor, and knelt in front of Kai, staring into his eyes. A drip of snot shone at the tip of his nose and he sucked it up. There was a smell of bubble bath and shampoo on him, Crystal's favourite, vanilla.

Everyone said their eyes were the same, dark gingernut; Dad's had gold blobs in. Seeing them made Kai want to cry, and he looked at his trainers – one of the soles was coming off; he'd tried to tape it together, but it hadn't worked. Only babies cried.

His breath knocked out of him when Dad grabbed him tightly. 'You all right, my boy?'

He nodded, not able to talk, holding his breath, keeping the tears in. Dad pulled Kai on to his lap and Mum sat next to them.

'You missed Dad, didn't you, my chocolate orange?'

Kai nodded. On TV there were wolves howling. They'd put it on for him. 'Please don't do it again, Daddy.'

His lips felt soft on Kai's temple and Kai grabbed the neck of Dad's sweatshirt and curled against him as Dad ground his fist against the top of his leg before rubbing his tummy.

'We got any painkillers?'

Mum nodded. 'You're going to stop, aren't you, Jesse?'

It was Dad's turn to nod.

'Say it,' said Mum. 'Promise.'

'I've stopped already,' he said.

'Promise,' said Kai.

'I'd never let down my boy,' he switched to look at Mum and gently poked her chin, 'or my woman.'

'Why?' She hesitated, taking his hand. 'Why you been doing it, Jess?'

He made a big big breath and Kai lifted up with his chest and he heard a wheeze inside Dad, then there was a bang upstairs. One of the girls in the bathroom. Leah. The pipes clanked.

'I'm a strange man living in a strange world.' He used his thumb to push hers away and stared at the crease lines of her palm. He kissed it. 'I've got you something, Sherry; I wanted to wait till Kai was home.'

Kai lifted up so Dad could reach in his pocket. He pulled out a rose-gold ring with a yellow stone. Mum placed both hands over her mouth. Was Dad asking her to marry him? She was smiling and water reflected in her eyes, making him think of Papa Grey when Kaos had him in his jaws. If only he could tell Mum and Dad the truth about Kaos dying.

'What finger?' asked Dad, pushing it down her first – too small – the middle one. 'Perfect.'

She folded her hands round his neck, kissing him with tongues, telling him she loved him and please don't do that to her again, she couldn't live without him. He'd not asked her to marry him. Kai knew she'd wanted him to, but she was still happy. All you had to do to make a girl happy was give them something special. Across the room, spread over the top of the settee, was his red cape. He eyed it up. It would suit Saffie.

In bed that night Kai stared out at the sky. A red and white light crossed it, a space ship or a plane. He imagined green aliens with black eyes watching him and then threw his pillow to the bottom of the bed so his head was near the door. From there he could see the silver moon planet. His and Saffie's. They had thrones and crowns up where they ruled the animal kingdoms protecting them from the furred hunters. Earlier, Mum and Dad let him run up to Nanny's on the promise he'd be back in an hour. Once up there, it was Saffie's blue door he'd knocked on. Boring Twin shouted for Saffie, Kai shut his eyes. She came running from the kitchen; flour whitened her hair like powdery snow and she'd shoved a tiny round cheese biscuit in his hand. Still warm. Its flakes tasted buttery. His mouth watered. So yum yum yummy.

'This is for you,' he said, holding out his shiny red cape.

She screwed up her face like tissue paper. 'What you going on about?'

'Because we're getting married. It's better than a ring.'

Sunshine shone out of her face; she nodded.

'Isn't it?' he asked.

'Obbiously,' she said. 'But it's your favourite.'

'It will keep you safe and you can wear it when you fly.'

Quickly, she held a finger to her mouth to shush him. She checked over her shoulder then she grabbed the cape with both hands and shook it before hugging it.

'Thank you,' she said, and then she yanked him to her for a jumpy cuddle. 'You're the bestest friend in the whole world ever.'

'Can you look after this until I bury it at the den?' Kai handed her the lock-picking set.

She nodded, staring at it as though she were holding the eye of the sky sword.

In bed Kai smiled and watched the almost full moon until his eyelids felt sticky and shut. That night he dreamed of Saffie flying in her brand-new red cape to the silver moon, where he was waiting in an astronaut suit.

CHAPTER 27

15 December 2005

My face is buried in Dad's sleeping bag; it stinks. I've never let anyone wash it. It doesn't smell like him any more but I want it to. There's a breeze. Middledown Woods whispers around me. My heart's as fast as a drum and bass beat. I have this thing where if I think about breathing, how to do it, I become ultra aware and forget how to do it so I have to make myself breathe, breathe, breathe. When that happens if I don't find something distracting, like counting or reading old text messages, then I get light-headed and my fingers and the whole surface of my skin feels electric. It feels like I'll explode. I wish I would.

10 December 2005

Soon as I got back from Dorset, I called Jord and we went to town. I wasn't ready to go home and felt scared to see

Yasmin. We had texted in the week and when I called her, she kept crying. It was the worst knowing it was my fault she was upset.

It was raining so hard everything looked misty and raindrops back-splashed in puddles. My Reebok Classic had a hole in the sole and my sock was wet. It made me think of the collection of small odd socks I had under my bed and that was a Chinese burn in my chest. I was glad it was tipping down.

Jord hated getting wet, though, so we stomped up the high street looking for cover. First we ducked into the kebab shop. It smelled of fried meat. The steps were wet and Sali told us to get out.

'I want a can of Coke,' said Jord.

Sali knew he was taking the piss and lifted the counter top to come out so we legged it up the road to Martin's because the steps were undercover, but when we got there three hundred kids had already thought of the same fucking thing and we squeezed under and pushed some of the eleven-year-olds out. They're cheeky shits. Usually I wouldn't have felt guilty when the rain got heavier and they started shouting; they were young, though, and this time I did.

'What now?' said Jord.

We needed somewhere dry where no one would find us so we could build a spliff. I thought of the Grey Tower. Thinking of that, and Saffie, of my baby and not loving Yasmin, wishing I could talk to Dad, and looking at the rain, it was all a riot in my head. A Land Rover sped down the high street. I could have sprinted in front of it to stop the noise.

'Bus stop?' I said. We chilled in there for an hour before a bus came to take us back to Middledown and once there we went to my bedroom. Luckily I'd left the window open; the room felt cold and smelled clean, even though my clothes were all over the floor. I pushed the chest of drawers in front of the door so Mum wouldn't barge in begging to go threes-up.

'Mate, I can't wait to break up,' he said. 'You're well lucky you got an extra two weeks off.'

'Innit?' I said. I turned on the TV and DVD player. *Pirates of the Caribbean*. I always left it in. I handed him the Kingers because I couldn't be assed to roll up and actually, he liked sprinkling weed.

'You seen that new girl?' Jord's concentration was hard as the mud in the den in winter and I wondered if he fancied her. It pissed me off, and that made me feel like a right shit-cunt.

Girls were girls were girls. Except some were special, like Saffie, like Leah. That Ammi girl had a different kind of energy, but I couldn't break up with Yasmin. Not when she was carrying my baby.

I'd be a good dad.

And what about my dad, should I see him? It scared the shit out of me thinking about how he would be. It had to be the drugs killing him off finally. It had to be.

'She's in my I.T. class,' I said.

'Tight little package, mate,' he said.

My face and neck went hot.

I took the joint after he sparked up. 'She loves Paris,' I said, remembering the 'I heart Paris' on her pencil case.

*

When we finished the smoke, I wanted to be alone.

'Mate, I'm tired.'

Jord was my best friend. 'You OK?'

I nodded.

'What did you do in Dorset, anyway?'

I felt like telling him I'd been out fossil hunting on the beach, but he might have asked to see a fossil.

'It rained all week.'

'Gutted.'

'Yeah. I spent most of the time listening to Nan and Betty talk about other holidays they wanted to go on.'

After a while Jord left. When I heard his back door go, I remembered how Kaos always used to bark, and missed the sound of him. That's when I turned off the DVD player and Mum pushed through my door.

'How's my youngest?' she asked.

I offered her the end of the smoke, hoping she would fuck off downstairs, but she came and sat next to me, so I turned the TV back on and the volume up. When I found it hard to sleep, I'd let the DVD play in the background, I knew the words off by heart. Instead of watching it, I thought of the Grey Tower. Desperately, I wanted Saffie here. Her socks under my bed. I wished Mum wasn't there so I could get them out. I liked to line them up. One day I would ask Nan or Leah to sew them together in a line so I could hang them up and they'd be like gremlin or leprechaun socks. I needed to do that. The first thing I wanted to buy my baby was a red cape. If I closed my eyes, I could see her, hair lighter red than mine, green eyes, freckles, lips the colour of Nan's marigolds in spring. I'd take her to the Great Oak to watch the starlings. In summer, we'd go paddling in Middle River and I'd teach her about the grey rabbits in the woods. The baby would be like me and Saffie, not Yasmin. I could feel it in me. Sure as I knew blood ran through my veins.

'What are you thinking about?' Mum asked.

'How ugly that cunt is,' I said. The bloke with the octopus beard filled the screen.

'Before that,' said Mum.

Part of me wanted to admit about the baby and another part wanted to ask why Dad didn't care about me, why he was only willing to see me now. That's another reason he had to be dying.

'Kai!' Mum said. 'You look so sad. Talk to me. I'm your mum. What's going on? I thought going away with your nan would cheer you up.'

I heard myself take a deep breath like I was going to talk.

I didn't.

My phone bleeped. It was Yasmin and I told Mum I was going to see her and when I started walking I was going to, to tell her I'd stand by her, we could do it. Instead, I walked to the Grey Tower. It was dark so I shone a torch along the cycle path, listening to the owls, and used my lock-picking set to break in. It was the first time I'd been there since I was a kid and went with Saffie. At the top of the tower I sat on the window ledge. Bats flapped in the roof.

The moon was a clipped-off toenail in the sky.

'I've fucked everything up,' I said. A bat darted past out into the night.

She stayed quiet, watching and wise.

'I want to go back and make everything all right.'

When I stood on the edge of the ledge with a hand either side of the frame, glass slicing into one of my hands, the pull to the grass outside felt so big that the landslide filled me again. This time it felt right.

The moon was bright.

She told me I had a baby coming.

The moon slammed a golden marble in my heart and I howled.

CHAPTER 28

THEN

Everyone was excited because it was Bonfire Night at the weekend, everyone apart from Kai. Saffie hadn't been to school, nor had her boring sister. He sat on the school bus with a belly full of bouncing tennis balls, ignoring the coach songs everyone sang like they were football fans, and stared out the window. The lanes were wet and muddy. They passed Farmer Reid's yard, where he was climbing on to a tractor. His black-and-white long-haired dog was in the yard and barked at the coach.

Something wasn't right. He just knew. Headmaster T had called him out of class at the end of the day and told him Nanny Sheila had rung and he was to get off the school bus at her house.

'It's very important you go straight to your grandmother's,' he said.

'OK,' said Kai.

'And when you're next here, well . . .' Mr T looked weird – his face twitched – for once he didn't know what to say. 'You know you can talk to me about anything you want.'

It was to do with Saffie, who never had time off school unless she puked or had chickenpox. Her mum was strict, saying education was the only way to good jobs, and Saffie said if she had to have a normal job she would be a pilot otherwise she was going to be an adventurer. It made Kai desperate to be a brilliant thing too, an Olympic runner, like Linford Christie, or another thing, he wasn't sure what. Nanny always said he should aim for the stars and that meant being an astronaut, which would take him to the silver moon. Going there without Saffie would be wrong, though. He remembered his dream. How it felt to float. He thought about Dad not being at home that morning when he jumped into bed with Mum and she'd said, 'I'm so sorry, my prince.'

The bumps in the lane were no fun on the coach without Saffie to laugh with and knowing Dad had disappeared again.

When the bus reached the top of Middledown, Nanny's and Saffie's estate was the first road on the right. The bus stopped. As he stood, Jade shouted from the back, 'You going to Nan's?'

'Yeah,' he yelled. No way was he going back to school without Saffie. Too boring. Before he went to Nanny's, he'd see how ill she was and then he'd pretend he was too.

House number 1 was painted green, the window frames were brown and in the summer the garden filled with flowers Nanny called dah-lee-as. Mr Wheeler's. Usually, he'd be watching Saffie's mum dig the garden, pointing her where to plant things and water. The garden gate was open; Kai stared at it. It was the only one in the street that was always shut. Kai started to jog. Past Nanny's house, he saw someone move in the living room; she didn't have net curtains because she liked to watch the goings-on. Nanny was nosy. Soon he was outside Saffie's, pushing the gate. All the curtains were pulled like everyone was asleep and there was a red ribbon on the path that he placed a foot either side of.

'Kai,' Nanny's voice called. When he looked two gardens over she was walking to her gate in a knee-length brown dress, saying, 'Kai, come here, Kai.'

He picked up the damp ribbon and shoved it in his pocket. Leah stood next to one of Nanny's pots he'd planted with Jordan; the poppies had come and gone. She wore her big-school's uniform, hair in long wavy ponytails, and her face was red and blotchy like Peperami. She'd been crying. Kai ran to the blue front door and started banging.

'Saffie!' he yelled as loud as a dinosaur at the bedroom window upstairs, the one with two panes. 'Saaaaaaffie.' Remembering the taste of her home-made cheese biscuit.

'Sssssssshh, Kai; come here.' Nanny Sheila caught hold of his arm. 'She's not there, love. Come on.'

'Where is she?'

Nanny pulled his arm and he followed, staring back at Saffie's bedroom window. Kai felt his knees go wobbly. 'Nanny, where is she?'

They walked through the front door, facing the yellow-carpeted stairs where photographs of Nanny in Malta and Tenerife with Betty cluttered the walls. She'd told the children that after she was widowed she learned to seize the day.

She took him into the pastel-coloured living room.

'Saffie had an accident, love.'

He closed his eyes. Leah was crying; she put a hand on his leg. She was wearing a silver ring with a little blue flower.

'Kai,' Nanny said. Her arms were solid as conker tree trunks. 'She hurt herself really badly yesterday, at the tower. She died this morning.'

The world went mixy. The ceiling became the floor, he was topsy-turvy. Died meant gone to sleep in heaven like Leah's dad, and that meant never seeing someone again.

'No,' he said. 'She must be—' He tried to stand up to go back to her house, but his legs were like jellyfish man.

Nanny held him tight. 'I'm sorry, my love. She was your best friend.'

In the tower, that's what Nanny said. The Grey Tower. Last time they were in the den – his breaths shortened, panting; he made tight fists of his hands – last time she'd asked if he'd ever gone to the Grey Tower alone. He'd given her his lock-picking set the day before. She must have gone there. How could she? How could she go without him? But he remembered the day she'd told him of her dream, where she was in the tower with her dad. The bouncing balls in his tummy started exploding.

'She isn't dead,' he shouted.

It was impossible because his best friend was little, like him. It was only fair for God to make old people go to sleep. 'She's my twin and I'm little.'

'Ssshhhhhhh,' said Nanny, holding him tight now, telling Leah, 'Call your mum. Tell her he knows and we'll be down soon.'

Where could she be? Kai struggled against Nanny's arms; she was old. Leah left the room.

'Kai!' Nanny shouted. He was out the door and running down the estate faster than Linford Christie. The football field met his toes; it was trimmed short, and muddy mole hills stuck out. Through the football field, past the goal posts, on to the cycle path, running, running.

'Come on,' he screamed at his feet. 'Saaaaffie.'

For the first time he ran the whole way to the gap in the stone wall into the woods, where he hopped and jumped over twisted roots, sticks and wet mud, frightening squirrels and rabbits as the birds sang happily above.

There was tape around the bottom of the tower, like nobody was allowed past, but he was alone. He walked around the tower, round and round. He'd given her his lock-picking set. It was his fault. Something caught his eye, a red ribbon. He tucked it deep in his zip pocket with the other.

Later, he was outside the den he and Saffie had covered with branches they'd snapped off needle trees so that it was hidden. There was a small hole where they'd crawled in. Opposite, next to the rabbit hole, he crouched. He was scared. A dog barked.

'Bruiser,' a voice shouted.

Kai quickly crawled into the hole, keeping low, through to the middle room. He looked into her room, the girls' room where fern grew along the sides in spring; it was empty. He made a big pufferfish breath before crawling into his room, then the biggest by the macky needle tree. He remembered how Saffie had watched him break into the Grey Tower.

Puffed out from fright, he stared at the palm of his hand at the scar they'd made together. One couldn't be there without the other and it was his fault. She was gone. He punched the floor and the tree.

Saffie was gone. It was his fault.

With a whack he smashed the back of his head against the tree and screamed, wanting to hurt himself all over. He cried. A lot.

Until he quieted, staring at the spot in front of the big green bush where she'd rubbed sticks to try to make fire. He put his hand in his pocket to squeeze her ribbons. He wished he was dead instead.

The funeral was in Middledown church. Hundreds turned up. People Kai didn't even realise lived in the village and who shouldn't have been there because they didn't know Saffie; only people who cared about her should be there. Mum said Kai was too young to go, but Nanny said everyone dies and the younger he learnt to accept it the easier life would be. Nanny always won. So Kai sat by her and his sisters and Betty in the second row from the front, where he stared at the tiny wooden coffin that locked his best friend away. How could she just be gone? There then disappear? He wanted to check the hiding places he'd forgotten – the bushes along the edges of the football field, the cornfields, people's sheds – he hadn't checked the top of the Grey Tower. He looked back at the arched door of the church and a million faces turned down their bottom lip at him. Sad clowns. They didn't know her. Hippie Mandy had folded tissue like two white bricks and held it under her eyes.

At the start, the cold room smelled thick in white flowers with long thin petals, but then sadness swept in like a mist through the valley during spring and his nose filled with snot. They should have ferns for Saffie, not white lilies.

Saffie's mum and sister made loud crying. It was lucky Nanny had thick tissues for him. There was a wet patch on her black dress where he laid his head next to her gold cross. Again, her arm wrapped round him. This time it was soft and her fingers squeezed his hand over and over as she whispered, 'Hush, now, hush.' Her hand held his with the scar. Each time he thought of Saffie sitting in the Grey Tower when they became blood twins the sadness hit him harder. When he thought of them playing dead lions in class, listening to stories and their fingertips buzzing next to each other, he squeezed his eyes tighter. How she'd jumped up to stand and lean out of the window in the Grey Tower and he'd pulled her back and they'd fallen on the floor and watched spiders crawl on the ceiling as the raven watched them. Who would he play with on the silver moon now?

He blew his nose. The silver moon, where she'd gone …

Every night he dreamed about her on the silver moon. He flew there, he couldn't land, and she waited, smiling in his red cape, before understanding he couldn't get to her. An invisible wall. He shouted to tell her, but no words came out, however much he moved his mouth, and then she looked sad and turned away.

Middledown village was ripe with whispers, wondering how, how, how? Johnny the Prawn had asked Bob-Cycle outside The Station pub when Denner carried him past and back to Mum's that horrible afternoon with Nanny and Leah following. Nobody knew. Kai desperately wanted to admit it was his fault. It was too scary. He couldn't eat or sleep, unless Mum gave him her special drink before bed and he was allowed to sleep with her because Dad wasn't home.

Now Saffie's mum was talking, 'Sapphire will always be my fluffy little princess.'

It wasn't right that Saffie was gone when he was still there. Why hadn't he buried the lock-picking set in his garden?

He dropped wet tissue on to the stone floor and opened his eyes when Nanny wiped his nose.

'Come on, darling boy, it's time to go home.'

CHAPTER 29

11 December 2005

The day after I climbed the Grey Tower I found Yasmin. I was going to tell her I wanted the baby – it gave me a happy feeling inside, if I'm honest, and I couldn't remember happiness till I had it again. I wanted the baby but not her. The last bit I wasn't allowed to say. We'd call the baby Sapphire Sheila Manners.

When I reached her house, I went round the back because I could see into the living room and the light was off, so she must have been in the kitchen or in her room. It surprised me to find Nan with Yasmin outside the back door. Both smoking. It made me sick that Yasmin was smoking.

'You taking the piss?' I took the fag from her hand and stamped it out on the ground. I kept scraping my foot over it.

Her mouth gaped.

'Yasmin's told me,' said Nan.

'Fuck!' I smashed my fist towards the back door. The window shattered. It shocked me.

'You idiot!' shouted Yasmin.

'I didn't mean to smash it!'

Nan grabbed my arm and pulled me down the rank; light from Denner's house shone on to his pond where the shed used to be. I could have pushed Yasmin's head into the water, held her face under. If she didn't have my baby.

'We need to talk,' Yasmin shouted.

'We do,' I said, 'but at the moment I don't want to look at your mug.'

I waved my hand out of Nan's grasp as she pushed me towards her door, thinking how controlling Yasmin was – she'd probably planned this baby to trap me. Bitch. 'You twist shit to Crystal, to Mum and now you're going on at Nan.'

'I'm fucking pregnant.' She wailed like a fighting cat. 'I don't know what to do.'

'Talk to me,' I said. 'It's ours; no one else's.'

'Not now,' said Nan. To Yasmin she called, 'Come round with your mum at eight,' then to me, 'Go inside.'

The kitchen was cold. Nan filled the kettle; I sat at the bottom of the stairs on the yellow carpet. The hallway paint looked shabby and needed redecorating. Actually, Nan's taste was mental. The older I got and the more houses I saw, the more I realised her taste was out there, like old Wheeler.

When Nan joined me with two souvenir mugs from Weymouth, she shuffled me over so that we were like primary-school kids sitting on a step watching woodlice. My eyes ran across the swirls in the carpet – there were darker bits like the bronze pollen in the middle of the lilies at The Station.

Nan started talking. A lot made sense and she said stuff I didn't want to hear: we should have been careful. I knew that. From now on she would make sure that I stood by Yasmin and did the right thing by her. It was the right thing to do.

On one of the photos going up the stairs, Nan and Betty were on a white yacht in bikinis holding cocktails.

Nan couldn't believe it.

Tell me about it.

We were so young.

No shit, Sherlock.

'But these things happen.' When Nan said this she held her palms up – there were calluses from gardening and housework – as though there was no way of changing the situation.

'Nan,' I said, 'it was an accident.'

'I know, love.'

'No,' I said. I felt awkward as ass with what I was about to say. 'I mean when we did, you know, the sex bit.'

The way she cleared her throat? She was listening. 'What do you mean?'

'I didn't want to. I was really drunk.' I stopped because I hated admitting that I was that drunk to her.

'And . . . ?'

'Yasmin kind of, not forced me, but she really wanted to and I just went along with it. I know it was stupid. I was drunk and not thinking right.'

'I was never keen on that girl.'

So much between me and Yasmin was poison. I told Nan she was controlling, but that I'd been a cunt to her.

'Watch your language,' interrupted Nan.

I kept remembering certain things, like persuading Yasmin to cut her hair; I felt ashamed.

'I hate it,' Yasmin had said at the time, rubbing clumps of it.

'It's never looked better,' I'd said, pressing a finger against her chin to turn her head. We were thirteen and her hair had been long. From the side, her nose and jawline had looked perfect. What a prick. I told Nan about making her cut her hair, waiting for her to hate me. She said nothing.

I rubbed the scar on my hand, wishing I was young again.

'How do you feel about becoming a dad, Kai? You know the Bible says abortion is wrong, but I know you're young and you never could concentrate when I took you to church, so I'm not sure the fear of God is in you. Do you want the baby?'

I knew I wasn't in a situation to keep a baby myself, like if she kept it, but it would give me a reason to push myself and see some light in all the darkness. I felt selfish because that was for me. I'd struggled to like life, so why would I want to put that on someone else, especially my own baby? I just thought I might be able to make it different and, strangely, I really wanted our family living on and to show Dad how good I could have been.

Did I want the baby?

I nodded. I did.

She put her arm round me.

'Good. She must keep the baby,' said Nan. 'Betty and I will help. We can redecorate Nicholas's bedroom so that whenever the baby is with you, you can stay here. What do you think? It might be easier here. Oh, love.'

Her cold fingertips found my face.

Nicholas was Leah's dad; Jade painted in there sometimes. It was a special room. Maybe things wouldn't be so hard if Nan helped and if my baby didn't have much to do with my mum and dad.

'Yes, please,' I said. My eyes closed and I felt her chin press on to my shoulder. She smelled of washing powder, and I swear I could smell Betty's perfume.

My phone rang. It was Leah, and before I picked up, Nan said I should tell her and ask her what she thought. What she said really hurt.

'You're getting rid of it, right?'

It.

My oldest sister; for the first time, she was a stranger.

'I'll be home on the twenty-second,' she told me. 'We'll talk properly then.'

We'd never hung up so fast and I honestly felt as though I'd rather never see her again.

Later, I waited in the living room. The clanging radiators hadn't warmed through the house so my hood was pulled over my ears; Nan said we'd light a fire after they left and the jacket potatoes would be ready by then. The main living-room light was too bright and the clock on the mantelpiece with golden arms ticked too loudly. The moment Yasmin walked in with her mum the room soured. Nan sat in the chair next to me and the others sat on the sofa, Yasmin's mum cooing over her like she was a cripple. For some reason, there was a plate of Bourbons on the coffee table. Nan was a joker.

'Well,' started Nan, 'this isn't the best of situations. Obviously.'

'Agreed,' said Yasmin's mum. It was going to be the worst conversation. I was glad it was Nan next to me.

'So, Kai and I have talked about it and Kai feels a certain way, but as Yasmin's the one whose body will change, we'd prefer you two to tell us where you stand first.'

Thank God. Nan was brilliant. I knew Yasmin wanted to keep it or she wouldn't have got us into this situation in the first place, and it would be best if she admitted she wanted to keep the baby first.

'We had a long talk today, didn't we?' She tilted her head towards her daughter.

'Yes.'

'Yasmin realised she's way too young to have a baby and so,' she paused, 'she wants to get rid of it.'

It.

How could this be real? Landslide slipped through my body, leaving my head spinning, letting the liquorice viper swell in my throat and chest.

'It surprises me you say that,' said Nan. 'They are young, yes, but the gift of a pregnancy is a miracle and I'd suggest you take a little longer to think on it. There are things we would do to help. Obviously, Kai would probably end up living with me and we could have the baby here half the time.'

Yasmin's mum laughed. 'Here? A baby should be with its mother.'

'I never thought you'd take such a traditional view on it.'

'Even if Kai had treated my daughter right, they're too young.'

'They aren't far off the age I was when I had Nicholas.'

'It's a different time. Yasmin wants a career.'

That was the first I'd heard of it.

'My daughter deserves better than a lad who's never at school who persuaded her to have sex.'

'What?' I frowned at Yasmin.

'Yeah.' Her mum's skin was orange leather, her lipstick and lips a bleeding gash, and there was a dent above the gash where she used to have her lip pierced. Gross. 'Yeah, I know. She told me. You're the one who got her into bed.'

As if she was saying this. There were nights I'd crashed there even when Yaz's mum wasn't at work and she'd always been fine with it. Split personality be fucked, the woman was a cunt.

'It wasn't really like that,' I said. 'Was it, Yaz?'

For the first time in her life, my girlfriend had lost her tongue.

'Yaz,' I said, stamping each word into the room, 'tell them the truth.'

'You made me feel like if I didn't do it, you wouldn't be with me.'

Un-fucking-believable. I didn't even know what to say. That was the point, there, when I saw the doubt in Nan's eyes and she didn't stand up for me. The anger sprung into me, but disappeared as quickly. If Nan lost her faith in me, what was the point in anything?

The doorbell rang, Nan stood. 'Who on earth is that?'

Carol singers.

The happy sound of 'Away in a Manger' burst into the house from the front door. Fuck sake. This weird thing happened: it was like my stomach had burst and a million bubbles were spilling and the feeling made me start laughing. I couldn't fucking stop.

'A kid with you would be the worst,' said the witch's mother. 'You're just a druggy, like your parents.'

It made me laugh even more. Nan marched into the living room to the cabinet and tipped a handful of pound coins into her hand before heading back out, sending the singers off and returning to the room. She shrugged her shoulders at me and shook her head.

'Incredible timing.'

'I've called the clinic,' said Yasmin's mum.

The sun was disappearing.

'Take some more time,' ordered Nan.

'It's not up to you.'

It was like me and Yasmin weren't in the room.

'Well, if you do go ahead,' said Nan, 'I'm sure Kai will want to come to the appointment with Yasmin.'

I didn't want to, but I knew it was right thing.

'*He's* the last person I want there.' Yasmin was back in the room and I'd never seen what a monster she was till that moment.

The words were bitter and hung like a dead body, swinging in and out, over and over, through my head. I knew she could be spiteful. This was something else. A pressure closing in from all sides.

The room was a cell. The door handle was painted silver.

'Just take a bit more time,' said Nan, but they were already standing to leave as she said, 'You'll live to regret it.'

CHAPTER 30

THEN

It was the Christmas holiday and Mum and Dad partied. At the kitchen table they drank, giggled and smoked. Fun because they laughed, danced and fooled around to Christmas carols on the radio. Mum had cooked sausage rolls and made egg sandwiches. Nanny's Christmas gift to Mum and Dad was a mini hi-fi for the living room. Kai, Crystal and Jade jumped around three boxes of tinsel and a Christmas tree in the centre of the living room. Leah lay on the settee reading Nancy Drew.

'Can I put the fairy on top?' asked Crystal.

'I'll put the trimmings up,' said Jade, pulling tinsel, climbing over Leah to reach a curtain rail.

Dad walked to the edge of Leah's settee next to the TV. With a cocktail sausage between his teeth, he bent and pushed it, Leah yelping, to create a gap in the corner of the room. 'Let's fling the tree up.'

Kai liked the tree. It was like having part of Middledown Woods in the house. He'd been too scared to go there since Saffie left. Together the family arranged plastic branches because in the attic it had bent lopsided, then Mum passed Dad the Coke can and they sat opposite Leah, sparking a lighter, sucking in, jumping up, grinning. At the table they poured vodka into glasses and built roll-ups. A bell tinkled over the radio and Mariah Carey's voice filled the room.

'Dance with me, then,' said Mum.

'Get your fine ass here.' Dad grabbed Mum round the waist. She threw her head back, he kissed her neck, and Kai felt happy watching them dance. Fag smoke twirled from their hands.

He hunted through silver and gold baubles, picking out turtle doves and a nutcracker. 'I'm putting my own things on the tree.' He ran to his bedroom and found the small picture he'd drawn of Papa Grey wearing a crown at Nanny's when the girls had been cutting snowflakes. Downstairs he used one of the green ribbons to attach the rabbit to a branch, sucking in the Christmassy smell of tinsel.

On Christmas Eve Mum and Dad started shouting because they'd run out of money. No Christmas presents poked from under the tree apart from the three Leah had wrapped. *A Christmas Carol* played on TV. Instead, the children watched Mum and Dad pushing and shoving. At the back window behind the sink stood Nanny Sheila; she'd just walked past the side window. Kai breathed better when he saw her. She watched for a minute then swung open the back door. Mum and Dad shut up. Ebenezer Scrooge howled at a ghost. Leah's hand drifted to the remote, lowering the sound.

Nanny Sheila's eyes hunted over dirty washing, plates, the empty trimming boxes that hadn't been put away, full ashtrays, empty cans of Special Brew, empty bottles of vodka. Her eyes widened at the home-made pipes.

'I knew it,' she said.

Mum followed her gaze, grabbed the can, opened the cupboard and threw it in the bin. 'Just rubbish,' she said.

'I know exactly what it is.'

'Sheila,' said Dad, 'it was nothing.'

Nanny Sheila moved to the cupboard. Dad stepped in front. She folded her arms. Her giraffe body as tall as Dad, she looked down her pointy nose. The red coat she wore bright against the grey T-shirt he'd been wearing for days, and Kai thought of Saffie wrapped up in his red cape buried in the graveyard. At least he hoped she was wearing it. A minute unravelled as long as the cycle path to Vells village.

'I've known men like you,' she said. Her voice never so serious or deep. 'I know what you're about.'

Nanny Sheila turned and everyone watched her. Calm anger burned. 'This is what I'm going to do.' She paused and looked at Leah. 'I'm taking the kids. They'll spend Christmas with me.'

Heat spread through Kai and he squeezed his hands into balls. What did she mean? To live?

'Sheila, no—' Mum started.

Nanny Sheila cut her off, pointing her hand like Bruce Lee. 'You have a week to sort this out.' She waved her hand and screwed up her face like she'd stood in fox pooh. 'I'll bring them back if you two and the house are clean.'

Dad's jaw rippled as he stared at the TV. He looked at Kai, who looked at Nanny Sheila. Kai felt relieved and wanted to cry.

'If I find you're both still using, I'll report you.'

'What the fuck?' Mum lunged towards Nanny Sheila. Kai flinched and watched, stunned.

Dad grabbed Mum at the waist. 'Behave,' he said, throwing her on to the settee next to Leah, who stood, crossed the room, took Kai's hand and pulled him towards Nanny Sheila.

'Come on, kids,' said Nanny Sheila.

Before she shut the door she turned to Mum and said, 'You'll thank me for this.'

In Nanny Sheila's pastel-coloured front room the fire was lit. Every other house on the Middledown council estates had gas fires, not Nanny's.

After they climbed out of the car, Nanny led them to the back of the house. 'You're going to have your Christmas present early, Kai. It's in the garden.' She held his hand through the narrow hallway and the kitchen, which stank of garlic, then out the back where the long lawn stretched to meet the field.

'Here.' She tugged his hand and he looked where she pointed; he felt like he wasn't in his body. Below the kitchen window there was a hutch. He knelt down; inside was a little rabbit.

'Is it mine?'

The girls had come out and were huddled behind him, making kissy noises. A long blonde ponytail, two brown plaits and two black bobbles of frizz.

'Yes,' answered Nanny.

He stood to run two doors down. 'I need to show Saf—'

Nanny's face crushed up when they both guessed he'd forgotten for a second. 'What are you going to call her, love?'

'Saffie.' He unclicked the latch and pulled out a yellow and white bunny. Her nose twitched. 'I love her. So would Saffie.'

Nanny owned her house. Recently, she and Betty had redecorated. The wooden coffee table in the middle of the floor, painted pale green, matched the mint settee, which clashed with the lavender walls and fluffy lemon rug that Kai lay on in front the fire, hypnotised by flames. A candle wrapped in holly shimmered above. The girls sat round the coffee table on 'powder-blue' cushions. Saffie the bunny hopped around the room and rested in Kai's armpit.

There was a display cabinet in the corner by the gramophone that Kai painted pale yellow in the summer when Dad was with Tony-teeth. Inside were fairy ornaments. The green queen of fairies was in the middle, she had long brown hair and Nanny Sheila said it was her when she was young. The clay fairy Kai had made for Nanny Sheila at school rested on the bottom shelf. Nanny Sheila took out board games from under the stairs and then popped warm mince pies on the coffee table in front of the children. The big gold gramophone by the front window played Frank Sinatra and Nat King Cole. The record sleeves were on top of the pile Nanny Sheila kept in the bottom of the cabinet. Sometimes Kai rummaged through, studying the singers' smiling faces. Not tonight.

'I have something for you all,' said Nanny Sheila, hiding her arms behind her back.

Kai turned from the flames. The three girls looked; none caught the smile Nanny Sheila encouraged. She tilted her head and revealed Christmas hats, two red like Santa's and two green elves. Leah cackled.

'Nan, you're mad.' Her laughter grew louder. She rolled on to her back and kicked her legs in the air until she could hardly breathe. The other three watched. She sat up. 'I'm hot.' Leah threw off her hoody. Kai looked at the pink scars on his sister's arms as she opened the Monopoly box and set up.

'Pass a pie, Nan,' said Jade, who wore a polar bear jumper that was tight around her pot belly. Crystal sat next to her, humming to the music; she looked like a rag doll.

Nan passed a plate and dished out four more. 'Before we start Monopoly,' she cleared her voice and dolloped ice cream into dishes, 'I'm going to tell you a story.'

'Yesssss,' said Leah.

'But before I tell you the story, I'm going to say something to you that you must all promise to remember.'

The girls nodded their heads, agreeing with Nanny Sheila, and Kai copied. It was obviously important.

'Your parents love you, but they forget to love you properly because they drink and do drugs. You lot are better than that. When you're older you will grow into beautiful and kind women,' she paused and nodded at Kai, 'and a young man. In the meantime, you must promise that if you're ever scared, or need somewhere to go or feel like running away, you must come here.'

She looked at each of them in turn as she spoke and said, 'I mean it.'

Kai and his sisters nodded a second time. He thought of how Saffie should be there while he stroked his bunny's fur. Since she'd left he only wore her socks and kept her ribbons in his china rabbit money box.

Nanny Sheila pointed at the candle above the fireplace. 'That's a Christmas candle. It's to remind us that in the deepest of winter when life is dark there is light and that spring is on its way. No matter how dark life may seem things will get better.'

Leah stared at the photo of her dad on the lavender wall. Kai moved over to her and rested his head on her lap, with Saffie the bunny in his arm. Leah stroked his matted hair. The fire felt warm on the bottom of his feet and he listened to the sounds of Jade and Crystal chewing.

'Do you know whose birthday it is tomorrow?' asked Nanny Sheila.

'Baby Jesus,' said Leah. Kai heard her voice deep in her tummy as he watched the fire lick, crack and spit.

'That's right.'

In Nanny Sheila's house Kai listened to the Nativity story. Every time he pictured Mum and Dad down home on their own, arguing because they had no smokes, his eyes prickled.

They stayed at Nanny's all Christmas holidays and Mum rang every day. Dad had already gone.

From the garden he could see Saffie's house. The seat of Saffie's yellow swing swung an inch in the breeze; he'd pushed her hard enough to make her scream once. Saffie's mum and sister must be at Mr Wheeler's; Nanny told Betty they'd been sleeping there since it happened.

Next door, Denner's shed door was open. Kai sat on one of Nanny's garden chairs by her green plastic table blowing breath clouds on Saffie the bunny. Jade sketched next to him.

Nanny had said maybe he'd like to change her name because he might feel sad more often if the rabbit was called Saffie, and Jade said to call her Rabbit. It made him angry. Sapphire was the best name ever and to call a rabbit Rabbit was stupid. Sapphire meant blue. Their hair was orangey and Hippie Mandy said ages ago that he was fire and Saffie was water. Hippie Mandy had got it the wrong way round. Specially as he had enough tears in his head to drown the sky.

'It's too cold out here.' Jade disappeared inside.

Denner had been in his shed a while and the faint smell of fags fingered the air. Saffie the bunny hopped over the table. He wished it was summer so there were lots of dandelions to pick.

'You all right, young'un?' Denner appeared, a fag burning in his pig-face mouth. Kai stared at Saffie the bunny. Denner closed his back door.

It was a wooden shed. Wood burned.

Denner put his hand up Mum's skirt.

A while after, Denner's car started up out the front; it had a grumbly engine that sounded angry when he drove off. Soon as the sound quietened, Kai walked towards Denner's garden and pushed through the shed door. There was a leather chair, a table with hundreds of newspapers on it. The floor was covered in tools, spanners, hammers, nails, a drill; the neon-yellow coat Kai recognised hung on the wall. The top newspaper had a picture of a safe on Weston-super-Mare beach on the front. Kai dug around in his pocket, drew out Dad's favourite Clipper with a spider on it and flicked it with numb fingers until the papers caught light, then he shut the door behind him and took Saffie the bunny into Nanny's.

CHAPTER 31

12 December 2005

At the end of school me and Jord were kicking a football at the side of the science block opposite the dining hall. The smell of chips and damp concrete stained the air. In the past we'd kick the ball hard because Mr Bridges, whose classroom was the other side, was a pillock. I couldn't be assed, though, so I stopped and sat on the wall, watching – there was half a shortbread in my pocket that I rubbed some scum off as Jord ran up to me and said, 'Don't turn round. Ammi's gonna walk past, ask her out for me.'

'Why do you want to go out with her?' I asked, biting the shortbread. It was soft.

'You mean, why wouldn't I?'

Ammi passed us, she smiled over at me – *me* – then headed towards the geography-block door where the lockers were. I followed. Her coat was orange with a black hood and pulled in at a tiny waist. She stopped at the lockers and didn't seem surprised when I leaned with my back against the cabinet next to her.

'Hey,' she said.

'How you finding it here?'

'School's school,' she said.

'I've got something I need to ask you.' I watched her face for a change. There, it was there, a glow in her cheeks.

'Oh yeah?'

'Will you go out with Jordan?'

'Oh,' she said, a crease flickered along her brow. 'Oh. Who's that?'

'The kid I was with out there.'

She walked back to the door, peered through the window. Back next to me she was careful choosing which books to leave and which to slide in her bag. The door flew open. Yasmin. Course it was.

'There you are,' she said.

I nodded. The look she gave Ammi was filth, but Ammi wasn't paying attention. The way Yasmin flung herself at me and planted a kiss on my mouth was pure Hollywood. I wanted to wipe my mouth, I tasted lip gloss.

'Walk me to the bus, babe.'

My girlfriend never cared about me walking her to the coach circle. With everything that was going on, though, I didn't dare say no. Couldn't risk her having an eppy.

As we walked off Ammi called, 'Kai? Tell Jordan I said OK.'

If everything wasn't so fucked up already it would have been a slap in the face.

*

I walked Yaz to the bus stop in total silence. We couldn't even look at each other. She got on the bus and I went to get my bike. I met Jord in the bike shed. He was psyched about his new girlfriend and said he was going to buy her lunch in the dining room the next day. Take in a flower and everything.

'Bullshit, mate,' I said, pulling on two beanies – one inside the other – that I'd left on the handle of my bike. 'She's only a girl.'

'Hottest girl in school.'

'Yeah, right.'

'Pull your head out your ass. You're just jealous because your girlfriend's a bitch.'

I coughed. What could I say? I coughed again.

The cycle path was smooth tarmac from school, past the nearby estates, alongside fields, until we hit Brewer's Lane in Hilcombe, where Jord wanted to stop off at Jonesies to get a Monster drink and Chewits.

'I'm gonna head on,' I said. 'I've got stuff to do.'

Into Middledown Woods, I cycled the path I knew better than any and was tempted to stop on the little bridge where the three paths met. It was best to avoid the memory of that place, so I sped up, raising my ass off the saddle before the bumps in the mud. All branches lifeless apart from the pines. Flapping of wings. A neigh from a horse somewhere in the distance. I passed Farmer Reid and his dog. I'd seen him my whole life and wondered if he'd ever even noticed me. Swung round the clump of silver birches till I saw her, green, tall and proud as a mafia boss. The largest pine in the woods. I slowed, rested my bike round the side of the laurel bush on the outside of the den, and then ducked down and crawled in quickly before Farmer Reid saw.

For years I'd worn thermals under my clothes, not only because I felt the cold but in case I ended up here. It was my spot in the world. Mine. The tent nylon helped keep the wind out and I tucked the bit by the gap that I called the door under some stones I'd nicked off a stone wall. Usually, here I'd feel OK. My gloves were in one of my coat pockets and I put them on, lying back with my hands behind my head. Before putting my headphones in I thought I'd listen to the woods for a bit, but I kept thinking about Yasmin and the abortion and Dad and that he was probably dying. Farmer Reid and his barking Collie passed. It was getting dark. I didn't know what to do. The whole of the universe was in my head and I wanted to bang it out. I sat up; the bark was rough as I scraped my forehead and nose. I banged it. It wasn't hard enough.

He's the last person I want there.

When we first found out Yasmin was pregnant I was shocked. Thinking about it now, she couldn't have wanted a baby by the look of her miserable face, but I'd kidded myself otherwise because I thought she'd set me up. I couldn't stand her and had to support her even if she had an abortion. Already I knew I'd end the relationship if she had one. A baby was a blessing. Nan taught me that.

When I was young all I wanted was to feel close to my dad, all the time; this was my chance to make that feeling for my own little girl.

Now it felt obvious Yasmin didn't want to be pregnant the whole time. I resented her. Why didn't she want my baby? Why did she feel so strongly that she didn't want my baby?

She obviously didn't love me either. Not if she could kill my baby.

I rammed my head against the trunk again and the crack of it felt good.

My phone rang. Leah.

'Kai!'

'What?' My words were grit as I pushed them through clamped teeth. The pain in my head thudded.

'Are you OK?'

'Yeah.'

'What?' she asked.

The phone was in my palm; her voice was far away – my palm was by my foot – I was kneeling. I lifted the phone to my ear.

'Fucking amazing,' I said.

'You're scaring me,' she said. 'You don't sound normal. I'm sorry I was so quick on the phone when you told me about ... when you told me about, well ...'

'That Yasmin's pregnant?'

'Yes.' She was going into her know-it-all voice. 'I just, you know, it was the last thing I expected. You're so young.'

There were a few seconds that felt like an hour and I yanked my head down the tree, feeling the pull on my skin.

'Kai! Kai!' Little faraway voice.

'Hmmmm?'

'You have your whole life ahead of you.'

For the first time in my life I hung up on my sister.

The nightmare, that nightmare, the suffocation of it was the viper through all my insides. It would burst. I'd be a pile of blood, bones and flesh. Organs. A stinking heart. The nightmare was in my head and it was Dad. On a sofa. Dad dying.

It wasn't a nightmare, it was Dad's omen.

I rubbed my forehead hard, as if I could rub the images out. It wouldn't work and the only way it would be OK was if Yasmin kept the baby. I had to persuade her. I had to. Everything depended on it.

Without my baby, there'd be nothing.

The screen of my phone lit up and there were dark trails of blood where my fingers hunted for Yasmin's number.

'What?' she answered.

'Please, Yasmin,' I cried. 'Please.'

'What's going on?'

'Don't do it, please. Keep the baby, I promise I'll do anything.'

Quiet, so quiet I heard a rustle in the leaves.

'Mum's away tomorrow night,' she said. 'Come round at seven.'

CHAPTER 32

THEN

It took Kai by surprise when Mum sat him down to say, 'Daddy's been locked up, he's going to be away for a long time.'

Like Saffie? 'For ever?'

She was knelt in front of him. He pushed fish fingers and eggy bread round a plate, wondering how long a person could live without food – a week? He would stop eating. It was his fault his best friend was dead, he'd given her the lock-picking set; the least he could do was find her on the silver moon to swap places. Each night he still flew to her in his dreams and they watched each other through the invisible wall.

'No,' replied Mum. 'Not for ever. For nine years.'

He counted on his fingers adding nine to his six. 'Fifteen.'

'We can visit him.'

'Are you OK?' asked Leah.

Kai shrugged.

'You should take him a book,' said Leah, scraping sweet-corn on to a fork.

The salt and pepper pots had small white lids. Kai grabbed the salt, not knowing what to say. Course he wanted to see him. It was scary, though. He poured salt into a pile on the table – it looked like the stuff Mum had sniffed off plates, which stopped a few weeks ago, the last time he'd seen Denner at their house.

Prison was the scariest place in England.

'Can Dad smoke in prison?'

'Yeah.' Mum pinched the material of his trousers and wriggled it. 'But only when he's behaved himself.'

'The smelly pipes, too?'

After the shed fire Nanny had questioned him and Kai had lied in front the girls: no, he'd not seen anything, except Denner had been walking round with a fag in his mouth. When Nanny Sheila took them home after Christmas Denner was with Mum, and Dad wasn't about. Mum said he was in town, probably with Tony-teeth and Elf, and Kai felt so angry he ran to his room and kicked his wardrobe as many times as he could so the door cracked. Leah ran in shouting, 'Stop!' He'd screamed, 'Make Denner go away' as Mum walked in to see what all the fuss was about and she'd listened. A moment later she told Denner to leave. When it was just him and Mum, Kai told her, 'He put his hand up your skirt so I set his shed on fire.' Since then it had been just him, Mum and the girls.

Kai was the man of the house till Dad returned.

Nine years.

*

At night Mum pounded her chest. 'My head's full of him. Breathing hurts.' The bedroom glowed dark yellow. Every night they slept with the lamp on; he stared at the crack in the ceiling and a smudged black moth. She hugged her knees facing him. The treasure chest on the dressing table was empty. He'd like to start a bonfire with it. It was the middle of the night; Mum had woken him making sounds like Kaos had when he was a brand-new puppy and cried for his mum when Kev and Shar turned the lights off and he was left in the kennel outside. It was mean to leave a pet outdoors.

When Mum was gone Dad lost his wings and when Dad was gone she couldn't breathe. Breathing was something Kai knew how to do.

'Put your hands on your legs,' he told Mum, 'and you have to do deep pufferfish breaths, like this, counting.' He showed Mum what Hippie Mandy had taught him. It was something he was good at. 'And,' he said, 'you have to think of happy things when you do it.'

'What do you think of?'

'When me and Saffie watched the rabbits from the top of the Grey Tower.'

She was quiet for a breath, then asked, 'The top?'

Since Dad went to prison and the only person to visit was Nanny, Kai told Mum all his secrets. It didn't matter any more, they were on the same side. 'Yeah, I broke in with my lock-picking keys. To take Saffie.' He thought about the silver moon he couldn't see from this side of the house and Saffie flying around it in his red cape. Maybe she'd wanted to be there all along.

Maybe. Maybe she thought she'd find her dad at the tower.

Mum curled around him, saying, 'I'm gonna look after you properly, I promise. It will be easier now.'

She meant because Dad was gone.

Mum said Kai could stay home from school with her because of Saffie and Dad, but Headmaster T wanted him back in class. Mum clicked on the loudspeaker so Headmaster T could speak to Kai.

'We'll make arrangements so you can leave class if you need to. Coming back to school and seeing your friends will help.'

Mum looked at Kai. 'Thanks for ringing, but my son hasn't eaten, slept or said a word to me for the past two weeks. And may I remind you that the only friend he wants to see has died.'

She never said the word 'may', she was being posh and bossy and telling Headmaster T that in this instance love was more important than school. It was another lie, about him not talking, it was a good one because he wasn't ready to play, remember spellings or swing from the monkey bars. How could he? Kai just wanted Mum, who let him stay off.

They hunted out the radio from the indoor shed, fixed the metal coat hanger back to it – she said that's how Dad worked it – and plugged it in in her bedroom so that it sat on the windowsill and they listened till lunchtimes, imagining what he'd be having for breakfast. They wrote him letters and Kai spelt out how he missed him – as high as the Grey Tower – and Mum wrote how she thought this was the best way to get clean for real.

On a Thursday morning – the day after some posh people had come round in suits to talk about 'children missing in education' – when Mum was heading to town to pick up her dole money and a bottle of brandy, which she now made last two whole weeks, she said, 'Come on, my prince, it's time to go back,' and he let her wash his face and pull on his *X-Men* T-shirt under his school jumper without fighting because he didn't want to be in the house on his own and he couldn't go to Nanny's who was in Wells for the day with Betty.

In class, Kai was given a new seat between Saffie's boring sister and Jordan, who sat at the back of the room next to the sink and its dripping tap. They were boyfriend and girlfriend. It meant Jordan pulled her chair out and said her boring yellow hair looked pretty when it was down. Bet she had nits. She lined her pencils up next to her pink ruler and rubber and she underlined the date and put hearts in the corners of pages. Saffie's writing had been so messy you couldn't read it because she wrote as fast as she could so they'd have more talk time. Why couldn't Boring Twin be dead instead?

Kai squeezed his eyes shut.

Saffie's sister lifted her head and made her mouth smile, her eyes looked really shiny. There was a mole by her eye like Saffie had, except hers was bigger and on the top lid so it looked like a mole not an eyelash. On her feet were Saffie's green Velcro shoes.

Why did he have such nasty thoughts? Her sister was kind and had loved her too and was the person in the world most like her after him. He was bad. All this badness was his fault. He was the worst person in the world.

'Kai, what did I just say?'

Miss Butterworth hadn't said it much the first week. As time pulled on, her bum-mouth kept asking and he'd look at her with a blank face because his mind was always out the window watching the colours of the sky. Without Saffie he couldn't listen or guess the answers. Nothing was fun any more. Writing in his exercise books felt like climbing up a mountain with hot coal on the floor, so most of the time he walked out when Miss wasn't looking, until Hippie Mandy found him and he'd cry in her lap that always smelled of oranges and soap.

How much did he miss Saffie? Further than the furthest planet away, the one that was called Pluto. They were being taught about the solar system and those were the only times it was easy to pay attention. He realised Saffie came to see him sometimes, in the evenings when the sun started to drop and the clouds lit up orange and red like her dragon's-breath hair. Miss Butterworth said Saturn was orange and red, and after that he saw Saffie riding on Dragon's wings along its rings.

One morning Jordan was off school and Kai sat next to Saffie's sister. He noticed that from the side her nose was like his best friend's. He said, 'You should cut your hair then you'd look like Saffie.'

At break time, Crystal told Kai that she had locked herself in a toilet cubicle and was crying like a baby; he didn't know if he thought she was stupid or if he was mean. What would Dad have said to Mum if he'd upset her? After lunch, he told her he was sorry.

'Yasmin,' he said, 'your hair's really pretty.'

CHAPTER 33

13 December 2005

Yaz and her mum called it 'the spare room', but to me it was always Saffie's room. I was stood in it, turning over the china seahorse, noticing how bright the blue and green scales were and wondering how the chip at the end of its tail happened. I wasn't expecting Yasmin to walk in. I thought she was still in her honey and vanilla bubble bath.

'You're obsessed!' The pink towel round her hair matched the one wrapping her body.

I placed the seahorse on Saffie's bedside table quickly, being careful not to break it; I think she'd named it Weed. Like Seaweed. I imagined that if Saffie was alive now, she really would have got that tattoo of a dinosaur climbing out of a volcano. Her bedroom hadn't been touched since she'd gone. I knew that her primary-school uniform was in the wardrobe, folded up on one of the shelves. I'd only ever pulled it out once. It felt too weird. The navy-blue sweater was tiny and it was like she was still a little girl. Miss Pan. I sometimes sat on her bed in the early hours, before sneaking out of the house, leaving Yasmin snoring. I'd hold the seahorse.

'Listen to me!' Yasmin ran at me with her hands up and I grabbed her arms. She wanted to strangle me. The towel slipped down. She was naked. Embarrassing. She jerked about, wet hair on my chin; when I held her, her ears went purple.

She screamed, 'Admit it. You're obsessed with my sister, you always have been.'

I was shitting myself, I really was, because if she knew that then I'd never talk her into keeping the baby. The right words wouldn't come.

Suddenly her mum was at the top of the stairs – I don't know why, she was meant to be in Swindon – the landing light made her cheeks look saggy as an American Bulldog. That needle sensation like I had the day Dad wrote stabbed into my temples.

'Get off her,' she shouted.

I let go of Yasmin, she swung at me, clunked my cheekbone. 'You're obsessed.'

'No,' I said. 'No.' The palms of my hands had mud stains on. I couldn't remember where from.

'Fuck you,' she squeezed the flat skin of her belly with both hands, 'and this kid.'

Pufferfish. Pufferfish.

As I slipped to the carpet, Saffie's green blanket felt like a kiss on my cheek.

'Kai!' Her hands shook my shoulders.

'Saffie?' I blinked. The white sky behind her made her a shadow.

Then her mum was there, dragging Yasmin away and phoning my mum, and it was over.

15 December 2005

The abortion happened yesterday.

Female owls are twenty-five per cent larger than males. The tawny owls are watching me now; I know it, even though I can't see them. They live in the trunk that my feet touch. The difference between males and females in the animal kingdom is like the one in humans, but opposite. Crystal reckons male ducks are prettier because of their green and blue feathers. How would she know? She's shallow and hadn't noticed that female ducks have a blue feather too. That wink of colour.

That was Saffie's life, the prettiest wink ever seen. My baby didn't even wink.

I'm really cold. I pull Dad's sleeping bag close to my face to rub my eyes, which are sore, and I imagine his voice the night he told me the bedtime story about Princess Sue. I have his letter in my inside pocket next to my heart. The nightmare I had about him really fucked with my head because it made me remember other things and I've tried my hardest to make the memories go away. I think that's why I've been drinking and smoking more, but the images are still there. It's mad how you forget things.

After school, before I came here, I went through the front door quietly. The door to the living room was shut. I could hear Mum's and Jade's voices and I wanted to barge in and tell Mum about the baby and how much I hated myself for fucking up. The way they were talking, though, steady and serious, made me stop. The edge of the door frame felt sharp on the centre of my forehead. Mum must have been cooking garlic with Jamaican allspice. I shut my eyes.

'When will he get here?' Jade.

'Any time this week, I think.' Mum. 'I thought he might be back tonight. That's why I want Kai here.'

The TV was on. They paused. How did Mum know when Dad was coming? Had he written to her, too?

'I just don't know what, you know, what he'll be like. Kai's so—'

'Oh, Mum, it's such a mess.' Jade.

The landslide feeling happened in my chest. I was fifteen, it had been nine years since Dad went down. He was coming to see us and he probably looked like a skeleton with bruises and dark eyes. I kept extra quiet, I knew she'd want to talk to me about it and my head just couldn't. I opened my mouth wide because I thought it would make my tight breathing quieter. I rested my foot on the second step of the stairs, the bottom one always creaked.

The whole time Dad had been in prison I never wrote back because he told Mum not to take me there after the first time. The cedar cigar box I made him when I was ten was hidden in my wardrobe waiting for him to get out; I wished I'd burned it. I swallowed, my throat felt dry.

'I've no clue what it's going to be like.' Mum.

There was a quiet pause, then Jade. 'How ill *is* he?'

There was quiet and then Mum. 'Kai's never wanted, you know—'

'We should go look for Kai.' Jade. She cleared her throat loudly. 'There's a place he goes – he might be there.'

'Now?' Mum. 'He'll be with Yaz.'

I started feeling dizzy. The dream I'd had suddenly shot to the centre of my forehead – Dad on the sofa – and there was something new, a moment. A real one.

Jade said, 'When Jesse gets here—'

I turned. As I reached for the door lock my hand shook.

I came to the den.

The walk here was as heavy as the Atlantic. Like I was laid on the ocean bed with its weight pressing on me. The images flashed like photographs.

When I was little, Dad didn't like to do smack alone and I remember sometimes he'd wake me up from sleep, take me to the living room. I'd watch him smoke and jack up. I think, usually, it must have happened in the early hours of the morning because of the look of the light that shone through the curtains and made a halo around his red hair. There was a sharp needle. It lived under the sink.

I didn't stop him or tell Mum.

Never told anyone.

I want to tell Dad about my baby. About Yasmin killing her. But would he even care? He was a shit dad.

Blim-burns on his sleeping bag feel scratchy on my face. I move my cheek to a dry spot. I don't understand why he never let me visit him after that first time. He must hate me and I know when he gets here, he'll be the same but worse. He's dying. The man in the nightmare dying on the sofa.

I couldn't stand the continual watching. Seeing him waste away; he'll die in front of me and I'll pay with my life anyway – he'll be all I think of. Like before.

Always he stared into the distance and I stared at him, wondering where his scary mind had landed. Sometimes he'd look at me, not smiling. There, but not.

I still feel the damp clouds of his sadness. I'd do anything to make him be OK, not even happy, just OK. If I couldn't make him stop then, now will be no different.

Mum's right. She knew him better than anyone. He won't have changed.

I can't live like that again.

The rope is from Kev's shed. Jord will go mad when he realises it was from his dad, but it makes me feel like Jord will be near me at the last moment and that's good because even Nan and Leah lost belief in me. I yank it over my palm, the one with the scar. Mine and Saffie's scar. I kiss it. Everything that was ever going to be good in life left when she went to the moon.

Me, Jord and Richie went to the meadow last summer. Jord asked, 'If you could go anywhere in the world, where would you go?'

Where would I go?

I put my can of Strongbow down and lay back, crossing one arm behind my head and feeling the tickle of grass on my neck, thinking of ants and worms below. I put my other hand in my pocket to hold the red ribbons. Somewhere untouched by people, where there were animals, trees and silver seas, and brown chicken curry, rice and peas like Mum makes on Sundays. There would be silver monsoons and honeycomb mountains. Bumblebees. Moon bees.

'I'd go to the moon, mate,' I said, and as he and Richie accused me of being high, I said in my head as I looked at the sky, *To find you, Saffie*.

The time's come to find her. To leave here.

I take her red ribbons from my pocket and knot them, before slipping them over my wrist like bracelets, then I curl the rope into a circle to carry. When I stand, my body is stiff. I lean towards the torch and yank it from the branch. I have to go quick in case Mum and Jade really do come looking for me. I say a last goodbye to my den and the grey rabbits. Suddenly I'm filled with peace as I point the torch in the direction of the Grey Tower.

ACKNOWLEDGEMENTS

Nina, whom I miss all the time and who taught me courage and so much about passion and the arts.

Lindsay, for ALL the things you've done for me the last few years. I don't know where I'd be without you (I certainly wouldn't have my quill).

Gavin, who made me believe my writing deserved to be on bookshelves, introduced me to JCO, and told me I had voice.

Lauren, Elijah, Ezra, Israel, my siblings; my favourite people in the world, without whom I wouldn't be. My constant sources of inspiration and love. Thanks for being pissed off, happy, and disappointed along with me. The best parts of all my writing are linked to you lot. Eli, you're still waiting for your cut for all the witty bits. Will a tenner do, or a pint down Spoons? Thanks for your hair on the front cover, Ez (it's my favourite part, you're a good luck charm). Is, I hope your two secret spots are of comfort (for me, they sparkle just like you). Lauren? Prawn cocktail crisps: thanks for forcing me to keep the faith and always, thank you for your fury.

Uncle Rog, of course you too, you bought me my first book! If it wasn't for you this beast probably wouldn't have happened.

Sam, Becky, Tish, Cat, Fran, Sasha; my best friends who have liked and endured me for years even when I haven't liked myself, and at times have been a spectacular prick. Sam, I love you dearly. You're allowed to read it now, but only because it's out of my hands.

Jason, for not letting me quit when I wanted to. That was the moment I trusted you actually liked it.

Rebecca, for repping my precious boy, Kai.